Rogues Rush In
A REGENCY DUET

His Bride for the Taking
Copyright © 2018 by Tessa Dare
His Duchess for a Day
Copyright © 2018 by Christi Caldwell

All rights reserved. No part of this book may be reproduced in any form by any electronic or mechanical means—except in the case of brief quotations embodied in critical articles or reviews—without written permission.

The characters and events portrayed in this book are fictitious. Any similarity to real persons, living or dead, is purely coincidental and not intended by the author.

This Book is licensed for your personal enjoyment only. This Book may not be re-sold or given away to other people. If you would like to share this book with another person, please purchase an additional copy for each recipient. If you're reading this book and did not purchase it or borrow it, or it was not purchased for your use only, then please return it and purchase your own copy. Thank you for respecting the hard work of the author.

For more information about the author:
www.christicaldwellauthor.com
christicaldwellauthor@gmail.com
Twitter: @ChristiCaldwell
Or on Facebook at: Christi Caldwell Author

For first glimpse at covers, excerpts, and free bonus material, be sure to sign up for my monthly newsletter!
Printed in the USA.

Cover Design and Interior Format

Rogues Rush In

A REGENCY DUET

TESSA DARE
AND CHRISTI CALDWELL

His Bride for the Taking

Tessa Dare

CHAPTER 1

It was the first rule of friendship among gentlemen: Never, ever lay a hand on your best friend's sister.

Don't do it. Don't even *think* about it.

Not. One. Finger.

Sebastian Ives, Lord Byrne, had never been one for following rules. But promises? He took those seriously indeed. His friendship with Henry Clayton had been the anchor in his turbulent youth, too valuable to risk. So he'd made a vow to himself, and he'd steadfastly held to it—as best he could, anyhow—for years.

Eleven years.

Eleven *long* years.

More than *four thousand days* of wrestling the temptation to take Mary Clayton in his arms and…

Well, from there the specifics varied.

Suffice it to say, aside from the casual contact necessitated by social convention, he'd never touched her—with one exception. After Henry's funeral, he'd held her for hours as she wept. That didn't count, surely.

But today, Sebastian found himself tempted to break his promise. No, "break" was too weak a word. He wanted to bundle his principles, snap them in two, and grind them to sand beneath his boot.

Damn, she looked lovely in her wedding gown.

Not only lovely, but inexplicably alone.

"Where the devil is your groom?"

"I'm not certain," she said.

He paced the floor of the chapel's tiny annex, averting his gaze from the slope of her neck and the gentle curl of auburn hair that adorned it. "How dare he keep you waiting, the bastard."

"Mr. Perry's not a bastard. He's the legitimate son of a barrister."

"I don't care if he's the Prince of Wales. The man made a promise to you, and he's not here to keep it. That makes him a bastard. A tardy bastard, at that."

"He isn't late, Sebastian." She paused. "He's not coming."

"Impossible."

"It's quite possible. In fact, it's evident. He's not here, and neither is his family." She released her breath in a defeated sigh. "He must have changed his mind at the last moment."

"Changed his *mind?* What sort of idiotic milksop would change his mind about marrying you?"

"One who wanted a different sort of wife, I suppose. Someone less opinionated, more amenable. You of all people know I can be difficult."

Difficult? When it came to Mary, his only difficulty had been keeping his distance.

He supposed he could see why a weaker man might find her intimidating. She'd always been more clever than Sebastian and Henry put together. She was strong and self-reliant, because losing her mother at a young age had given her no other choice.

And she was passionate. If she believed in something, she would argue her case with everything she had, and never back down. She believed that women should have the vote, that prisoners should have better rations, that war widows should have pensions.

And that sons of violent drunkards should never spend Christmas alone.

Any man who'd let her go was a bloody fool.

"It's done," she said. "I'll have to find the curate and tell him the wedding has been called off."

"Oh no, you won't. I'm going to go out and find that blackguard and drag him here."

"I don't want to marry a man who needs to be dragged to the altar. Even in my current state of bruised pride, I think I deserve a bit better than that."

"Of course you do. You always deserved better than Giles Perry in the first place. But he proposed to you, and you accepted him. And I'll be damned if he'll get away with this."

"Sebastian."

He relented. "Very well. I won't drag him back. I'll *invite* him to make good on his word to you."

"And if he doesn't accept that invitation?"

Sebastian stopped pacing and turned to her, staring directly into her brilliant blue eyes. "Then I'll call the bastard out."

"A duel?" Mary's heart missed a beat. "Oh, no. You can't."

"Oh, yes. I will."

He gave her the classic Sebastian look, commanding and stubborn in equal measures. She'd watched grown men wither under that glare. It didn't help that he was built like a Viking warrior, tall and broad-shouldered, with features struck from bronze. There was nothing soft on him, anywhere.

Not on the outside, at least.

"That look doesn't work on me," she said. "I know you too well."

"You don't know everything, Mary."

"I know I've watched you cradle a sparrow hatchling in your hand and feed it from a tincture dropper."

He tipped his head back and groaned. "That was ages ago."

"Mashed worms, three times an hour, for *days.*"

"Rescuing the thing was not my idea. It was Henry's."

"But you were the one who saw it through. The dear little bird thought you were its mother. Remember?" She hooked two fingers and skipped them up his arm. "Hop, hop, hop…"

"Stop."

She withdrew her hand. "I'm just saying that if you ever had any hope of intimidating me, it disappeared that summer. So don't even think about dueling. You're not a man who'd kill another in cold blood."

"Your honor must be defended. Perry's already put off this wedding twice."

"He put off the wedding once," she corrected. "The other time I was in mourning. That wasn't his fault."

"No, that wasn't his fault," Sebastian said in a low, bitter voice.

"It was mine."

Mary silently cursed herself. She never should have mentioned it. "You must stop blaming yourself. It was war; men die. You weren't responsible for Henry's decision to enlist."

"Perhaps not. But when he was killed, I became responsible for you."

"I'm nearly twenty-eight years old. I should think by now I'm responsible for myself. And I may have been jilted, but I'm not heartbroken. Giles and I held each other in esteem, but it wasn't a love match. I'll survive."

"Yes, but your reputation will not. You know the things people say when a long engagement is broken. They will assume that you've… Well, that the two of you…" He churned the air with one hand. "Help me here. What's a polite way to say it?"

Mary was suddenly curious about the impolite ways to say it. But that wasn't a conversation for the moment. "They'll assume we anticipated the wedding vows."

"Yes," he said with obvious relief. "That."

"I can't help it if people gossip."

"You'll be ruined. You don't have the money or connections to overcome even a hint of scandal. If you don't marry Perry today, you might never wed anyone at all."

"I'm aware of that." *Painfully so.*

Spinsterhood wasn't an especially appealing prospect—not only because she'd always dreamed of falling in love, setting up house, and having children—but because with Henry gone, the modest family fortune had passed to a third cousin. Thus far, her cousin had been both sympathetic and generous, but should he change his mind, her financial situation could quickly turn grim.

"And what about your political causes and all those charitable organizations?" he asked. "I know how important they are to you. If you lose your good reputation, you'd lose a good measure of influence, too."

Yet another blow, and one that struck nearer her heart.

She shrugged, trying to appear nonchalant. "Perhaps I'll have to surrender my membership in the Ladies' Social Justice Society. The meetings were rather a bore, anyhow."

"I'll take care of this," he said. "Once I have him staring into the end of my pistol, he'll reconsider. Don't worry."

Don't *worry?* The only emotion she could feel at the moment was worry. The chances of Giles killing Sebastian in a duel were slim, but they weren't nonexistent.

"Sebastian, I won't let you risk your life for me. Not over this."

"I'd *give* my life for you. Without a moment's thought."

Goodness. For once, she was caught without a response. He'd taken her breath away. She'd already lost her father, then her only brother.

Mary couldn't bear to lose him, too.

"Listen to me. I'm not going to wed Giles. Ever. Even if you found him, reduced him to pleading at gunpoint, and brought him back to this chapel within the next quarter-hour, I would refuse. Do you mean to threaten me with a pistol, too?"

"Of course not," he grumbled. "I can't force you to marry him."

"Well, then. That's settled. Spinsterhood it shall be." She steadied herself. "If you'll excuse me, I'll go explain to the curate."

He caught her by the arm. "No, I will not excuse you. You will not go explain to the curate. You will not be ruined, and you are not going to be a spinster, either. You're going to marry me."

CHAPTER 2

SEBASTIAN DIDN'T EXPECT THAT SHE would take his declaration well.

And he was right.

"*What?*" she exclaimed.

"You need to marry someone, and if you won't wed Perry, you will marry me. It's the only way."

Her brow crinkled. "It's not the only way."

"It's the only way I'll allow. I know how small your dowry is. You're not going to be an impoverished spinster if I can help it. And I can."

"If it's the money you're concerned about, you could settle a few thousand pounds on me. You certainly have it to spare."

"And make you a target for unscrupulous fortune-hunters? The devil I will."

"My goodness. What a low opinion you have of my ability to choose suitors."

He stepped back and made a show of searching the room. "The last man you chose to wed isn't here."

He saw her flinch, and he regretted his harsh tone. He didn't want to hurt her. She deserved to be courted by scores of men and worshipped by the lucky fellow she chose. But the world they lived in wasn't fair. That damned Perry would go on to have a fine life, and Mary would pay the price—with her prospects, her reputation, her friends, her influence.

She sighed. "I know you see this as your problem to solve, with

Henry gone. But Henry cared about you, too. He wouldn't want you to throw your future away out of misplaced loyalty."

"My loyalty is not misplaced. In fact, there is nowhere else my loyalty *could* be placed. I don't have anyone else." He forged on, wanting to escape the softness in her eyes. "As for the suggestion that I'd be throwing away my future, I won't even dignify that with a response."

"I'm not helpless, Sebastian."

"I know you aren't. But it's what's best. No one will fault you. It's exactly something society would expect me to do, kidnapping a bride from the altar. I'm a shameless rogue."

"No, you're not."

He refused to take up that argument. "You'll be a lady. A wealthy one. I've always known I'd need a wife eventually."

"But…I'm too old," she blurted out.

"You're not old."

"I'm older than you."

"By two years."

"Closer to three. Most men want a younger bride."

"I'm not most men."

She looked at him and sighed. "Yes, I'd noticed."

Well, he'd done more than notice Mary. She'd captured his attention from the very first, and all *because* she was older. She was more worldly and interesting than the girls his own age. Not to mention, her womanly figure had been a source of both temptation and torment.

And on that subject…

"There's one thing you should know," he said. "I am a lord, even if a disgraced one. There's still an entail on the family property." He paused. "I'll need a son. And that means we'll have to…" He searched once again for a polite term.

"Share a bed."

"Do you know what that involves?" He assumed that someone would have given her some idea, but he wanted to be absolutely certain that she knew what she'd be undertaking.

For Sebastian, of course, the bedding would be no chore. He'd imagined making love to her more than once.

Who was he fooling? He'd imagined it hundreds of times. He'd even *dreamed* about her, long after he thought he'd ceased dreaming of anything.

"I understand the marriage bed," she said in perfect innocence. "The husband kisses the wife on the lips, and then she becomes pregnant."

He stared at her, quietly panicked.

She broke into laughter. "I know how intercourse works, Sebastian. Even if I haven't experienced it yet."

Thank God. "So you understand that in order to create a child, we'll need to … do that. At least once. Possibly several times. Even then, the child could be a girl. In which case, we'd have to begin all over again. But I promise, I'd impose on you no more than necessary, and only when you're ready."

She shook her head. "You are running so far ahead of yourself, you're a vanishing dot on the horizon. Right now, I need to announce that *this* wedding isn't happening. After an appropriate interval—a few months, at the least—we can discuss this again. If you still feel the same, and if I agree, we can announce an engagement then. Maybe a wedding in October."

"Unacceptable."

"Christmas, then."

"Definitely not." He'd managed to talk her into this. He wasn't giving her months of time to change her mind. "We're getting married today."

"Today?" Mary echoed. He'd flown past determined, straight into the realm of deranged.

He made a circuit of the vestry, gathering her things. Flowers, veil, wrap. "Your trunks are packed, I assume."

"They're outside, in the coach that Giles hired. We were going to leave for the honeymoon directly after the wedding." Thank goodness they'd planned for a small ceremony at the church, with no wedding breakfast. At least there weren't many witnesses to her humiliation.

"So that's sorted. And you're wearing a gown."

"We *can't* marry today," she declared, having recalled that she was the daughter of a solicitor and claimed more than a passing familiarity with the law. "We don't have a license, and no banns have been read. It simply isn't possible. So there you have it."

He stopped and considered this. "You're right, we'll need a special license. Which means we'll go to Canterbury and be married there."

"Oh, Lord. You've taken leave of your senses. This explains so much."

"My parents are both dead, as are yours. And now Henry, too. We don't have families to attend the ceremony. Or to object."

"*I* object." She spread her arms. "Here I am, standing right in front of you. Objecting."

"You're not objecting on any reasonable grounds. You're just being contrary."

"Well, you're just being hot-headed."

"I'm not hot-headed. I make swift decisions, often ruthless ones. The estate would have gone insolvent years ago otherwise. But when I heed my gut, I've never had cause to regret it."

She raised an eyebrow. "Yet."

He took her by the hand and fairly dragged her out the vestry's side door, hurrying her toward the waiting coach. "I have a seaside property. A mere cottage, but it's situated nicely on the cliffs near Ramsgate, just a few hours' journey from Canterbury. It's the ideal place to spend a week or two away from London. Less gossip that way."

The gossip.

Heavens, there would be so much gossip.

Well, if there was going to be gossip about her, Mary supposed she would vastly prefer gossip about how she'd been kidnapped by a shameless, sensual rogue, rather than gossip about how she'd been abandoned at the altar by the milquetoast son of a barrister. Passionate was better than pitiful.

"If we leave now," he said, "we'll arrive at the cottage by nightfall. I came here on Shadow, so I'll ride out. But I'll be alongside the coach every step of the way."

He handed her into the carriage, then conferred with the coachman. Bribing him handsomely, she supposed. He was always a man who acted decisively, but she'd never seen him so resolved. Not since he'd declared that he'd purchased a lieutenancy and meant to go off to war.

She flung open the carriage door. "Sebastian, wait."

He reluctantly turned back.

"What about love?" she asked him quietly. "Don't you want to marry for love?"

"I'd rather marry someone I trust."

"Love and trust go hand-in-hand."

"Not in my family, they didn't."

Mary's heart ached for him. The first time he'd come home with Henry from school, he'd been so mistrustful and withdrawn. Wearing so much invisible armor, it practically clinked as he walked. Over the years, he'd grown comfortable in their home, revealing more and more of himself. Letting down his guard.

But after the war—after Henry died—everything had changed. He'd walled himself away again. She didn't know how to reach him, and she worried he'd never let anyone else draw close enough to try.

"You're being so good to me," she said. "I appreciate it, more than you know. But you needn't do this. I may find I'm well-suited to being a spinster. Or perhaps someone will care enough to wed me despite the scandal."

"Someone already does, Mary. You're looking at him."

In the silence that followed his words, they were both very still.

"If you think I'm being selfless, let me assure you I'm not. I could not keep Henry alive, and that failure will haunt me until I die. You *must* allow me to protect you, or I won't know how to live with myself. You'll have my title and my wealth at your disposal. As a lady of means, you can champion any cause you desire. Aside from giving me an heir, your life will be your own. Let me protect you. That's all I ask."

How could she say no to that? Mary rummaged through her mind for one last objection, but came up empty-handed.

No, not empty-handed. Sebastian's hand was in hers. If she married him, she wouldn't be alone. And neither would he.

Good heavens. She was truly going to be Mary Ives, Lady Byrne.

She gave his hand a squeeze before releasing it. "Take care on the road."

It wasn't quite the wedding Mary had expected.

No, it was much grander. And far more romantic.

Even with a rushed elopement, no guests, and a wedding gown

crumpled from travel, the setting was undeniably enchanting. The soaring beauty of the cathedral, the solemn priest in his vestments, the spicy fog of incense. Fading sunlight shone through the stained glass windows, sending crescents of blue and red gliding across the floor.

The scene felt magical, timeless.

And she had the handsomest groom. Sebastian had never looked finer. He fit right into the medieval setting. Like a knight in invisible armor, ready to take on an impossible quest. Mary wasn't certain of her role in this story. Was she the fair maiden he sought to please, or was her broken engagement merely a dragon he needed to slay? His hardened jaw gave no clues.

As the priest began the ceremony, the words washed over her in a hushed murmur.

Sebastian's part came first, and he nearly stepped on the priest's words with his firm, "I will." No hesitation.

Then the priest turned to her. "Mary Elizabeth Clayton, wilt thou have this man to thy wedded husband, to live together after God's ordinance in the holy estate of matrimony?"

She nodded. Thus far, everything sounded acceptable.

"Wilt thou obey him…"

Oh, dear.

"…and serve him…"

She cringed.

"…love, honor, and keep him, in sickness and in health; and, forsaking all others, keep thee only unto him, so long as ye both shall live? If so, answer, 'I will.'"

Mary hesitated.

"If so," the priest repeated, leaning on the words, "answer, 'I will.'"

She couldn't say it. Not quite yet.

She addressed Sebastian directly. "I don't have to do this, you know. I do have a choice."

"What choice? To be a ruined spinster surviving on a meager income?"

"It wouldn't be so bad as you're implying. At least I'd be free to do as I like."

"Mary," he said in a low voice, "this is not the time to argue for the sake of arguing."

"I'm not arguing. Just listen to me for a moment, will you?"

"I don't see the point in discussion."

"Well, I see the point in it," she said, affronted. "When I have something to say, I'd like to be heard. Especially by the man who'll be my husband."

"There's no way in hell I'm taking you back to—"

"Ahem." The priest looked perturbed. "Shall we return to the ceremony?"

"I'm paying for a new chapel," Sebastian snapped. "You can wait until my bride and I are finished speaking."

Mary found his gruff protectiveness oddly endearing, especially since it came under the imminent threat of damnation.

"I'm making a choice, Sebastian. That's all I meant to say. When I make these vows, I'm choosing to do so freely. I'm choosing this." She lowered her voice to a whisper. "I'm choosing *you*."

The casual observer would never notice it, but Mary knew her words had a profound effect. The tension left his shoulders, and suddenly his flinty eyes weren't quite so stern.

For the moment, at least, the warrior had lowered his shield.

She looked at the priest. "I'm ready now."

"If so, answer, 'I will.'"

She looked into her groom's eyes. "I will."

The remainder of the ceremony was brief, in part because there were no rings. Sebastian didn't even have a signet ring. He would have never worn anything of his father's, and most especially not that.

There were vows and a prayer or two, and before Mary even knew it, the thing was over.

"I pronounce you man and wife."

It was done. They were married.

Sebastian leaned forward as though he would kiss her, but then he seemed to change his mind. She might have suspected he'd lost his nerve, if she didn't know Sebastian to be entirely composed of nerve to begin with.

Instead of kissing her lips, he brushed a kiss to her cheek and then rested his temple against hers. A tender gesture, somehow more intimate than a kiss.

"I'll take care of you," he whispered. "Always."

"I know you will," she whispered back.

Mary had no doubt in her mind whatsoever that Sebastian would provide for her every need and guard her with his life.

But it was probably going to knock him on his arse when he learned that she intended to do the same. He needed understanding, warmth, family, love—and she needed all those things, too. This was not going to be a practical arrangement, nor a way for him to satisfy his conscience.

This was going to be a marriage.

And that marriage started tonight.

CHAPTER 3

By THE TIME THEY LEFT Canterbury, daylight was fading and thunderclouds had gathered on the horizon. The coachman was not pleased when Sebastian told him they'd be traveling on to Ramsgate in foul weather, but a few guineas made a marked improvement in his mood.

Halfway through the journey, both night and rain were falling. Then Sebastian's horse threw a shoe, slowing their progress to a walk. When they finally arrived at the cottage, the windows were dark. No one came out to greet them. Country hours, he supposed. Perhaps folk went to bed at sundown hereabouts.

Sebastian dismounted Shadow and saw the weary gelding settled in the stable—which looked and smelled as though it hadn't been used in years. Fortunately, the horse had been fed and watered in Canterbury. Any hay in the loft would surely be rotted.

After seeing to his horse, Sebastian pounded at the cottage's front door.

No answer.

Naturally, he had a key to the place, but he didn't carry the thing on his person. It was in a strongbox underneath the desk in his London town house. When he'd left the house this morning, he'd expected to sit quietly seething in a church while he watched Mary wed another man. He never could have imagined that by nightfall he'd be standing in front of this stone cottage on the coast of Kent, having married her himself.

When another round of knocking produced no response, he

rattled the door to judge the strength of the bolt. It was already loose—a fact that would have angered him, had the circumstances been different. Tonight, however, this particular instance of shoddy upkeep was a gift. One swift kick, and the bolt gave way.

That accomplished, he darted back to the coach. First he needed to untie Mary's trunks from the carriage and bring them in before they were completely drenched. After he'd stashed her luggage inside the cottage, he returned to the coach for her.

"Put your hands around my neck," he shouted through the rain. "I'll carry you."

"I can walk."

Sebastian didn't have time for this. He hefted her out of the coach without further discussion, tucking her against his chest and carrying her into the cottage.

"You didn't have to do that," she said, once he'd set her down.

"The ground was wet and muddy."

She smiled wryly. "I'm not too concerned about the hem of my gown. It's not as though I'm going to wear it again."

"It's our wedding night," he said. "On the wedding night, the groom carries the bride over the threshold. As hasty and patched-up as the whole thing has been, and considering that you didn't have so much as a ring, I thought I'd do that one thing properly."

"Sebastian. That's terribly sweet."

Sweet, she called him? Good God.

Outside, the coachman snapped the reins and drove off into the night.

Sebastian shoved the door closed and propped it shut with a chair. Mary located a flint and used it to light a candle, giving them their first proper look around the cottage.

Sebastian cursed. It was a shambles. He'd seen henhouses in more habitable condition.

"How long has it been since you visited this place?" she asked.

"Years. But there's supposed to be a caretaker living here with his wife. At least, I've been paying a caretaker's wages. I didn't expect the place to be sparkling, but this?" He batted at a cobweb.

"At least we're out of the rain."

Except that they weren't truly out of the rain. When he looked up at the leaking thatch roof, a cold rivulet of water hit him square in the eye.

Not a few hours ago, he'd stood before a man of God and vowed to keep and protect Mary for so long as they both shall live. He wasn't off to a smashing start.

"We'll go to an inn for the night," he said.

"How? The coachman already left. Shadow's thrown a shoe. And I don't recall seeing an inn when we passed through the village."

"Well, we can't stay here."

"It's only a few leaks, some dust and cobwebs." She scouted around the place, holding her candle high. "This room off the kitchen isn't so neglected. It's dry, at least. And there's a bed. I have fresh bed linens and a quilt in my trunks. They're part of my trousseau."

He slicked back his wet hair. "At least let me walk to the village and find us something to eat."

"Oh, no you won't. You are not leaving me alone in this place." She picked up a hamper he'd unloaded from the coach and set it on the kitchen table. "Giles's sister said she'd packed us a little something. Well, not *us*, but you know."

Yes. Sebastian knew. And he hated the thought that if she'd married that prig she'd be warm, dry, and fed right now.

She opened the hamper. "We have a bottle of wine. That's promising. And…" She unwrapped a packet of brown paper. "Cake."

Sebastian looked at it. That wasn't merely cake.

That was *wedding* cake.

Suddenly, he wasn't hungry.

She broke off a hunk of cake and took a healthy bite. "We'll survive until the morning," she mumbled with a full mouth. "It will be fine."

He supposed they didn't have much choice.

"Are you sure you don't want some?" She took another bite of cake, then licked her fingers. "It's good."

He shook his head. "I'll lay a fire. You make up the bed."

While she unbuckled the straps on her trunk to search for the bed linens, Sebastian removed his coat and undid his cuffs, turning his sleeves up to the elbow. He searched the kitchen for firewood and found a paltry number of logs. Nowhere near enough to keep a blaze fueled through the night.

He ventured out into the rain and made his way around the cottage's exterior until he found a depleted woodpile beneath a crumbling lean-to. The wood atop the stack was damp. Much of the rest was rotting.

When he got his hands on that caretaker, he would make the man pay for leaving his property in such a state of neglect.

He scavenged a few of the driest logs from the heap, carried them to the chopping block, and gripped the ax handle to pry it free. He braced his feet in the mud and gave it his best one-handed pull. Instead of the blade coming free of the block, the handle broke off in his hand. Sebastian stumbled backward and fell on his arse.

Brilliant. Now he was soaked with rain *and* coated with mud. He carried his armful of unsplit wood back into the cottage and stood in the entry, shaking himself like a dog and sending muddy droplets in all directions. He pried off his boots before crouching at the hearth to make a fire.

With a bit of work, he'd built a respectable blaze. Toasty warmth spread through the kitchen. If they left the door to the bedchamber open, the heat ought to be sufficient to warm that room, too.

"The bed is ready," she said from behind him.

He added a log to the fire, then rose and turned.

Christ.

Mary stood before him wearing a sheer, lacy, snow-white negligee.

He couldn't speak. The cat had got not only his tongue, but every other part of his body that wasn't his eyes, heart, blood, or stiffening cock.

Eleven years, four thousand days. And on how many of those four thousand nights had he imagined her naked? More than he'd ever admit. And here she was, standing before him, wearing the silk equivalent of a branch and a fig leaf.

More beautiful than in his wildest imaginings.

She'd unpinned and brushed out her hair, and the glossy auburn locks tumbled about her shoulders in waves. The wine had stained her lips claret red.

And her nipples were a blushing, rosy pink. He'd always dreamed they'd be pink. He'd also always dreamed they would taste like custard tarts, which now struck him as oddly specific.

"What," he finally scraped out, "is *that?*"

"It's…a nightgown."

"It's a cobweb. There are more holes than thread. You're shivering already." *Not to mention, your rosy nipples are hard as darts.* "Don't you have something more drab and sensible?"

She wrapped her arms about herself. "They're all like this."

Of course they were all like that. She'd packed for a honeymoon. A honeymoon with someone else.

He was a monster. She had to be cold, exhausted, and awash with conflicted emotions. Even if her heart wasn't broken, it must have been bruised. From the looks of that negligee, she might have even been looking forward to her wedding night with Perry. Instead, she was here in an infested, rotting hellhole. With him.

And he was berating her about her choice of sleeping apparel.

Well done, Sebastian. Well done, indeed.

She crossed the room to him. "Come, then. Off with your clothes." She yanked the hem of his shirt from his trousers.

"Mary." He took a step in retreat. "I'm not… We're not… Not tonight."

She tipped her head to the side and regarded him. "You are soaked to the skin and spattered with mud. I'm not being a brazen hussy, I'm protecting my embroidery. I worked hard on those bed linens, you know. So take off your things and leave them to dry by the fire."

He shook his head. "I'll sleep on the floor."

"Don't be absurd. I won't let you sleep on the floor."

"It's nothing. I slept in much rougher conditions while on campaign."

"This isn't the army, Sebastian. There's a perfectly good bed."

"Exactly. Bed, singular. Not beds."

"We *are* man and wife," she teased. "The priest said so."

Wife.

She was his *wife*.

"I know you mean to take care of me," she said. "But now that we're married, I get to take care of you, too. You're not sleeping on the floor." She touched his wrist. "Besides, it's cold. I don't want to be alone."

Very well. She had him there.

And in that negligee, she had him hard as granite.

This would be a very long night.

"You go ahead and get in the bed," he said. "Take the side nearest the kitchen. It will be warmest. I'll join you in a minute."

He waited until he heard her slip beneath the quilt before disrobing hastily and draping his wet clothing over two chairs near the fire. As he crept into the bedchamber, he tried to stay in the shadows. Not out of modesty, but so she wouldn't be alarmed. He was a rather hulking fellow, big in all sorts of ways. Experienced women seemed to like his body just fine, but he wasn't certain how a virgin would react.

He stretched out beside her on the bed, crossed his arms over his chest, and closed his eyes.

She nestled up against him.

He wriggled a few inches away.

She snuggled close again. "Hold me. You're so warm. And I can't stop shivering."

With a heavy sigh, he draped one arm around her shoulders, still careful to keep their bodies apart from the navel down. "I don't want to crush you."

"How could you crush me? You're next to me, not atop me."

He groaned. *Don't give me ideas.*

"You're inching away again," she accused. "Am I so objectionable?"

"The furthest thing from it."

"Then what's the matter?"

Fine. Don't say you didn't ask for it.

He rolled onto his side to face her, pulled her close, and thrust his rampant arousal against her belly. "There. I hope that answers your question."

She swallowed hard. "Oh. Were you wanting to—"

"Engage in politely phrased activities? No." He released her. "Not at all."

"You don't have to be so vehement about it."

"A man's body has a mind of its own. Especially when the man in question is naked and in bed with a beautiful woman. One clad in nothing but a wisp of lace, who keeps wriggling her body against his." He exhaled heavily. "But I don't want you to be anxious. We'll wait until you're ready. Whether that means weeks, months, even years. I won't rush you."

She was silent for a moment. And then she started to laugh.

"What?"

"You won't rush me?" The bed quaked with her laughter. "This from the man who kidnapped me in the morning, married me in the afternoon, and installed me in his remote seaside cottage by evening. But you won't *rush* me. Oh, Sebastian. That is too much."

He didn't know what to say.

"Look at that furrow in your brow." She rubbed the space between his eyebrows, as though attempting to iron it flat. "Don't look so stern. I'm only teasing you. But perhaps you're not ready to be teased. I won't rush you, either."

Without thinking, he reached out to stroke her hair.

She laid her head on his chest. "I've worried about you in the past year. You're too stubborn to let on, but I know you've been hurting. Whether it's Henry or the war, or something I can't even comprehend. Even when we're in the same room, you've seemed so far away."

He didn't know how to answer that. It was true, he'd been grieving. Not only for Henry, but for so many of his brothers in arms. But it wasn't something he knew how to talk about. And he could scarcely complain to Mary about it. She'd lost her only brother. With both her parents gone, Henry had been her only family remaining. She was alone.

Or rather, she'd *been* alone. Now she was with him.

"Go to sleep," he told her. "At first light, I'm taking you away from this miserable place."

She tilted her head to look up at him. "Kiss me goodnight?"

He hesitated.

"It's our wedding night. It seems we should at least have that. For tradition's sake, if nothing else."

Very well. He touched his lips to hers, giving her a chaste, sweet kiss.

And then, Devil take him, the kiss became more.

His first taste of her was a rich, buttery sweetness. Like cake. That cursed wedding cake that was meant for her to share with another man. He wanted to steal that taste from her mouth and burn it to ash.

He swept his tongue between her lips. Exploring, claiming. He slid his hand to the back of her head and wove his fingers into her hair, tilting her face to his to deepen the kiss. She pressed closer, and the exquisite softness of her body made his skin tighten and his blood pound.

Within him, desire sparked and spread like a blaze.

Natural. Wild. Uncontrolled.

This was meant to be a goodnight kiss. A sweet brush of lips against lips before drifting off to sleep. Instead, his long-buried desires were waking and stretching. Roaring to life with a ferocity that startled even him.

He yearned to explore every part of her with his hands. Cup her breasts in his palms, run his fingers along her sweet, hot cleft. He wanted her beneath him. Astride him. Pressed against the wall. Bent over the table, with all that frothy lace pushed up to her waist.

He wanted her calling his name, holding him tight. He wanted to fall asleep tangled with her, and wake up with her in his arms.

He wanted all she had to give him, and more.

Mary, Mary.

A crash of timber and iron jolted them both. The kiss came apart, but he kept Mary close.

Two human silhouettes filled the doorway between the bedchamber and the kitchen.

"Whoever ye are," came a menacing voice, "ye'd best prepare to die."

CHAPTER 4

In the chilling darkness, Mary clutched Sebastian tight. Her heart trilled like a rabbit's in her chest.

Pushing the quilt aside, Sebastian let her slip from his arms and quietly swung his legs to the side of the bed. She sensed his muscles coiling with tension.

He was preparing to fight.

"Don't be frightened," he murmured. "I'll keep you safe."

She exhaled shakily. Of course he would fight to keep her safe—he was so damnably selfless that way—but she needed *him* to be safe, too.

As she blinked, her eyes adjusted to the dim, flickering firelight. The two silhouettes in the door belonged to a man and a woman. The man brandished a long, round-barreled weapon. A rifle.

Be careful, Sebastian.

The man leveled his weapon.

Sebastian rose to his full, imposing height, moving between Mary and the door. Into the line of fire.

He gave the intruders a single, thunderous word. *"Begone."*

"Lord preserve us." The man's weapon shook. Out of fearful trembling, she suspected, not anger. She squinted and peered around Sebastian's torso. For heaven's sake, it was nothing more dangerous than a broom handle.

"What sort of devil be ye?"

"I should be asking you that."

"'Tis a demon, to be sure," the woman said. "Naked as sin.

Formed like Lucifer 'imself."

"Get the hell out," Sebastian said, each word a distinct threat. "Both of you. Or I'll snap your miserable necks with my bare hands."

For a tense moment, no one moved.

Finally, the broomstick-wielding man broke the silence. "Have at 'im, Fanny."

The woman rushed forward, wailing like a Valkyrie and raising a blunt cudgel over her head—one that appeared, from Mary's eyes, to be a rolling pin.

She thwacked Sebastian in the arm. "Take that, ye foul devil's spawn. Back to the fire and brimstone with ye."

Sebastian, clearly unwilling to strike out at a woman, ducked and raised his arms to protect his head. He turned his back to her.

Fanny skittered around him in circles, battering him about the shoulders. "Have that." *Thump.* "And that." *Thwack.* "I rebuke thee."

Meanwhile, the man remained in the doorway, apparently content to let his female counterpart do the fighting for them both.

Well, Mary decided two women could play at this game.

She leapt from the bed and launched herself at the woman, tackling her against the wall. "Stop that, you shrieking harpy."

"Get off me, ye demon's consort. Cavorting with the Devil in my man's and I's bed."

"That's no devil." Mary found the woman's ear and gave it a tweak. "That's your master you're bludgeoning."

Fanny gasped. She flung aside the rolling pin, and from Sebastian's pained shout, Mary deduced the thing had bounced off his toes.

"God keep us," Fanny breathed. "Dick, 'tis Lord Byrne 'imself."

"Y-yer lordship." The man in the door—Dick, she supposed—pulled the hat from his head and bowed. "Dick Cross. I'm the caretaker. And this is the missus, Fanny. We hadn't expected ye. A thousand apologies, milord."

"A thousand isn't nearly enough." Sebastian whipped the quilt from the bed and wrapped it about his hips. "Try multiplying that by a factor of a hundred."

Dick shuffled his feet. "Ciphering were never my strong point, milord."

Ignoring him, Sebastian went to Mary. "Are you hurt?"

"No. Not at all."

He turned to the caretaker and his wife. "That's a stroke of luck for the two of you."

"We'll leave ye alone, then." Fanny gathered up her rolling pin and inched toward the door, tugging her husband with her. "Ever so sorry to have interrupted yer night of sin."

"It's not a night of sin."

"We'll leave straightaway and let you be with yer lady of the evening."

Sebastian puffed with anger. "What are you—"

"Now, now. No shaming from our quarter," she added. "Only God can judge. Perhaps fornication's forgiven for the upper classes. Special dispensations from the Church, no doubt."

"Must say, she's a fair one," Dick put in. "A sight better than the wenches what walk the docks."

Fanny whacked her husband with the rolling pin. "What would ye know about the wenches what walk the docks?"

"Let me alone, woman. 'Tis no concern of yours. The master wouldn't truck with that sort. Got the quality goods, he has."

"Enough." Sebastian grabbed the caretaker by the shirt and lifted him onto his toes. "Insult my wife one more time, and I will shove that broomstick up your arse."

"Y-yer..." His eyes flicked to Mary. "Yer wife?"

"Yes. My wife. Lady Byrne. As of today."

"Beggin' apologies, milord. Milady. We didn't receive any word that ye'd married. Nor a notice that ye planned to be in residence."

"I can see by the state of this cottage that you didn't. Not that it's any excuse. Imagine my displeasure when I bring my bride for a seaside honeymoon, only to find the place in complete disarray. You ought to keep the house in readiness at all times. Instead, we arrived to find this place filthy and in disrepair."

"We've been feelin' poorly."

"Oh, I'll teach you what it is to feel poorly."

Mary decided to intervene. She laid a hand to his arm, gently. "Sebastian."

It was enough.

His demeanor softened. He gestured toward the door. "Begone, the both of you."

"Aye, aye. We'll jes' be in the kitchen, then."

"You'll be in the barn," he said. "We'll discuss the state of your employment—or lack of it—tomorrow."

After the couple had left, Mary and Sebastian returned to the bed. He turned her so that her back rested against his chest, spooning his body around hers. Keeping her warm and safe.

Her eyelids grew heavy. Heavens, what a day. It seemed impossible to bend her mind around it all. A jilting, an elopement, a decrepit honeymoon cottage.

And one fiery, passionate kiss. If a single kiss could create such a whirlwind of sensation, she could only imagine how their lovemaking would be. It boded well for the honeymoon, she thought. If only they hadn't been interrupted.

Mary pressed her lips together, trying not to giggle. In the end, she couldn't help it. She dissolved into laughter.

"What?"

"The rolling pin. The ciphering. Everything."

"It's not amusing."

"To the contrary. It's highly amusing. I've never been called a demon's consort before. You'll be laughing about it tomorrow."

"Doubtful."

"Very well. Perhaps you'll be laughing about it next year." *Or maybe the decade after that.*

"Go to sleep," he grumbled.

Just this once, she decided to obey his command.

CHAPTER 5

MARY WAS FIRST TO WAKE. The fire in the kitchen had gone cold, so she wriggled backward, curling into the heat of his body. He growled a little in his sleep. The hard, hot ridge of his erection jutted against her thigh. Apparently, one part of him was awake. A large part.

Her own intimate places softened. She felt a keen, hollow ache of curiosity.

Slowly, stealthily, she turned to face him, trying to muster the courage to steal a peek under the quilt. However, her carnal investigations were set aside when she glimpsed his face.

He looked so different in his sleep. Less troubled, more vulnerable. She stroked the thick, tawny hair back from his brow.

There it was, the tiny sunburst scar just beneath his hairline.

She remembered the night he'd been given that wound. Mary had been the only one awake, sitting in the kitchen with a cup of tea and reading over some papers. Sebastian had stumbled into the house well past midnight, his eye blackened and blood streaming from his hairline down to his chin.

Mary had set her work aside at once. She'd cleaned his wounds and applied a poultice to his blackened eye. He'd told her he'd been in a fight—someone he knew from Cambridge. But the story was just a story. He knew she'd noticed the remarkable similarity between the sunburst cut on his brow and the sunburst shape of his father's signet ring.

And she knew Sebastian had noticed the work that kept her up late. She'd been correcting the errors in contracts her father had drawn up for a client. That was the time when his mind had just begun to fail.

They had these little secrets, the two of them. Always unspoken, and yet always understood.

She pressed a kiss to his scar.

He stretched and yawned, then turned to stare up at the roof above. "I was hoping this cottage had been a nightmare." He rose from bed and went to retrieve his trousers. "I'm going to walk Shadow into the village and find the smithy. Once he's been shoed, I'll ride back and we'll leave for Ramsgate at once." He pulled his shirt over his head. "Stay abed. Get some more sleep."

Mary nodded in drowsy agreement and drew the quilt up to her chin.

However, the moment the door closed behind him, she jumped out of bed. She excavated her simplest, plainest frock from the depths of her trunk, dressed in haste, and had a look around the cottage.

Last night, she hadn't explored any of it, aside from the kitchen and the small room she now understood to be Dick and Fanny's bedchamber.

The cottage wasn't large, and it had been sorely neglected, but with a bit of work it could be a charming home. Downstairs, she explored a parlor with a large fireplace ideal for cozy nights in, and a dining room nowhere near large enough for a party, but more than sufficient for two.

A library rounded out the ground floor, and it was Mary's favorite room yet. Bookshelves covered the walls from floor to ceiling, and a massive mahogany desk lodged by the window, issuing a dare: *Just you try to budge me.*

She'd no desire to make the attempt.

Instead, she took a seat at the desk and ran her palms over the glossy wood. When she inhaled, her lungs filled with the scents of leather and tobacco and old books. A powerful wave of memories crashed through her.

The library was so much like Papa's.

Henry had never taken an interest in the law, but Mary had loved watching their father work. She'd steal out of bed on nights when she couldn't sleep, tiptoeing through the house to his study.

There, she'd find him poring over a legal reference or a making notes on a contract. He didn't scold her or chase her back to bed. Instead, he'd take her onto his lap and explain whatever task lay before him—in simple, but never condescending, language.

Her father had believed girls should be educated in all the same subjects as boys, and he'd encouraged Mary to form her own opinions and share them with confidence.

Most importantly, he'd always made time for her.

Sadly, his time on earth had been much too short. She missed him every day.

Swallowing back the lump in her throat, she left the study and made her way up the stairs to explore the cottage's bedchambers. There were three in total. Two small rooms, and a larger one for the master and mistress of the house.

She went to the window and opened it wide. A breathtaking view greeted her. The blue-green sea, frosted with whitecaps and sparkling with sunshine.

Beautiful.

She pressed a hand to her heart. In no time at all, she'd fallen in love with this cottage. It was the perfect place for a honeymoon.

They would not be leaving for Ramsgate today. Not if she had anything to say about it. However, if she meant to convince Sebastian, she had no time to waste.

She went outside and found the well. Once she'd drawn a full pail of water, she took it in both hands and—rather than carrying it inside the cottage—proceeded directly to the barn, where Dick and Fanny Cross lay snoring atop a mound of straw.

She dashed the water over them. "Wake up."

The caretaker and his wife jolted to life, sputtering.

"You will not find me an easy mistress to please," Mary said, "but at the moment I am your best friend. If you want any hope of keeping your posts, you'd best rouse yourselves and prepare to work your fingers to nubs. Do you understand me?"

The caretaker struggled to stand. "Yes, milady."

"Good." She set the bucket at the caretaker's feet. "You can begin by drawing more water and bringing it in to the kitchen. Fanny, gather up brooms, rags, soap, and some vinegar."

Fanny nodded.

"This cottage—or at least a fair part of it—*will* be presentable by the time your lord returns." Mary arched an eyebrow. "Or prepare to face the wrath of the demon's consort."

Within an hour, they had the kitchen swept and the cobwebs knocked from the corners. Mary had scrubbed the panes of the windows with vinegar and a drop of lemon oil. Dick brought in eggs from the henhouse, and Fanny produced bread, a slab of bacon, and some butter. In the cupboard, Mary found a jar of preserves and a locked tea caddy. She broke the rusted lock with a knife and was rewarded with a small stash of serviceable, if a bit stale-looking, tea.

By the time she had the kettle boiling, eggs and bacon frying, and bread sliced for toasting, her hair had begun to come loose, and perspiration dotted her brow. She meant to wash her face and pretty herself before Sebastian returned, but she didn't have a chance. The clop of Shadow's freshly shoed hooves on the lane told her he'd already returned.

She patted her hair, hastily untied her apron and cast it aside. At the last second, she adjusted the bouquet of wildflowers she'd picked on a whim earlier and crammed into a crockery vase.

As Sebastian came through the door, she clasped her hands together and tried not to appear as anxious as she felt inside. How silly, that she'd be nervous. But perhaps it was natural. This was her first morning as a wife, and she found herself eager for her husband's approval. Maybe he'd be impressed by everything she'd accomplished in only a few hours, and then he'd embrace the idea of domestic bliss.

My darling, you've worked a miracle. I can't imagine how I ever lived without you. Truly, you are the best of wives.

"Good morning." She smiled and prepared herself to receive his praise.

Instead, he shook his head. "Mary, what have you done?"

Sebastian gestured broadly at the kitchen. "What is all this?"

As he watched, the smile faded from her face. "It's breakfast," she said. "And we did a bit of tidying up."

The kitchen hadn't merely been "tidied up." It had undergone a complete transformation.

The spiders had been evicted from the corners, and the thick layer of dust had vanished from the fireplace mantel. The smell of fresh sea air breezed through the open window, and a pair of lacy curtains fluttered in the wind. Everything in the place had been scrubbed and polished to a gleam. Even the floor looked to have been scoured.

She must have worked every blessed minute he'd been away. Yet more impressive, it would seem she'd convinced Dick and Fanny Cross to do some labor, too.

The prettiest thing in the room, of course, was Mary herself. She was lovely as a Dutch painting. She'd dressed in a sage-green frock with cap sleeves and delicate lace edging. Her skin seemed to glow in the morning light, and her cheeks had a fetching blush. She wore her auburn hair in a loose, haphazard knot, and stray wisps had curled at her temples and the nape of her neck.

"You look as though someone stomped on your new hat," she said. "Don't you like it?"

"It's not that I don't like it. You shouldn't have put yourself to all this trouble, that's all. We're leaving for Ramsgate this morning."

"Yes, about that…" She chewed her bottom lip. "Let's at least have breakfast first. I'm hungry. And if I'm hungry, you must be starving."

Sebastian *was* starving. He hadn't had a bite to eat since breakfast yesterday, and that might as well have been last year. But since that kiss last night, another sort of hunger was tormenting him. He was ravenous for his wife.

While she loaded a plate for him, he washed his hands. Then he sat down to a feast. Fried eggs, bacon, toasted bread with butter and jam. How had she managed all this?

Eat first, his stomach growled. *Talk later.*

He attacked his food, downing four eggs, two rashers of bacon, and six points of buttered toast in a matter of minutes.

She filled his teacup for the third time. "Feeling human again?"

"Mostly."

When she bent over the table to pour his tea, he could glimpse not only the sweet, abundant curves of her breasts, but the dark, secret valley between them. If he didn't know better, he'd have thought she *meant* to give him the tempting view.

"I've been thinking." She propped an elbow on the table and rested her chin in her hand. "Instead of going on to Ramsgate, perhaps we could stay here."

"No." He drained his tea and set down the teacup with authority. "We're not going to spend another night in this cottage."

"But—"

"I'm taking you to an inn. Or a hotel. The finest establishment Ramsgate has to offer, whatever that might be."

And wherever they stayed, he would demand the best room. Not merely a room, but a suite. An apartment with a soaking tub and a private dining room.

And, most importantly, separate bedchambers.

Last night, that simple goodnight kiss had nearly been his undoing. This morning he was slavering like a dog, after just one glimpse of her breasts. If he shared a bed with her again tonight, he'd risk losing all control.

"But Ramsgate is so popular this time of year. It will be full to bursting with ladies on holiday. Too many prying eyes. Someone will recognize us, and then the rumors will be all over England."

"Unless we're visiting the shops or the seaside, we won't attract notice."

She laughed to herself. "Sebastian, you are like a walking exhibition of Grecian sculpture. Wherever you go, you attract notice. Once we ride into town together, we may as well put a notice in the *The Times*. Can't we remain here and avoid the gossip? In just one morning, I've already improved the kitchen. Give it a few more days, and this cottage will be positively charming, you'll see."

He relented. "Very well. If that's truly what you want."

"It's what I want. If it weren't, you know I wouldn't hesitate to tell you."

"This is true." He tapped a finger on the table's edge. "But I have one condition. We must do something about our sleeping arrangements."

"I wholeheartedly agree." She pushed back from the table. "Which is why I've something to show you upstairs."

CHAPTER 6

SEBASTIAN FOLLOWED HER UP THE stairs, feeling strangely wary. Just what sort of surprise did she have in mind?

"I found it in the attic," she chattered on the way. "It must be centuries old. We dusted it off with rags, and Dick carried it down to this room. It's the largest." She led him into a bedchamber branching off the corridor and made a sweeping arm gesture toward one corner. "See? It's a bed."

Sebastian blinked at the jumble of timbers. "That's not a bed. That's firewood."

"It's a disassembled bed. And I think you'd have a difficult time burning it. It's heavier than bricks." She lifted one end of a plank. "I don't even know what kind of wood this is."

He ran his fingers over the surface and examined the grain. "I'm not certain, either." He picked up a lathe-turned wooden leg. Or was it a finial? Time had coated the wood in a dark, impenetrable patina that he couldn't even gouge with his thumbnail.

"I don't think it's English. What style of carving do you make that out to be?" She leaned close to him, offering a piece decorated with a chain of stylized wildflowers.

He shrugged. "Swedish, maybe?"

"Well, wherever it came from, it's going to be slept in tonight. I already told Fanny to stuff a mattress tick with fresh straw. We just have to put the frame together. All the pieces seem to be here." She took hold of a board and lifted it, eyeing the dimensions. "Do you think this is a slat, perhaps?" She tipped her head to regard it from another angle. "Or a rail?"

With a shrug, she carried it to the center of the room and laid it flat on the floor.

Sebastian poked through the stack of planks and pieces. "Simple mortise and tenon joints. Shouldn't take long." He chose two pieces that looked as though they'd been hewn to fit together, and the tenon slipped into the mortise like a hand into a fitted glove. "That's one joint connected."

Mary paused in the act of laying a second plank next to the first, lining up their bottom edges for comparison. "Oh, no. We're not going about it all higgledy-piggledy. We don't know if those two pieces belong together."

"Of course they do. They were made to fit."

"You can't be sure of that."

He held up the joint for her, sliding the tenon in and out of its slot a few times. "Is that not proof enough?"

"Perhaps there are two that would fit the same hole."

"Well, I don't know how you propose to complete this bed without joining pieces together. Did you find a leaflet in the attic with instructions? In Swedish?"

"Of course I didn't. That's why we need a plan. Now, we're going to arrange all these pieces neatly in rows first, laying them out on the floor so that we can count and compare. We'll put a little mark on the similar ones. Plank A, plank B, and so on. Then we'll chalk up a diagram on the floor and—"

"I thought you wanted to sleep in this bed tonight. Not next week."

"What's wrong with planning first?"

"You're making it more complicated than it needs to be." He lifted the wide, flat headboard and placed it against the wall. "Is this where you want it?"

"A little to the left." She waved him to the side. "No, back to the right a touch. There."

He set the piece down, then returned to the stack of timbers and selected the largest. "This goes at the foot of the bed."

"Are you certain?"

"Yes." He lifted the board with a grunt, swung it about, and positioned it parallel to the headboard. "Hold that in place."

She sounded skeptical. "So you've done this before. Assembled beds."

"Loads of them."

"Loads of them? When and where was that?"

He gave a strangled groan of impatience. "Just trust me, Mary. I have it all under control. This won't take but a few minutes."

One hour later

Mary pulled to a standing position and massaged the wrenched muscle at the small of her back. "It's still not right. That one doesn't go there."

"Yes, it does." As she stood observing, Sebastian tried once again to shove the wooden tab of one rail into the slot carved into a leg.

"See? It doesn't fit."

"It will fit. There aren't any other pieces left that it could be."

"It's probably one of the pieces we've already used. It could be anywhere." She gestured at the half-finished bed frame. "Or maybe the right piece was never here to begin with. This was why I wanted to make a plan, you know."

He gave her a look. "Don't be that way."

"Don't be *what* way? Right?" She huffed a breath, blowing a wisp of hair off her cheek. "There's nothing else to be done. We'll have to take it apart and start over."

He swore with passion. "We are not taking the thing apart. And this piece does fit." He glared at the wood, as though he could force it into submission through the sheer power of masculine brooding. "I just need a mallet."

"I think *I* need a mallet," she grumbled.

"What?"

"Nothing," she chirped with bright innocence. "I'll find you that mallet straightaway."

Two hours after that

Mary sat in the corner of the bedchamber with her knees hugged to her chest.

With a grimace of effort, Sebastian gave the bed-key one final twist to tighten the ropes. *"There."*

Mary watched as he dragged the freshly stuffed mattress tick onto the frame.

She would have offered to help. But by this point, she knew better than to touch—or even breathe on—his work in progress. And God forbid she make a helpful suggestion.

He stood back, straightened, and used his sleeve to wipe the sweat streaming off his brow. "Finished."

She stared at the bed, biting her tongue.

"Well…?" He propped his hands on his hips. "I told you I'd have it put together."

"Yes, but—"

"But *what*, Mary? But *what*?"

"But there are three boards left over." She stood and pointed. "Where do they go?"

He gave a one-shouldered shrug. "Must be surplus."

"Surplus? What centuries-old bed comes with surplus pieces?"

"This one."

She rubbed her temples.

"It doesn't matter." He took a pace backward. "It's sturdy enough to hold an ox. Just watch."

"Sebastian, wait."

He took two running steps and launched himself at the bed, twisting in midair so that he landed on his back. All sixteen stone of him, squarely plunked in the center of the mattress.

"See?" He folded his hands under his head and gave her a smug look. "I told you it was st—"

Crash.

One side of the bed frame collapsed beneath his weight, tipping the mattress at an angle and shunting him to the floor.

Mary stood very quietly.

He stared blankly at the ceiling. "Go on. Say it."

"Say what?"

"I know you're thinking it. You may as well have out with it."

"I'm not sure what you mean," she lied.

"Yes, you are."

"Let's go downstairs for some tea."

"For the love of God, Mary. I know it's coming. Just say it now."

"I don't—"

"*Say it.*"

"I told you so!" she shouted. "Is that what you want to hear? I told you this would happen. I told you you were doing it wrong. I. Told. You. So."

He stared up at the ceiling, infuriatingly silent.

Mary, however, was only getting started. "I wanted to make a plan. But noooo. You don't need a plan. You've assembled loads of beds. You know exactly which pieces fit where. Because you, like all men, have a magical nugget of furniture-assembly expertise dangling in your left bollock." She flung a hand at the unused boards. "*Surplus?* You're telling me sixteenth-century Swedish artisans made *surplus?*"

He finally pulled himself off the floor. "I"—he jabbed a finger in his chest—"told you"—the finger turned on Mary—"that we should go to Ramsgate. Where they *have* beds already. Assembled beds. Comfortable beds. Beds just sitting there in well-appointed rooms, waiting for someone to use them."

"I don't want to go to Ramsgate."

"Yes, so you told me. You're very keen to avoid the gossip. God forbid you be seen with me in public."

Her chin jerked. "What?"

"I mean, you could have been married to Giles Perry, a barrister's son with a promising political career. Instead, you're with the disgraced Lord Byrne. The one who dirties his hands in trade, because his father drove the estate straight up to the brink of insolvency and only failed to take it over the edge because he drank himself to death first. Those ladies on holiday would cluck their tongues, wouldn't they? All of England would be shaking their heads."

"Sebastian. You can't think I'm ashamed of having married you."

"Of course not," he said mockingly. "You prefer to spend the week squirreled away with me in some ramshackle cottage, scrubbing floors and assembling furniture, when you could be staying in the finest seaside resort."

"I *do* prefer it."

"To be sure." He rolled his eyes to the ceiling. "Why wouldn't you? Just look at all the fun we're having right this very moment."

She shook her head. "I can't believe this."

"Well, I can't believe you. It's clear you're trying to persuade me into remaining here. Vases of flowers on the table, breakfast." He gave the unfinished bed a disgusted look. *"That."*

"Well, pardon me for attempting to make our honeymoon cottage just the tiniest bit romantic."

"It's not supposed to be romantic. You were jilted by your groom. I stepped in to marry you out of loyalty to your brother. It's not as though we clasped hands and ran away into the sunset, Mary." He swept her with a cold look. "We're not in love."

His words struck her in the chest with such force, she couldn't breathe.

And she hadn't any logical reason to feel hurt. He was only speaking the truth. She simply hadn't realized, until this moment, how much she wished the truth were different.

"I…" She blinked rapidly, forcing back a hot tear.

He pushed his hands through his hair and cursed. "Mary, don't listen to me. We're both exhausted, and—"

"It's all right, Sebastian. You don't need to explain." Mary backed her way toward the door. She had to escape this room. The walls were closing in on her, squeezing at her heart. "We can leave for Ramsgate whenever you're ready."

CHAPTER 7

It took Sebastian about five seconds to realize what a bastard he'd been. However, he forced himself to wait a few hours before attempting to tell her so. She needed time and space to breathe, and so did he.

As penance, he did exactly as she'd suggested from the start.

He took the whole damn bed apart, sorted the pieces by size and function, chalked an outline on the floor, and wouldn't you know. It all fit together as it should.

When he finally went looking for her, she wasn't in the cottage. He searched through every room, growing increasingly concerned, until he returned to the master bedchamber and happened to look out the window. She was down by the water, walking along the sandy shore.

He picked his way down the winding path to the beach. As she came into view, he paused a moment to recover his breath.

Her lovely profile was to him as she stared out over the ocean. The breeze whipped at her filmy summer frock and toyed with the loose strands of her hair. Before she walked on, she stopped and bent to gather something from the sand, adding it to a collection in her palm.

"Mary!" He jogged down the beach until he reached her side. Once he'd reached her, he searched his brain for the right words. Only three came to mind. "I'm a jackass."

She ducked her head. "You're not alone."

They walked on together.

"What is it you're collecting?" he asked.

"Cockleshells." She held them up for him to see. "Couldn't resist."

Mary, Mary, quite contrary, how does your garden grow?
With silver bells and cockleshells, and pretty maids all in a row.

Whenever she dug her heels into an argument, Henry had teased her with that rhyme, even long past the age when they should have outgrown it. Sebastian supposed that was what brothers did.

She poked through her little collection with a fingertip. "Perhaps I'll put them in the garden, with some silver bells and pretty maids all in a row. It would be a nice remembrance, wouldn't it?"

"I think he'd like that. A chance to tease you from beyond the grave."

"Henry did have a point. I've tried to temper my inclination toward contrariness, but it never seems to work. I'm my father's daughter, and it's in my blood. A bit of rousing debate was like a game for us. One we both enjoyed." She gave him a cautious look. "But I know it's not that way in everyone's family."

It certainly hadn't been that way in Sebastian's home. No good-natured arguments between his parents. Only threats and accusations and the sound of china shattering against the wall.

"I'll try to be more patient," he said.

"I'll try not to be right all the time," she teased. "I suppose this means our first argument as a married couple is out of the way."

The knot in his chest unraveled. Apologies accomplished, just like that. He'd learned so much from his time spent in the Clayton house. It was in that house he'd learned to be a man.

Henry had taught him what it meant to be a friend.

Mr. Clayton had taught him what it meant to be responsible.

Mary had taught him what it meant to yearn. To sense there was something more beneath the surface of a friendship. To wish he knew how to bring that into the light. To wonder if he could ever deserve it.

She stopped to gather another cockleshell and turned it over between her fingers, inspecting it. Dissatisfied, she cast it away. "Imagine if I'd married Giles. I would have been 'Mary Perry, quite contrary.' How dreadful."

He pulled a face. "Dreadful, indeed. Why did you accept his proposal if you didn't love him?"

"Considering his political aspirations, I told myself I could do some good as his wife. That was before I realized he was only motivated by ambition. He didn't truly care about serving the people. I'd have gone mad as his wife, trying to hold my tongue in company and support his bland political positions without expressing my own thoughts. I'm so relieved that I didn't have to marry him."

"Are you?"

"Yes. In fact, I'm more than relieved. I'm happy."

Happy.

The word made Sebastian's brain spin.

Naturally, he agreed with the assessment that she and Perry would have made a disastrous match. He'd known that from the first. Differences of opinion aside, the man simply wasn't good enough for her.

But could she truly be *happy* to have been jilted?

That was too much to believe. In all likelihood, she was merely soothing her own feelings. Telling herself it was for the best, in order to ease the pain.

In time, he'd do his best to make her happy in truth.

"I have something for you." He reached into his breast pocket, fishing around for his small gift. "I brought it back from the village, but I forgot about it earlier, what with all the—"

Her eyebrows lifted. "Surplus?"

"Exactly." He smiled a little. "While I was at the smithy with Shadow, I had the blacksmith make this." He withdrew the tiny circle of polished silver and placed it in her palm. "It's only temporary. You'll have something much finer at the first opportunity. But for now, it's the best I could do."

She regarded it wordlessly.

Sebastian shifted his weight from one foot to the other. At the smithy, it had seemed a good idea. Now that he saw it resting in her delicate hand, the ring looked crude and paltry. "You don't have to wear it."

She clamped her fingers over it, closing the ring in her fist. "Certainly I'm going to wear it. Don't think I'll give it back now."

He exhaled with relief.

She slid the thin, humble band onto her third finger. "It was thoughtful of you to bring it." She stretched up to kiss his cheek. "Thank you."

As she pulled back, he wrapped an arm around her, keeping her close. His gaze dropped to her pale-pink lips.

Irresistible.

He kissed her, and she leaned into his embrace. Her frock was wonderfully thin, and her breasts melted against him. He explored her mouth with possessive strokes of his tongue, taking more, and then yet more. She offered everything he asked, and then began to take from him, too. She laced her fingers together at the back of his neck and clung tight, making him her captive.

Love, never set me free.

His hand began to wander of its own accord, sweeping down her spine and over the flare of her hip, coming to settle on the curve of her bottom. He flexed his fingers, claiming a plump handful of flesh and drawing her body to his with a firm, swift motion. His cock grew and stiffened, pulsing against the softness of her belly.

He bent his head and kissed his way down her neck. Her little gasp of pleasure made him swell with triumph.

More. He wanted more.

He stroked her breast through the thin muslin of her frock, palming and kneading her softness. Her nipple tightened. He strummed the sensitive peak, brushing his thumb back and forth in a teasing caress. She moaned faintly, and he covered her mouth with his own, drinking in the sound of her pleasure.

When the kiss ended, he readied an insincere apology.

I was carried away, didn't mean to press you too far, we'll go as slowly as you please, et cetera…

But she spoke first.

"Sebastian." She wet her lips. "Make love to me tonight."

Mary held her breath as she gazed into his eyes.

Sebastian was silent for so long, she began to grow self-conscious. And confused. He'd just explored her body as shamelessly and thoroughly as a Viking plundering a medieval village. How could he be shocked by her request?

He shook his head. "It's too soon."

"We're married. This is our honeymoon," she said. "Once we leave, you'll have your business affairs, I'll be settling into a new home. There seems no better opportunity than now."

In fact, she worried that this might be the only opportunity. If they didn't forge a strong connection before leaving Kent, she might be waiting a very long time for another chance.

"It's only been one day," he said. "You're not over your disappointment."

"I told you, I didn't love him. Perhaps I ought to be heartsick, but I'm not. I'm relieved."

"That doesn't mean you're ready to leap into bed with me."

"No doubt it will be awkward the first time. But that's always going to be the case, no matter how long we wait." She turned her gaze around the empty beach. "Besides, there's little else to do for amusement. Unless you'd rather play cards all night."

He groaned. "Playing cards with you is like trying to hold back the tide—there's no way to win."

"Fair enough," she said. "No cards. Which brings us back to bed."

He stared into the distance.

"Sebastian, even though I wasn't expecting to wed you, I've always found you attractive."

In fact, she'd never grasped the strength of that attraction until she realized how her feelings toward Giles paled in comparison. Giles didn't make her hot all over with just a simple glance. He didn't even make her lukewarm.

She hesitated. "Of course, I don't expect you to say you feel similarly about me."

He caught her chin and tilted her gaze to his. "You," he said darkly, "make me ache with wanting."

Oh.

Sweet heavens. She'd known he'd say something kind. He'd compliment her eyes, maybe, or possibly her complexion. Call her pretty, perhaps. But his intense confession of desire had caught her entirely unawares.

She'd gone fishing for a few small compliments, and somehow she'd harpooned a whale.

He took her by the arms. "I know you enjoy arguing, but this is one matter where I will not be moved. We had a rushed wedding, but we're not going to rush this. I've too much pride to make it a hurried, joyless affair. I'm going to learn every inch of your body, and you're going to learn every inch of mine. And when I know you're ready…when you're aching for me every bit as fiercely as I'm aching for you…that's when I'll make love to you. Not a moment before."

Oh, Sebastian. That won't require nearly so much effort as you think.

Her own body needed no further coaxing. But how was she going to convince *him*?

"We'd better go back." He turned them in the direction of the cottage and offered his arm. "Dick and Fanny are preparing us a proper dinner, I'm told. Four courses, to be served in the dining room."

"Oh, my. I think they're scrambling to please you so they can remain in your employment."

"As well they should be."

As they neared the cottage, they spied a coach coming up the lane.

"It's here. Thank God." Sebastian strode toward the house with renewed vigor.

"Whose coach is that?"

"It's mine. I sent an express from Canterbury, telling my housekeeper I'd be here. I asked her to send the carriage with some of my belongings from Town."

Mary lingered behind him as he went to greet the coachman. Together, the two men unstrapped a trunk from the back of the carriage. Sebastian carried it inside, undid the latches, and opened it.

"It's a miracle. I am now in possession of clean shirts, a razor, shaving soap and tooth powder… All the modern necessities of a civilized life." To her, he added, "And *we* have a coach and driver. We can go wherever you like. If Ramsgate doesn't suit you, you may have your choice of destination. Bath. The Wye valley. The Lake district. The Cotswolds. Hell, why not Paris?"

Mary laughed at his last suggestion. Inside, her feelings were conflicted.

She was running out of excuses to stay in this cottage. She loved this place, but she had to admit she would love it better after a few months of repairs and deep cleaning. And to be truthful, she'd always wanted to see the Cotswolds.

But what she wanted more than anything was to prevent Sebastian from pulling away. He'd made it clear that he felt compelled by honor to observe an irrational, indefinite waiting period before they consummated their marriage. And yet he'd confessed to desiring her, just now.

You make me ache with wanting.

A shiver traveled from her scalp to her toes.

Knowing Sebastian as well as she did, Mary could easily guess what self-sacrificing compromise he'd arrived at to ease his conscience. He'd keep his distance from her, in whatever way he could. Sleeping in separate beds. Pursuing different interests. Burying himself in whatever work he could find.

"We can't leave until after dinner," she said. "Dick and Fanny will be sorely disappointed, after going to all that work."

"The horses need to be watered and fed, as well."

Mary gathered her courage. "You're now in possession of evening attire. And I have a full trunk of gowns I've never had the chance to use. Since Mr. and Mrs. Cross have promised us a formal dinner, why don't we dress accordingly?"

"If you like." He scratched his jaw. "I need a bath and a shave, anyway. Shall we say dinner in an hour, then?"

"Perfect."

CHAPTER 8

WHILE MARY DISAPPEARED UPSTAIRS TO bathe and dress, Sebastian adopted the study as his own dressing chamber. He took more care with his appearance than he had on the day he'd been presented at Court. He scrubbed, lathered, shaved, combed, brushed, dressed, and buttoned. He even polished his boots to a mirror gleam. Beau Brummel he was not, but he didn't want to let Mary down.

He'd always thought it a shame that she never had a proper Season in London. It wasn't something her father could have afforded, he supposed. The Claytons were an established and well-respected family, but the second son of a fourth son of a landed gentleman didn't come into much, if any, inheritance. So no social debut for Mary, and now she'd missed her own wedding day—which was meant to be a bride's chance to shine.

She deserved to have been admired by scores of gentlemen, on any number of occasions. Life and circumstance had prevented it. So Sebastian was going to smarten up, stand at the bottom of those stairs, and admire her enough to equal a hundred men put together.

Almighty God.

Perhaps a thousand men put together.

She descended the stairs in a shimmering gown of sapphire blue that precisely captured the brilliant hue of her eyes. Pearls studded the elegant upsweep of her auburn hair, in much the same way that charming freckles dotted the pale shelf of her décolleté.

"You're beautiful," he said, stating it as a simple fact. Because it was.

Her blue eyes widened with surprise. But she shouldn't have been surprised.

"I've always thought you were beautiful. From the first time I saw you."

"Oh, come now. I won't believe that. I was your best friend's irritating older sister."

"You were my best friend's irritating and *beautiful* older sister. And I was the typical adolescent boy, unable to think about anything else. There were summers when just being in the same room with you nearly drove me out of my skin."

Her eyes softened. "I never knew you admired me like that."

"Oh, I admired you." He looked her over. "I admired you a great deal, and often. Sometimes more than once a day."

She gave him a playful punch on the shoulder. "Se-*bas*-tian Lawrence Ives."

By God, he was a selfish bastard. She'd spent more than an hour readying herself for his eyes alone, and all he wanted was to turn her about, lead her straight back up to the bedchamber, and give her a ravishing that would undo all her effort in a matter of seconds.

Sebastian dragged his thoughts back to proper gentlemanly behavior. He should not, would not make love to her tonight. He would banish the thought entirely.

Naturally, the next words from her mouth were, "I notice you assembled the bed."

So much for banishment.

He took her hand, bowed over it, and kissed her fingers. "Lady Byrne. May I have the honor of escorting you in to supper?"

"Thank you, Lord Byrne. You may."

Mary sent up a quiet prayer as he led her into the dining room, where the table had been set with the finest chipped plates and mismatched cutlery the cottage had to offer.

Please, let this work.

The gown seemed to have been a good start. If Dick and Fanny had managed a dinner that was the tiniest bit romantic, and if she plied him with a few glasses of wine, perhaps he would set down those shields composed of misplaced duty and loyalty, just for the night.

To the side of the room, Dick stood at ramrod-straight attention, holding a rather shabby-looking towel draped over his left forearm. His coat was buttoned, and he'd tied a red kerchief about his neck as a cravat. A severe part divided his hair into unequal halves—save for an errant cowlick that bounced with every mild stirring of the air.

He bowed deeply at the waist. "Milord. Milady."

"Good evening, Mr. Cross," Mary said, as Sebastian helped her into her chair. "This all looks so lovely. You and Mrs. Cross must have worked very hard."

"Oh, aye." Dick poured wine into their glasses. "But we're not afraid of hard work, milady. Never did you meet such devoted servants as me and my Fanny."

Sebastian reached for his wine, clearly sensing the theme of the dinner unfolding. *One-Hundred-and-One Reasons Not to Sack Your Caretaker.*

Dick brought out a tureen and a woven basket, over which had been draped a small square of linen. "Yer first course, milord and milady. Soup and pain."

"Soup and *what?*" Sebastian echoed.

"Pain." Dick ladled soup into Mary's bowl.

Mary looked at the greasy beef broth. Then she met Sebastian's inquiring gaze and shrugged in response. *I have no idea.*

"Don't make no sense to me either, milord. But the missus says everything's French tonight." He waggled his fingers in a mocking gesture. "La-di-dah."

As he left, he whisked the cloth off the basket between them, revealing the contents.

Bread. Or, as the French would call it, *pain.*

"Oh, dear." Mary pressed a hand to her mouth. "This does not bode well."

"Let's just eat." Sebastian raised his spoon and sipped from it once, then set it down. "On second thought, let's not eat this." He nodded in her direction. "How do you find the pain? Tolerable?"

"Stop," she pleaded. "Don't make me laugh. They'll hear it."

Once the soup had been cleared away, Dick returned with a

covered oval platter, which he placed on the table with a flourish. Mary crossed her fingers and her toes, hoping for better this time.

"Second course, milord and milady. Poison." He bowed. "Enjoy."

After Dick had retreated, Mary stared at the covered platter. "Tell me he didn't say 'poison'."

"I believe he did." Sebastian tilted his head. "Do we dare lift the dome for a peek?"

"I'm not looking. You look."

"Maybe we should just ask for more pain instead."

"Oh, you." She plucked a roll from the basket and lobbed it at him. "I'll give you pain."

He lifted a finger to his lips. "Shh."

In the kitchen, Dick and Fanny could be heard having a squabble of their own.

"Woman, what do ye have me sayin' out there? Servin' poison to his lordship."

"I told ye, 'tis right here in the cookery book. P-O-I-S-S-O-N. Poison. That's what they call it."

"Oh, aye. That's what the Frenchies *want* ye to believe. *That's* how they get you."

Sebastian lifted the lid from the platter, revealing precisely what they both now expected: a steamed fish.

"*Voila*," he said. "*Poisson.*" He reached for the fillet knife. "Shall I serve you some, my lady?"

"You try it first."

"I *am* known for living dangerously." He took a bite. Chewed. Sat a moment in thought. "It's not poisoned. But it's also not good."

By the time Dick returned with the third course, the dining room was thick with suspense. In lieu of eating, Sebastian and Mary had spent the past several minutes placing bets on what disastrous dish they'd be served next.

"'Ere we are." Dick plunked two shallow serving bowls on the table. "Stewed chicken and mash."

"Really?" Well, that was disappointing.

"*Cocky vein!*" Fanny stormed out from the kitchen. "Lord above ye, man. How many times did I say it. It's cocky vein and pumpery." She swept her husband with a withering glance. "Have a bit of class, ye old fool."

"Oh, I'm the fool, am I?" Dick followed her back into the

kitchen, carrying on in a loud voice. "Yer the one what'll have us sacked before I even serve the chocolate mouse."

The shouting and arguing continued, interspersed with the banging of pots and pans.

Cringing, Mary poked at the *coq au vin* and gave the dish of *pommes purée* a cautious stir. It was the consistency of paste.

So much for a romantic dinner.

"Perhaps we'd be better off in Ramsgate after all," she said, resigned. "I'd best pack my things. Do you think they'd notice if we just slipped upstairs?"

"Not for another hour or two, at least." He threw down his serviette. "Come along, then. Let's make our escape."

Together, they crept up the stairs to the bedchamber and shut the door behind them. Once they were alone, she couldn't help but laugh. "The worst part of it is, I'm so hungry."

"Take heart. If we make haste, we're less than an hour's drive from a proper meal."

She turned her back to him. "Will you help me with the buttons and laces? I need to change for the journey."

He hesitated. "I'm not adept with those things."

"I'm sure you'll manage."

He hadn't been joking about his ineptitude. As he plucked at the hooks and wrestled with the buttons, Mary was strangely encouraged. It was comforting to know he hadn't amassed *too* much practice disrobing women.

Once he had the back of her gown undone, the tapes of her petticoats unknotted, and the laces of her stays untied, he stepped back a few paces. "There you are. I'll step out into the corridor while you—"

"Don't be silly."

She turned around, hastily shoving her gown and petticoats to the floor, and setting aside her corset. She stepped out from the mound of silk and crinoline, standing before him in only a lacy, light blue chemise. One she'd taken in at the seams an inch here and there, so that it clung to her breasts and hugged her hips.

Mary pulled the pins from her hair one by one, then shook out her upsweep with a sensuous toss of her head. A motion that not coincidentally pushed her breasts high.

She'd come this far. She might as well be completely shameless.

Neither wifely homemaking or romantic dinners had succeeded in changing his mind. She had only one strategy left: seduction.

And she had absolutely no idea what she was doing.

His reaction wasn't quite what she'd been hoping for. He frowned at her body as though it were an arithmetic problem he couldn't solve.

"What is it? Don't you like what you see?"

"I can't say that I do, not entirely. You're a vision of beauty, but you're standing there in a negligee meant for your honeymoon with another man."

"Oh, is that the problem?"

She slipped the chemise over her shoulders and drew her arms out of the sleeves. The garment dropped to the floor in a lacy puddle.

"There," she said. "No more negligee. Problem solved."

CHAPTER 9

NO, SEBASTIAN THOUGHT TO HIMSELF.

No, his problem was definitely not solved. His problem was growing by the moment, hardening against the placket of his trousers.

"Don't play games," he warned, keeping his distance a few paces away. "If you don't truly want this…"

"I want this." She crossed to him, reached for his hand, and placed it on her breast. "I want you."

That was it.

Restraint, depleted. Argument, over. Decision, made.

There was only so much temptation a man could take from the woman who'd been the center of his every torrid fantasy. If she wanted him, she was going to get him. Every last, aching inch.

He grabbed her by the backside and lifted her straight off the floor so that her legs wrapped around his hips. Then he carried her toward the bed.

"Wait," she said. "Are you sure it will hold us?"

In answer, he simply tumbled with her onto the mattress. She tensed and held her breath.

When the bed didn't collapse, he arched an eyebrow in chastisement. "You know, you should have a little more faith in your husband."

"You're right. In the future, I will."

"Good."

She didn't need to know that the bed was now sturdy because

he'd followed her instructions. He'd keep that to himself.

Now that he had her beneath him, he brushed a light kiss to her lips and then trailed his mouth downward, making an arrow-straight path for her hardened left nipple.

He'd been waiting more than a decade to taste her there.

He swirled his tongue over the tight pink peak, and then drew her nipple into his mouth, suckling her lightly. She bucked and moaned beneath him, and he pulled harder still. He transferred his attention to the other breast, licking over her nipple and then painting her breast in widening circles.

She was so soft, so sweet. He could have spent a full night treasuring and nuzzling her bosom alone—and someday, he vowed, he would—but tonight, his body clamored with impatience for more.

He rose up on his knees to yank at his cravat and wrestle out of his topcoat. She helped him in the effort, unbuttoning his waistcoat and tugging his shirt free of his trousers. When he was finally bared to the waist, he lowered himself atop her. His blood sang when their bodies met, skin to skin.

He slid a hand down her body, reaching between her thighs to explore her silken heat. She gasped and bit her lip. He held her gaze as he caressed and explored. With his thumb, he covered the swollen bundle of nerves at the crest of her sex, rubbing gently back and forth. Her breathing quickened, and her eyes glazed with pleasure.

"Good?" he asked.

She nodded. "Very."

He bent his head to kiss her neck, then dipped lower to her breasts and belly, making his way to her mound.

Her thighs clamped down on his shoulders. "Wait."

Sebastian waited. He'd waited more than a decade already. What were a few minutes more?

She pushed up on her elbows, looking down at him. "What are you doing?"

"I mean to kiss you." He pressed his thumb against her. "Here."

"Are you—" She broke off, distracted by his touch. "Are you sure?"

"Yes." He clucked his tongue. "Not three minutes ago, you promised to have a little more faith in your husband."

"I should know better than to say such things." She lay back and flung her wrist over her eyes. "Very well. Do what you like."

He smiled with devilish intent. "I'm going to do what you'll like, too."

When he laid his mouth to her…well, to *her*…Mary nearly jumped out of her skin. The pleasure was so keen, so unspeakably bright. One flutter of his tongue against her most sensitive place, and she writhed beneath him.

The sweetest torture.

Within moments, he had her responding to him with startling intensity. Her pleasure mounted at an unprecedented pace. She began to gasp and moan, lifting her hips to seek more contact. Then he slid a finger inside her, and the blissful stretch sent her over the edge. She cried out and convulsed with release. Her intimate muscles pulsed around his finger.

When the pleasure had left her wrung out and panting, he slid back up her body. He reached between them to unbutton the falls of his trousers. Then he found her hand and brought it to his erection. "Touch me."

She explored his full length with her fingertips. The softness, the ridges, the smooth skin at the tip, and the hardness that underpinned everything. She encircled his shaft, stroking lightly up and down. His resulting moan was immensely gratifying.

He lowered himself atop her, and she felt the broad crown of his erection prodding at her entrance. "Are you ready?" His voice was hoarse, strained.

She nodded, unsure if it was the truth.

He pressed against her, and then inside her, stretching her body to accommodate his. She winced with the pain of it, but tried not to cry out. The last thing she wanted was for him to stop.

He loved her in slow, gentle, steady strokes. Even when his arm muscles trembled with tension, and his breathing was harsh. He took care of her, guarding her even from the strength of his own need.

Until the very end, when his pace faltered for a moment. When he resumed, it was in a faster, harder rhythm. His gruff, masculine sounds of pleasure thrilled her. She clutched his shoulders tight.

With a final, deep thrust, he collapsed atop her, shuddering with release.

Afterward, they held each other tight. No talking or kissing. Just breathing and existing together in the most simple, essential of ways.

He drew in a deep breath and released it as a growl, wrapping his arms around her and squeezing tight. "You."

She smiled. "You."

He lay back on the bed, and she rested her head on his chest.

"It's quiet downstairs," she said. "Fanny and Dick stopped arguing."

"Do you think they killed each other with rolling pins, or poisoned themselves?"

"More likely they went out to the stables and fell asleep. But whichever it was, I hope they cleaned the kitchen first."

As he held her, tenderly stroking her hair, Mary's conscience began to needle her. "There's something I should tell you," she said, hoping he'd take the revelation well. "Something I should have told you before we married."

"There's something I should have told you, too."

"What's that?" She was happy for him to go first.

"I want a family. I should have told you this before you agreed to elope with me. But it's not only that I need an heir. I want our child—hopefully, our children—to have a true home."

Oh, Sebastian.

He rolled onto his back and stared up at the ceiling. "My youth was a string of broken promises. You know that. You were there. How many Christmases did I spend at your house when my own father failed to collect me from school?"

"I don't know. But we were always happy to have you."

"You pitied me," he said. "The worst part was, you expected my presence, every year. Always a place set at the table, small gifts wrapped and waiting. Packets of sweets, fishing lures. I always assumed you scavenged a few odds and ends from about the house to give me, so that I wouldn't feel left out. Until the year you knitted me a muffler. You probably don't recall."

"Of course I do. I made Henry one, as well."

"I still have it, you know. Blue and gold stripes, my house colors at school. That's when I finally understood. A muffler in my house colors couldn't have been produced on a moment's notice. You had to have knitted it in advance, and you had it wrapped and waiting."

"Sebastian…"

"You knew. You all knew what I didn't want to believe. That my father's excuses were inventions, and his promises meant nothing. He would never keep his word to come for me. I should have realized it myself." He passed a hand over his face. "I'd never felt so stupid."

Mary sat up in bed. "You should not have felt stupid," she told him. "You were a boy who wanted to believe in his father. There's no shame in that. I'm only sorry he never lived up to your hopes."

"You can't know how it feels. It's like being tied to a cartwheel, tumbling from hope to disappointment over and over again. Eventually, your spirit is simply crushed. I won't put a child through that." His eyes met hers. "Can you understand?"

She nodded.

"So it's not enough for me to simply sire an heir and be done with it. I want to be a good father. To be there for every Christmas, every birthday. Teach our children to ride and fish, patch up their scrapes, put them to bed at night. I know it's more than I let you believe when we eloped. I was selfish. Because I knew if I had any chance at that life, it would have to be with you. If you not for you and Henry and your father, I wouldn't know what family is."

"You darling man." She leaned over and kissed his lips. "Nothing would make me happier than a family with you. Nothing."

"You're certain?"

"Have you ever known me to be otherwise?"

"I suppose not." His mouth tipped in a lopsided smile. "So what was it you wanted to tell me?"

She stroked the space between his eyes. For once, there was no furrow in his brow, and she couldn't bear to carve a new one.

"I wanted to tell you that I love you."

His expression shuttered. "You don't have to say that."

"I think I do have to say it. Because I've been keeping it to myself for years now, and it's burning a hole in my chest. You don't believe me, do you?"

He shook his head. "Not for a moment. That is, unless you mean it in some sort of friendship or fondness way. There are different sorts of love, and—"

"Wait." She sat up in bed, reaching for the edge of the rumpled bed linens. "I'll prove it to you. You know I worked on my trousseau for years. Every girl does. But I hemmed this particular set of bed linens the year I was one-and-twenty, I believe." She skimmed her fingertips along the side until she found what she was searching for. "Here." She showed it to him. "What does that say?"

He peered at it. "I don't know."

"Yes, you do. It's 'M.C.I.' I was dreadfully infatuated with you by that time, and in a sentimental moment, I embroidered your initial at the end of my own. Nearly seven years ago."

"But you say you were infatuated. Infatuation isn't love."

"No, it's not. I told myself the same thing. So after you'd purchased your commission and left for war, I put my feelings aside. I told myself to be practical. Giles asked to court me, and then he asked me to marry him. I said yes. Even though I knew I didn't love him, could never love him."

She closed her eyes and steeled herself. "But it wasn't until I lost Henry that I truly knew. The rector came to call. And I knew—I just knew—it meant one of you had been killed. When he told me Henry had died, I was devastated. Not only because I'd lost him—but because I'd had this terrible flash of relief in the same moment. I'd thought, Thank God it wasn't Sebastian." A hot tear fell to her cheek, and she impatiently dashed it away. "Can you imagine? I hated myself. But after that, there was no denying it. I was truly in love with you."

He caught her in his arms and rolled them over, so that she was beneath him. His disbelieving gaze searched hers. "Mary."

"I love you." She took his face in her hands and kissed his cheek. "I love you." Then his chin. "I love you." Then the pounding pulse under his jaw. "I love y—"

He covered her mouth with his, kissing her forcefully. As if to forbid her from loving him, and at the same time beg her to never, ever stop. They tangled tongues and limbs and hearts and souls.

He buried his face in her neck. "I need you," he whispered hoarsely. "Can you take me again?"

She nodded. "Yes."

This time it was different. Not slow and tender, but desperate, urgent. He raised up on his arms and stared down at her, never breaking his intense gaze as he took her in deep, powerful thrusts.

This wasn't lovemaking. It was possession.

"You're mine now," he said through clenched teeth. "Do you hear me? You're mine."

He moved harder, faster. As if he meant to pound at her body until he became part of her, sharing the same blood and bone, and pulling away would tear them both in two.

She held him tight, arching her hips to match his rhythm. His every motion drove her higher. Closer to her peak. Closer to him.

Somehow they found each other in the feverish storm of climax, holding each other in every possible way.

He slumped atop her, and she caressed his hair and shoulders as he recovered his breath. His back was slick with sweat.

"You're mine now," he whispered. "Don't even try to argue it."

"I won't argue it," she said. "Just as long as you understand that you're mine, too."

CHAPTER 10

THEY WOKE TO THE SOUND of someone pounding at the cottage's front door.

Mary sat up in bed. "Who on earth could that be, at this hour? Surely not Dick or Fanny."

Sebastian gave a derisive chuckle. "*Certainly* not Dick or Fanny. They would never knock."

"You have a point."

"It would seem they've gone away," he said after a minute. "We can go back to sleep."

"I don't know if I can return to sleep. Not after being startled awake."

"Well, then." He slid his arm around her, drawing her close. "I suppose we could amuse ourselves in some other way."

The pounding resumed.

With a groan, Sebastian let his head drop to the pillow. "Stay here. I'll see to it." With a light kiss to her lips, he rose from the bed and slid his legs into a pair of breeches. He plucked his shirt from where it lay discarded on the floor and dragged it over his head and arms. Then he reached for the candlestick and stumbled his way down the stairs.

"Whoever you are," he bellowed as he slid back the bolt, "you had better have a good reason for knocking at my door in the middle of the night."

He opened the door.

"Believe me, I have an excellent reason." Giles Perry stood on the threshold, holding a lantern in his left hand. He wore a dark cape flung over his shoulders and a murderous expression on his face. "I've come to do this."

He drew back his fist and punched Sebastian square in the ribs.

Oof. The blow took Sebastian by surprise. But that was about all it did. Perry hadn't the bulk or strength to deliver a bruising punch. Sebastian didn't even reel a step backward. Looking into Perry's pitifully disappointed face, he almost felt a bit sheepish about his lack of response. He wondered if perhaps he ought to double over and feign a dramatic groan just to be polite.

But then he recalled that this was the man who'd left Mary waiting at the altar—and Sebastian had no further inclinations to pity.

"How dare you come here," he growled.

"How dare you *be* here," Perry replied, indignant.

"This is my house. I've every right to be here."

"You don't have any right to be here with *her.*" Perry ducked under Sebastian's arm and entered the cottage. "I've come to rescue Mary."

"Rescue her from what? A surfeit of orgasms?"

"From you, you…rutting blackguard."

Oh, now that was too much. "Listen, you puling jackass. You have no claim on Mary any longer. That ended when you abandoned your promises and left her waiting at the altar alone. The only reason you don't have a bullet hole through your chest is because she begged me to spare your miserable life."

"What are you on about? I didn't abandon her."

"I'm fairly certain you did. I was there, and you weren't."

"Because I honored her request. Mary broke it off. Not me."

"You lying little—"

"He's not lying." Mary stood at the top of the stairs, dressed in one of his shirts. "He's telling the truth. I'm the one who called the wedding off."

Sebastian shook his head in disbelief. "That can't be. It doesn't make any sense."

Perry moved to confront her directly. "You ran away with this brigand? Willingly?"

"He's not a brigand. How did you find us here?"

"The coachman told me, when he finally returned. I'd hired that carriage by the hour, I hope you know." He shook his head in irritation. "This was supposed to be a discreet agreement. You become a spinster, I get a seat in the House of Commons."

"You'll still be an MP. It's not as though you need to win votes. You're buying a rotten borough. With my dowry, I might add."

Sebastian couldn't have heard that correctly. "You gave him your dowry?"

"Yes." She descended the remainder of the stairs. "In exchange for releasing me from the engagement on such late notice."

"I should have never agreed," Perry said. "I've a promising future in Parliament, you know. I could be Prime Minister one day. Many people are saying it. When this news gets about, you will have made me the laughingstock of London."

"Oh, Giles. Please. No one thinks about you half as much as you believe they do."

"I beg your pardon. I'm in the newspapers at least twice a year."

"You're a man, from an influential family. You'll weather the scandal, buy your seat in Parliament. From there you can make your reputation in politics—and, I might add, a far better match. If anything, people will believe you had a close escape. They'll assume it was my fault, and that you were well rid of me."

Sebastian pinched the bridge of his nose. "Help me out here, Mary. If you'd called off the wedding that morning, why did you come to the church? With all your belongings packed, no less?"

She looked everywhere but at him.

"Oh my God. You *planned* this?"

"In a way. I couldn't be certain you'd suggest we elope. But I prepared for it, just in case you did."

"You told me you didn't *want* to elope. You argued against it."

"I argue against everything. It's in my blood." She bit her lip. "If I'd agreed too easily, you might have been suspicious."

He turned away, pushing a hand through his hair. "This is unbelievable."

"I'm so sorry. It was wrong of me. But for a year now, I've been so worried about you. You never called on me anymore. I realized I couldn't go through with the wedding months ago and—"

"*Months* ago?" Perry squawked.

Sebastian wheeled to face him. "Why are you even still here?"

"Because." Perry tugged on his waistcoat. "I believe I'm owed an apology, too."

"You're sure as hell not getting one from me."

"I'm sorry, Giles." Mary approached him. "Truly sorry. I should have broken it off ages ago. But I would have done you a greater disservice by becoming your wife. I think we both know that we weren't suited to one another."

"Perhaps not, but—" Perry made a disgusted gesture in Sebastian's direction. "Of all men, did it have to be him?"

"Yes." She glanced at Sebastian. "Of all men, it had to be him."

Emotion gripped his heart like a fist.

"You heard my lady," he said to Perry. "Now you can leave. Go back to London and amuse yourself by further corrupting Parliament."

Perry finally moved to leave the cottage. "I'll have you know," he said, hand on the door latch, "that I have several plans for the benefit of the poor and infirm."

"Just get *out.*"

At last, the man was gone.

Sebastian turned to his deceitful bride.

She clutched her hands together in front of her. "I owe you a great many explanations."

"You can offer all the explanations you like, but there is no excuse for this."

"Will you at least hear me out?"

First, he had a few things to say of his own. "You lied to me. You led me to believe you were jilted, alone, vulnerable. When Henry and I went off to war, I made a vow to protect you if he didn't come back. The past few days, I've tortured myself. Knowing that I kept that promise to guard you as best I could, and at the same time believing it came at the cost of your happiness. Now I learn that was only a falsehood. How much of the rest of it was lies, too?"

"None of it. I swear. Everything else was the truth." She approached him. "I know I lied about being jilted. That was wrong of me. But if you care for me, and want to raise a family together... Is it really so terrible to learn that it was you I loved all along?"

"I don't know if I can believe that now."

He could scarcely believe those three words when she'd spoken them the first time. How the hell was he supposed to accept them now?

"You think I would lie to you? About the day I learned of my own brother's death?" Her voice shook with emotion. "If that's how little you think of me, we can annul the marriage. No one knows we went through with it, save for the coachman and Giles. And Dick and Fanny, but who would they tell?"

"The Church knows. I know. We said vows. We've had…" He motioned impatiently. "…marital relations."

Well, look at that. He'd come up with a polite term all on his own.

"A marriage can be annulled on grounds of fraud," she said. "If that's what you allege, I won't fight it."

"Oh, I'll be damned if I'll annul this marriage. You're not getting off that easy." He inhaled slowly, trying to steady himself. "I'm far from a perfect man. But if there's one thing I value above all else, it's keeping my promises."

"I know that."

"Precisely, Mary. You know that. You *know* that. And you used it against me."

She nodded slowly. "You're right, I did. I see that now. Perhaps it is unforgivable."

She turned and quietly climbed the stairs.

Sebastian didn't follow her.

Mary spent the rest of the night pacing, weeping, and hoping against hope that she might hear his footfalls on the steps. That he might come to her, allow her to apologize, consider giving her another chance.

Before Giles had arrived, they'd been on the verge of something truly wonderful. And because of her stupidity, she'd set them back years. She didn't know how she'd convince him to trust her again. But no matter how long it took, she wouldn't give up.

As dawn broke, she finally heard the sounds of stirring downstairs. She ran to the door and pressed her ear against it, holding her breath.

No footfalls.

Instead, she heard the sound of carriage wheels crunching on the gravel drive. Heading away.

No.

Mary looked about the room, panicked. Good Lord, she was still barefoot and dressed in nothing but his shirt. She hadn't been able to bring herself to change out of it.

There was no time to find something else.

She flew from the room, hurrying down the stairs on bare feet and reeling around a corner in her mad dash for the front door. "Sebastian! Sebastian, wait! Don't le—"

Oof. As she opened the door, she collided with something.

Something tall and strong and wonderful.

"Sebastian." She threw her arms about his neck and hugged him tight. "Thank God you're still here. I thought you'd left me."

"I told you I wouldn't leave you. What would make you think that?"

She pulled back and searched his eyes. "The coach. I heard it leaving."

"Ah, yes. That would have been Dick and Fanny making their departure."

"You don't mean that you sacked them? I know they're terrible, but they meant well."

"I did not sack them," he said. "I've sent them away on holiday. To Ramsgate."

She blinked at him, stunned. "Sebastian, you didn't."

"I did. They're to have a room at the finest establishment, with full board and all expenses paid, for a week. And we"—he put his hands on her waist—"are on our own."

"Just the two of us?"

He nodded.

"For a whole week?"

"I'm afraid so." He shook his head, as if in dismay. "We'll have to prepare our own food. Split our own wood. Nothing to do but stroll on the beach in the afternoons and sit by the fire in the evenings with a glass of wine." His eyes darkened. "Well, that and go to bed early."

"Oh, dear. What a trial." She put her hand to his cheek. "Does that mean you've forgiven me?"

"I'm not sure. I'm still put out with you, and I spent the whole night thinking on it. You lied to me."

"I know."

"But then, you also gave up your dowry and the chance at a

secure marriage, risking ruin and spinsterhood for me. Which seems as though it ought to count for something, too."

"I only did it because I loved you so much. I hoped perhaps you felt something for me, but I knew you'd never do anything about it. If I told you how I felt, you would have fled as quickly as Shadow could carry you. You would never have married me unless you believed you were coming to my rescue."

"I wish I could contradict that, but I suspect you're right."

"I'm always right."

He gave her a look.

"Often right," she amended. "If it helps, my first plan didn't feature deceit at all. I was going to simply seduce you. But I didn't have the confidence that I could pull it off."

His mouth quirked at the corner. "Oh, you could have pulled it off."

"Really?"

"Without a doubt." He drew her close, resting his forehead to hers. "Mary, Mary. Can you truly love me that much?"

"More. You should have seen my third plan if this one didn't work. There were highwaymen."

He laughed.

It was a warm, unburdened laugh that made her heart soar.

She'd disarmed him now. He couldn't keep her out any more.

"I love you," he murmured. "God, it feels good to say that at last. I love you, Mary."

He bent to kiss her, then stopped. "I've just thought of something. If your trunks weren't packed for a honeymoon with Giles Perry, does that mean all those negligees were truly—"

"For you?" She smiled. "Yes."

"Are there more of them?"

"Take me upstairs and find out."

She didn't have to ask twice. He bent down, lashed an arm around her thighs, and flung her over his shoulder before mounting the stairs.

Mary hoped he'd pieced that bed together correctly. Because it would be put to the test all week long.

EPILOGUE

"Come away from the window, darling," Mary said. "You're leaving nose prints on the glass."

Henry pouted. "You said Papa would be here in time for tea."

"He will be. He promised, and your father always keeps his promises."

Mary was eager for Sebastian to arrive, too. Tending all four of their children during his absence had left her frayed at the edges. When they were in London or at Byrne Hall, she had a nursemaid to help, but when they took their annual holiday here in the cottage, they preferred to keep it family only. With the addition of Dick and Fanny Cross, of course.

She shifted Molly, her youngest, to the other arm and wiped the spittle from her chubby face. The poor dear was cutting a new tooth. At least William had gone upstairs for a nap, but Jane and Henry wouldn't cease bickering.

Someday, Mary would finish her latest strident letter to the editor of *The Times*—but it wouldn't be today.

"Papa will most likely be late," Jane said.

"No, he won't."

"He will be. On account of the rain."

"It's not raining," Henry objected.

"Not now, not here. But it was raining hard an hour ago. The clouds have shifted since. So it's likely raining on him now. He may even have to stop over somewhere."

Mary shushed them both. "He'll be here. He'd never miss one

of your birthdays."

"It's an easy enough promise to keep, considering three of our birthdays are all in the same month. Henry's the only one left out." Jane crinkled her nose in thought. "It's rather a coincidence, isn't it?"

Mary only smiled. It was no coincidence at all that three of their four children had been born in March. Not when one considered that they spent a holiday at the Kentish seaside every June.

There was just something about that bed.

Mary dearly hoped she wasn't around when Jane finally puzzled out the truth. She was far too clever, that one.

She set Molly down on the floor to play, then invited Henry to sit on her lap. "Henry, have I told you about the night you were born?"

Jane rolled her eyes. "Only hundreds of times."

Mary ignored her eldest's complaint and wrapped her arms around Henry. "You came early. I was at Byrne Hall, and your Papa was in London. I sent a message to him by express, but I thought he couldn't possibly arrive before you did. I should never have doubted. Your father rode all night—in the rain, mind—and arrived just in time to welcome you into the world. He was there for your first birthday, and he'll be here to see you turn six. Never doubt it."

Molly pressed a sticky hand to the window. "Papa!"

"See?" Henry gave his older sister a superior look. "I told you he'd be here in time for tea."

"And I told you it was raining," she replied.

Sebastian came through the door, dripping with rainwater and stamping the mud from his boots. "I heard there's a young master here who's six years of age. Who could that be?"

"It's me!" Henry rushed to give his father a hug.

He was closely followed by Jane.

Molly toddled over and made grabby hands. "Papa, up."

William scrambled downstairs, rubbing the sleep from his eyes, and jumped on his father's back.

Mary exchanged amused glances with her husband. "You look like a children tree."

An exceedingly handsome children tree. Even all these years later, he never failed to take her breath away.

"Come have cake, Papa."

"Can we go sea-bathing tomorrow?"

"Did you bring us sweets from Town?"

"Papapapapapa."

She came to his rescue, shooing them away. "Give your father a rest, all of you. Go help Mrs. Cross set the table for tea."

Once they'd all run off, she was finally able to greet Sebastian with a kiss of her own. "In case you couldn't tell, you were very much missed." She helped him out of his coat. "Was the road terrible?"

"Shadow and I have been through worse."

"I'm so glad you're here. Your children are exhausting."

He chuckled. "I'll take them down to the seaside tomorrow so you can have a rest."

"You don't have to do that."

"Oh, I do." His arms went around her, and his voice went dark. "You're going to need a rest tomorrow, because I mean to keep you up late tonight."

The kiss he gave her was one of boundless love and intense passion, and it conveyed an unmistakable message:

She'd better not make any plans for next March.

The End

COMING IN AUGUST, 2018

The Governess Game
(Girl Meets Duke, Book 2)

He's been a bad, bad rake—and it takes a governess to teach him a lesson.

The accidental governess
After her livelihood slips through her fingers, Alexandra Mountbatten takes on an impossible post: transforming a pair of wild orphans into proper young ladies. However, the girls don't need discipline. They need a loving home. Try telling that to their guardian, Chase Reynaud: duke's heir in the streets and devil in the sheets. The ladies of London have tried—and failed—to make him settle down. Somehow, Alexandra must reach his heart . . . without risking her own.

The infamous rake
Like any self-respecting libertine, Chase lives by one rule: no attachments. When a stubborn little governess tries to reform him, he decides to give her an education—in pleasure. That should prove he can't be tamed. But Alexandra is more than he bargained for: clever, perceptive, passionate. She refuses to see him as a lost cause. Soon the walls around Chase's heart are crumbling . . . and he's in danger of falling, hard.

MORE BOOKS BY TESSA DARE

Girl Meets Duke series
The Duchess Deal
The Governess Game (coming August 2018)

Castles Ever After series
Romancing the Duke
Say Yes to the Marquess
When a Scot Ties the Knot

Spindle Cove series
A Night to Surrender
Once Upon a Winter's Eve
A Week to be Wicked
A Lady by Midnight
Beauty and the Blacksmith
Any Duchess Will Do
Lord Dashwood Missed Out
Do You Want to Start a Scandal

The Stud Club series
One Dance with a Duke
Twice Tempted by a Rogue
Three Nights with a Scoundrel
The Wanton Dairymaid series
Goddess of the Hunt
Surrender of a Siren
A Lady of Persuasion

Novellas
The Scandalous, Dissolute, No-Good Mr. Wright
How to Catch a Wild Viscount

ABOUT THE AUTHOR

TESSA DARE IS THE *New York Times* and *USA Today* bestselling author of more than twenty historical romances. Blending wit, sensuality, and emotion, Tessa writes Regency-set romance novels that feel relatable to modern readers. Her books have won numerous accolades, including Romance Writers of America's prestigious RITA® award (twice) and the *RT Book Reviews* Seal of Excellence. *Booklist* magazine named her one of the "new stars of historical romance," and her books have been contracted for translation in more than a dozen languages.

A librarian by training and a book-lover at heart, Tessa makes her home in Southern California, where she lives with her husband, their two children, and a trio of cosmic kitties.

To receive updates on Tessa's new and upcoming books, please sign up for her newsletter: tessadare.com/newsletter-signup

His Duchess for a Day

Christi Caldwell

CHAPTER 1

Surrey, England
1821

TO ALL THOSE IN WALLINGFORD, Mrs. Elizabeth Terry was just any other miserable dragon at Mrs. Belden's Finishing School. Her days consisted of instructing equally miserable students on ladylike deportment and skills to catch a husband. And then beginning those same lessons in the following days for other young women unfortunate enough to find themselves students in this dreary place.

The irony was never lost on any that the leading ladies of Society who were in this establishment received lessons from women who had a false "Mrs." attached to their names to create an air of respectability. When the truth was, they were all nothing more than spinsters or poor women required to work to survive.

Well, not *all* of them.

"Why should we possibly take lessons on husband hunting from *her*?"

Standing at the front of the parlor that served as a classroom, Elizabeth's cheeks burned hot under that less-than-discreet whisper.

At six and twenty, however, and on her own for more years than any person ought, she was made of far sterner stuff. "What was that?" she challenged, the remarkable cool of her tone hopelessly ruined as her wire-rimmed spectacles slipped down her nose.

The other young ladies seated beside the habitual insulter, Lady Claire Moore, all fell silent, diverting their stares to their laps.

A duke's daughter and goddaughter to the queen, Lady Claire had an icy demeanor that all the instructors at Mrs. Belden's and the harpy headmistress herself couldn't muster. "Marriage," the ten-and-seven-year-old student drawled out in slow, enunciated syllables.

The girl at her side giggled and then swiftly concealed that expression of her mirth.

Lady Claire scraped a condescending stare over Elizabeth, lingering her focus on the gray skirts. Gray skirts that hung large on Elizabeth's small, shapeless frame. "I asked how you could *possibly* instruct us on how to find a husband."

She couldn't. Elizabeth wasn't so foolish to believe that she knew a thing about flirting or enticing… anyone.

"Hush. Don't be unkind," Lady Nora snapped in a shocking defense. After all, there was some manner of code, either spoken or unspoken, that no one defended the dragons.

"You'd defend her? A dragon?" Lady Claire quipped. "But then, with your parents gone now and your brother off chasing skirts, you'll likely be the next drag—"

Exploding to her feet, Lady Nora came out of her seat and launched herself at the other woman.

Oh, blast.

Elizabeth surged forward and swiftly placed herself between the pair. "That is enough," she said in perfectly modulated tones.

She'd learned early on that yelling had little effect on recalcitrant students. The same for drawn-out lectures. If one truly wished to penetrate a tense situation, one was best to meet it with calm.

Lady Nora instantly fell back, but hovered alongside the other woman.

An ashen, trembling Lady Claire burrowed in her seat.

Elizabeth looked to the recently volatile young woman, feeling a kindred connection to this woman who'd recently lost her parents. "If you'll please sit?" she murmured. Angry, scared, and lost, Elizabeth knew precisely what Lady Nora was feeling. Only, where the young woman had a rogue of a brother, Elizabeth had… no one. Of course, a rogue of a brother who didn't see his own sister might be the same as having no brother at all.

With stiff, reluctant movements, Lady Nora returned to her seat.

"Now, as I was saying…" She puzzled her brow. Blast and damn. What had she been saying?

"The gentlemen who we should set our caps on?" Miss Peppa March piped in helpfully. Heavily rounded, with large cheeks and limp brown hair, the six-and-ten-year-old girl, a recent student, looked up from the little journal and pencil she clutched in her fingers.

"No advice Mrs. Terry or anyone gives is going to help you secure a husband," Lady Claire muttered.

Lady Nora shot a foot out, catching the young woman in the ankle.

A cry burst from the other lady's lips. "How dare you?"

"Oh, I'd do it again, dare or not," Nora answered with a mocking smile.

An argument immediately broke out with each girl firing insults and hateful words at each other.

Bloody hell. Elizabeth slapped her palms over her face. She'd forever been rot at this. It was the miracle of this century that the intolerable Mrs. Belden hadn't figured out the sham Elizabeth had perpetuated—she was a dreadful instructor.

"Enough," she said through her palms. When the bickering pair continued on through that command, Elizabeth raised her voice. "I said, enough."

Her voice echoed around the parlor, bringing the room to a screeching silence. She'd also learned that raising one's voice did have some effectiveness if rarely used. This was one of those instances.

A sea of startled eyes stared back.

Elizabeth stretched that moment on. Steepling her fingers before her, she passed a hard stare around, touching it upon each girl.

Ultimately, she settled her focus on the one young lady clinging to that pad and pencil. One who still had hopes that Elizabeth might have some wisdom about how a young woman might catch a husband. She didn't. Nothing, that was, that she knew from any real experience, but rather, what she'd gathered from the dull texts Mrs. Belden insisted the instructors use in their tutelage.

"Now," she finally said, smoothing her palms along her skirts. "The art of finding a husband is the finest of the arts." A little giggle met that silly pronouncement, also insisted upon by the headmistress. And were she seated on that powder-blue sofa and the roles reversed, Elizabeth would have had a like reaction. But she wasn't. She was a woman dependent upon her role here.

As such, she leveled a look on the girl, who immediately went silent.

"But before one employs any effort on finding one's husband, a lady must identify the manner of man she wishes to spend the remainder of her days with."

Until death do part you…

And with that deviation from Mrs. Belden's usual script for the husband-hunting course, every student went silent and sat on the edge of her chair—which was saying a good deal indeed, given Lady Claire and Lady Nora hadn't managed that feat in all the years she'd served as their instructor.

Reveling in that newfound attention from her students, Elizabeth wound her way around the room, drawing out the silence, increasing the anticipation.

"Who does a lady wish to marry? A gentleman who is titled?"

"Of course," Lady Claire put in.

"One who is wealthy?" Elizabeth continued over her.

"A wealthy husband is essential," another girl interjected.

"Yes, money is essential and a title desired." Elizabeth paused alongside the arm of Lady Claire's sofa. "But what about the man himself? Should one marry a fool for a fortune? A faithless philanderer for a title?"

Each pair of eyes in the room rounded in like manner.

"Or should one choose a devoted gentleman? One who is clever enough to discuss text and matters of import and challenge you to use your mind in return?"

"Is she saying we should become… bluestockings?" That scandalized whisper came from somewhere in the corner of the room, penetrating Elizabeth's senses.

Bloody hell. *I'll find myself sacked.*

Clearing her throat, Elizabeth rushed to the front of the room and gathered the journal in which she'd written the lectures six years earlier. She flipped through the pages, seeking, seeking, and then finding.

"What you require in a husband," she forced herself to read.

For, God help her for being selfish, even as she would rather school the young ladies present on using their own minds, to do so would see her cast out. She'd faced the peril of having nothing and no one years earlier. It was a life she'd no wish to go back to.

And so, she read, "A titled gentleman is the ideal one. The greater the title, the greater your security and status in Society." Oh, God, what a lot of rubbish. A ducal husband didn't mean rot. "A husband with noble lineage is noble because…" She grimaced, struggling to make her tongue move to get those words out. "Because of his pedigree."

"Like a dog," Lady Nora grumbled.

Yes, most of them were. Noble dogs, but a dog was a dog.

Elizabeth cleared her throat. "It behooves a lady to find one with close connections to one's own family." More rubbish. "But that does not mean…" Footsteps sounded in the hall, a pair of them, one heavy and one light. "You should fail and consider other valuable attributes such as"—Elizabeth paused in her rote reading to flip the page—"a gentleman's willingness to support your aspirations to become a leading societal hostess." She choked a bit. *Hell, I am going to hell for propagating this information.* "Furthermore…" Elizabeth glanced up from her reading and froze. Her gaze collided with that of the hated headmistress who controlled the fates and futures of too many women and girls, Elizabeth included. Swallowing hard, she spared a brief glance at the less relevant, less threatening figure at the harpy's side—

The book fell from Elizabeth's fingers, landing with an indignant thump upon its spine.

She tried to swallow, tried to breathe, but remained incapable of either or both. For she'd been wrong. For the first time, the harpy headmistress was *not* the most dangerous figure present.

A pair of more than slightly mocking, twinkling blue eyes met hers. They'd always been twinkling. When he was a boy of twelve bent on making his parents' lives a misery through his mischief making and as the man who'd chucked pebbles at her window to urge her out to study the stars.

Nine years later, several stone heavier, the gentleman before her was broader, more muscular, more powerful… more everything than he'd been when last she'd seen him.

He sent a black eyebrow slashing up.

Elizabeth recoiled.

The velocity of that movement brought her head whipping back with such force her glasses tumbled from her nose. The wire-rimmed frames landed on the detestable book at her feet and then clattered noisily on the hardwood floor.

"Ladies, please rise for our distinguished company," Mrs. Belden called, thumping her cane in that decisive manner that marked her words not to be debated. All the young women sprang to their feet.

As if anyone *would* challenge the dragon.

Except now… now… Elizabeth's heart knocked wildly as she contemplated making for the window in the opposite corner of the parlor. She squinted, the faces before her blurred and the room a kaleidoscope of shadowy images as she searched for her spectacles. Nay, she'd merely imagined him. Of course, she'd not given any thought to him since the last scandal sheet had been passed around by the other dragons in desperate need of something to read other than dull books on propriety.

Dropping to her knees, she fished about, because surely she'd not seen correctly. Surely she'd imagined him. Surely…

Oh, bloody hell… surely she could find her dratted glasses.

The floorboards groaned, slightly depressed by the tread of approaching footfalls.

Not Mrs. Belden's mincing, practiced ones. But rather, sure, steady, determined, and very masculine ones.

On her hands and knees, Elizabeth froze in midsearch. Through the murkiness of her horrid vision, a pair of black boots drew into a blurry focus.

Her stomach lurched.

Squeezing her eyes shut, she made herself go as still as possible. Willing him gone. Willing the entire room away. Willing the floor to open up and swallow her, sparing her from this long overdue exchange that she'd managed to convince herself would never come.

"I believe these are what you are looking for?" There could be no mistaking that voice, a slightly husky, melodious murmur. Familiar, and yet foreign for the amount of time that had passed since she'd last heard it. The gentleman placed her spectacles in their proper place.

Crispin Ferguson, the Duke of Huntington, smiled back. "Hello, *Duchess*." A hard glint iced once-warm eyes. "We meet again."

CHAPTER 2

The last place Crispin Ferguson, recently the 9th Duke Huntington, would have ever searched for Elizabeth Brightly over the years was a dreary, straitlaced finishing school.

Which was no doubt why the young woman—his *wife* of nine years—had remained so damned elusive.

Of course, her disappearance and her absolute ability to remain hidden hadn't surprised Crispin in the least. After all, this was the same girl he'd once played hide-and-seek with in the far-distant corners of Oxfordshire. If Elizabeth hadn't wanted to be found, she had had him searching from the moment the roosters crowed until the moon shoved back the sun for its time in the sky.

"Their Graces, the Duke and Duchess of Huntington," Mrs. Belden announced in the same obsequious, fawning tones that had dogged him the whole of his time as ducal heir and now his ducal life.

Like dutiful little ducks, the seven young ladies present dropped into respectful curtsies.

A bespectacled Elizabeth looked about, perplexity brimming from behind her lenses. Did she seek escape? Or confirmation of the person now addressed by the crowd?

Having grown up alongside her and read her like the pages of a journal written in his own hand, Crispin would have ventured it was the former. But with time having carved them into strangers, she was unreadable in ways she never had been.

"And all this time, you fortunate young ladies have been schooled by a duchess." The headmistress' voice shook with pride and honor.

That seemed to snap Elizabeth from the shock that gripped her. She shot a hand up. Rushing past Crispin in a whir of skirts, she presented herself before Mrs. Belden. "No. That isn't necessary." She spoke to the room at large, pointedly leaving Crispin out of her announcement. "You needn't... address me so."

Her absolute indifference should have smarted. And yet, after a lifetime of fawning women vying for his attentions and affections, Crispin was... intrigued by this more composed version of the girl he'd called friend. With a grin, he perched his hip on the arm of the nearest unoccupied sofa and observed the proverbial show.

"But... but... are you saying you are not a duchess?" The headmistress' face fell.

Seven rabidly curious stares whipped over to the lady in question.

Folding his arms at his chest, Crispin joined in, staring expectantly at Elizabeth.

"I... I..." She'd never stumbled over her words. She'd always been remarkably in control, when he'd been brash and reckless in every way.

For the first time since he'd entered the room and interrupted her lesson, Elizabeth looked at him. Crimson color splotched her cheeks, rushing to the roots of her like hair.

"It is... *complicated*," she finally settled on.

No truer words had ever been uttered.

Nonetheless, the headmistress who'd greeted him with a fanfare usually reserved for a king beamed, as Elizabeth's words seemed to be all the confirmation she'd required. Raising her cane, she clapped the head of it against her palm. "Ladies."

"No!" Elizabeth squeaked, darting between the girls now filing from the room. "You needn't leave. His Grace was just leaving."

"No, I wasn't," Crispin called over, layering that jovial assurance with ice.

Elizabeth shot him a withering glare the likes of which his terrifying mother, the dowager duchess herself, couldn't manage.

Yet, when a duke spoke, the world listened, just as the rapidly departing ladies before them did.

And a moment later, Crispin found himself alone with Elizabeth.

"Hello, Duchess."

She spun about. "*Stop* calling me that, Your Grace," she hissed, jerking her head back toward the open doorway.

Yes, no doubt, the headmistress listened from the other side.

Elizabeth ducked her head outside.

"My apologies," the headmistress squawked, her footsteps growing distant as she retreated.

Elizabeth yanked the door closed and then spun back to face him. "You need to leave. Now." She continued speaking in a rush, not allowing him to get a word in. "You should have never come. *Why* did you come?"

And that brought them to the reason he was here.

Crispin straightened from his negligent repose. "Do you know you're the only woman in the whole of England who'd turn away the life of a duchess to live a life of drudgery?"

Several furrows creased the space between her eyebrows. "I don't live a life of drudgery," she declared, a defensive edge creeping into her tone, belied by the liar her eyes and miserable gray skirts made her out to be.

"Indeed?" he drawled, drifting over. "Nine years may have passed since we last saw one another, but we were friends far longer than that." He stopped so only a handbreadth separated them. "This is your reveal, love." He dusted the tip of his index finger between her eyebrows.

Gasping, Elizabeth tripped over herself in a bid to escape his touch.

Which was also a ducal first for one who'd had every woman from maids to maidens and matrons hurling themselves into his path.

"What do you want?" she demanded, all fire and fury.

Elizabeth Terry—nay, Elizabeth Brightly hadn't changed a jot. She was still the small, slender imp with outrageously curled hair and cream-white cheeks. No, that wasn't altogether true. Her eyes had changed. They were more wary than the fresh innocence of her then seven and ten years.

Was it a product of life's natural progression? Or the effects of their failed *marriage*?

For the first time since he'd stepped inside this establishment and found that the woman he'd spent years looking for was here the whole time, regret needled around his chest. For what might have been. For their lost friendship. For a *marriage* that could have been.

Unnerved by that maudlin musing, Crispin clasped his hands behind him. "My father is dead."

"My apologies," she said softly. "I loved His Grace very much."

Yes, everyone had adored his father. As cold and ruthless as the dowager duchess was and always had been, her late husband had been jovial and warm.

"He always liked you a great deal, too, Elizabeth," he said quietly.

Something passed in her eyes, but she dipped her gaze, and he was left to wonder at that brief flash of emotion.

Her family had lived on a parcel of land in the Fergusons' Oxfordshire properties. Despite the station divide between her father, a struggling merchant, and Crispin's, the duke, the men had been friends, and their children—Elizabeth and Crispin—had become even greater ones. Until the day her parents had taken ill, within a couple of weeks of each other, and in that short time, she'd found herself orphaned. When Crispin had proposed marriage to a friend to provide her security, his father had proven a duke would always be a duke where matters such as marriages were concerned.

"I haven't come to speak about the past," Crispin finally said. The scholar in him, who'd spent years as a fellow delivering lectures in Oxford, knew that logic and reason said no good could come from any such talks. They wouldn't erase anything that had passed between them.

"The thing about the past, Crispin..." she said in governess tones, stealing the use of his Christian name when no one had done so... since her. To the world—his mother included—he'd only ever been a title. "One cannot divorce oneself of one's past when it is responsible for one's present and future." She started for the door.

Why...why... she was dismissing him? Just like that?

He rocked back on his heels.

"You are my wife," he called, halting her in her tracks and bringing her back around. God, how he hated to put any favors to her, the traitorous friend who'd accepted his offer of marriage and then abandoned him. He curled his lips up into a slightly mocking, indifferent grin. "And, you see, I am in need of one." A pretty blush splashed her cheeks with pink color. "A wife, that is," he purred.

A strangled, choking sound escaped her.

Despite the gravity of their reunion, Crispin's grin deepened. "Not for… those reasons." Eventually, there would be the need for an heir. "That is not why I'm here."

That assurance did nothing to ease the tension from her small frame. Rather, she narrowed her gaze on his face, sizing him up the way she might a London footpad who stepped too close. "Wipe that false rogue's smile from your lips, Crispin Ferguson."

That grin she took as fake, however, was the first real expression of mirth he'd formed with his lips in… longer than he could remember. And this person who'd once known him better than anyone couldn't even tell. She didn't know the difference.

This, their meeting, was spiraling out of his control, the control he had on his emotions. In a bid to restore a semblance of calm, Crispin grabbed a pair of mahogany rope-twist armchairs and positioned them so they faced each other.

"Perhaps we should sit, Your Grace."

Elizabeth remained planted to her spot close to the doorway. He set his jaw. God, she was as stubborn as she'd always been. Crispin settled his frame into the small, mustard velvet chair. He looped an ankle across his opposite knee, and the delicate wood groaned under that slight movement. "I've no intention of leaving, Duchess."

She elevated her chin. "I asked that you stop calling me that, Your Grace."

"But that is what you are now." He flashed another smile meant to rile, meant to infuriate, meant to shake some of the bloody calm out of her. "What was it we pledged? Hmm?" He lifted an eyebrow. "Until death do us part?"

"Funny you should remember that part," she noted in droll tones, completely unaffected. "There was the whole 'to live together,' love her, comfort her, honor, and keep her in sickness and in health." Elizabeth shot him an arch look. "*Forsaking all others.*"

He sat back, celebrating the first real triumph since he'd stepped into this schoolroom and faced her. Despite her seeming indifference, she'd revealed her hand for a second time now. "You kept up with gossip on me," he noted huskily. Those gossip rags were forever speculating about which widow or actress he was linked to at any given point.

The hard, tense set of her lips strained her cheek muscles and was going to give the minx a deuced megrim. "Hardly," she said too quickly.

She'd always been rubbish at lying. It was an inadequate skill set that continued to this day.

"I would be remiss if I didn't point out, *Duchess*"—she winced—"that you were the one who left me." The memory of that night slipped in. He'd been informed she'd been feeling unwell, but when he'd visited the guest rooms she'd been given as his bride—they were empty. She was gone. All that had remained had been three curly strands of her red hair upon a blindingly bright white coverlet.

"Is that why you are here, Your Grace? Did I wound your pride?"

God, the chit could drive the patience from a saint. As it became increasingly clear that the lady had no intention of taking the seat across from him, Crispin stood. "I'll get 'round to why I'm here. Since my father's death and my ascension to the dukedom, there have been…" He searched for the words.

Elizabeth crossed her arms. A study in annoyance at his presence? His telling? All of it? "I've been the recipient of attention from many ladies."

"How dreadful for you," she declared, her expression deadpan. Just then, her glasses slipped down the bridge of her nose.

Crispin stilled. They were the wire rims she'd donned when last he'd seen her nearly ten years ago. The fact that she still wore the same pair was an inconsequential detail. Or it should have been.

He frowned. And yet it was not. It was a material telling about Elizabeth and the state of her affairs these past years.

Noting his attention, Elizabeth pushed her glasses back into place and jutted her chin at a defiant angle.

As for the first time since he'd entered the room, Crispin took in those details, which had escaped him until now: the heinous gray skirts that hung, shapeless, on her slender frame. The painfully severe chignon that could never tame those crimped red curls. She *should* be attired in garments fit for one of near royalty, as she, in fact, was. The idea that she'd gone all these years without, choosing a life of work over a life with him, stuck odd in his chest.

They, after all, had been friends, and this was the life *she'd* sought instead. She'd always been prouder than most—including him.

Including anyone he'd ever known in his thirty years.

He cleared his throat. "As I was saying—"

"Your bride problem."

"I only ever had one bride problem," he muttered. And it had been this fearless minx before him.

Understanding lit Elizabeth's eyes. "I see."

Crispin puzzled his brow. "You do?" Of course. With her head in a book for as long as he'd known her, she'd always been clever enough to see everything.

The first eagerness he'd caught in her expressive moss-green gaze flared to life. She sailed over in a whir of loud, rustling skirts. "You require an annulment." A smile, one that still dimpled her cheeks and lit her eyes and turned her lips up, transformed her from the ordinary girl of his past to someone... quite... enthralling. He stared back, transfixed by the sparkle in the glittering green depths of her eyes. "Do you have papers for me to sign?"

Reality seeped back in. "What?" He raced through his mind for whatever last words had been spoken before he'd noted the entrancing color of her intelligent eyes.

"Papers." Her smile slipped, and he mourned that fleeting light. "For the annulment?" Hope threaded those three words and stuck in a pride he hadn't realized he had.

"You think I want an annulment?"

"You don't?" She answered another of his questions with one of her own.

"I don't."

She looked so crestfallen that, if he weren't so offended, he would have laughed outright. "But then you can marry whomever you wish," she persisted.

"I understand the implications of a church-granted annulment," he said with false drollness. Crispin made a show of studying her. "You'll do just fine."

Splotches of color tinged her cheekbones again.

Her mouth moved.

Before she found the right words and skewered him, Crispin hurried on with his reason for being here.

"I'll need you to return to London... as my wife."

CHAPTER 3

He'd found her.

How, after all these years?

Or perhaps he knew long, long ago and was content to let you live here?

Something in that pinched at Elizabeth's heart. A silly, nonsensical hurt.

As a creature of reason and logic, she'd recognized the power afforded him. As heir to one of the oldest titles in the kingdom, he possessed both the resources and capabilities to find her in whatever corner of England she chose to hide.

But now, after all this time apart, he'd actually *wanted* to find her.

A marriage conceived by him had, in the moment, seemed like a solution to each of their individual problems. But that was the folly of youth. They'd thought of the immediacy of their circumstances and the benefits in that very instant… but hadn't truly considered… the after.

Until it had been too late.

"*It was a mistake marrying her. I know that.*"

Hating the hurt of that echoed in her memory all these years later, Elizabeth fought it back and adopted the same veneer of aloofness she'd mastered at Mrs. Belden's.

Now, he required her to return to London with him, on a matter that by his accounts had nothing to do with an… heir. Of its own volition, her gaze went to the towering, figure. One broad shoulder propped negligently against the wall did nothing to diminish the power of his frame. Nearly six inches taller and two stone in muscle greater when they'd last met, he bore only the faintest trace of the lanky, wiry friend of her youth.

From her place at the center of the parlor, Elizabeth forced her spine straight, a futile bid to make herself taller. An impossible feat. Even more impossible around this bear of a man.

Crispin sent one dark brow slashing up over a sapphire eye that twinkled. "Nothing to say?" He flashed a dangerously enticing half-grin that dimpled his left cheek. "That's not like you, Elizabeth."

No, it wasn't. She'd once been garrulous and free with her words, particularly around this man. Mrs. Belden's Finishing School, however, watered down a woman's temperament. "You don't know me," she said calmly, smoothing her palms over her skirts. The reminder effectively quashed his smile, restoring a ducal veneer of ice. *Not anymore.* "And my name is Mrs. Terry." She tacked on that important afterthought.

He shoved himself from that wall and stalked forward with steps to rival the sleek panther who'd been part of his late father's menagerie. The primitive glide of his steps sent a lone butterfly fluttering in her belly and spiraling throughout her being. "I would have never ventured you'd gone off and used that, of all names."

Fighting for control, Elizabeth slid behind the ivory sofa, placing it between them as a weak, but necessary, barrier. "There is nothing wrong with the name Terry," she said tautly, hating that he continued to knock her off-balance. It was why it was easier to fight him on a "name" than on his intentions for her. How dare he upend her fragile, but once stable, existence and remain so infuriatingly calm through it?

Crispin stopped at the opposite end of the sofa. He lowered his hands to the scalloped mahogany trim. "No," he concurred. "Your mother's previous name was Terry. You were always Brightly."

It's a splendid name for a girl with your wits, Elizabeth. Another whisper of a memory about a friend who'd once found a gangly, awkward girl in the country as special as she'd found him.

They, however, had together gone and destroyed that special bond. She was as much to blame as he was. "What do you want, Your Grace?" she asked quietly, calling forth the distinguished rank as a reminder about the barrier that existed between them. Except, it was a warning given too late. They'd traveled a path that could not simply be undone...

He straightened. "Tsk, tsk. As we're husband and wife, I never took us for a couple who'd refer to each other by our titles and surnames."

She shook her head. "We're not husband and wife." Elizabeth lifted a finger. "Not truly." To him, she'd only ever been his best chum Elizabeth. *Only, I yearned for something more...* "A marriage is brought to completion through sexual intercourse." A garbled choking built in his throat. His disquiet helped Elizabeth find her footing. "And given there's never been any penetration of your peni—"

Crispin shot a hand out. His gloveless palm covered her mouth, muffling the remainder of that word. His ears an impressive shade of red, he glanced at the door then back over to Elizabeth. "Enough."

"What?" He'd become a duke in every way, then. It was an image that didn't fit with the rogue written about in the gossip columns that ultimately found their way to Surrey. But then, that transformation, too, had been inevitable. Dukes might be rogues with their mistresses, but invariably they became stuffy bores for the rest of the world. She and Crispin together had jested about it long ago, and through his laughter, Crispin had vowed to never follow that path to pomposity. For reasons she couldn't understand, she mourned that change. "It's an opinion that goes back to Boccaccio. A marriage without consummation is no marriage. It's a universal acceptance across *all* cultures."

He snorted. "That was a *story* set forth in ancient Greece, hardly modern England."

Damn him for being as clever as he'd been all those years earlier. Powerful peers weren't supposed to know obscure writings on the sacrament of marriage. "Modern England," she corrected, refusing to back down, "still states coitus determines the validity of a union. And the truth remains,"—she patted the back of her head in a bid at nonchalance—"we've not shared so much as a kiss." *But I wanted to. I wanted him to want me in all the ways a man desires a woman.* Hers had been foolish, hopeless musings of a girl who'd had the misfortune of falling in love with the last person she ought.

"That's not true, love," he dangled, flicking the tip of her nose the way he might a younger sibling. That only sent her frustration up a notch.

"I'd hardly consider a kiss between two children anything significant." That sloppiest of kisses had come when she was a girl embarking on a quest for knowledge about the "human kiss" with him, a like-minded scholar of six and ten.

"And yet..." He stalked around the sofa with sleek steps. "You recall it all these years later." Crispin hooded his gaze, the long, thick, black lashes she'd envied as a girl sweeping down. Only, there had never been anything primal in the way he'd stared at her before.

I said too much. "H-hardly for any reasons that matter," she squeaked, cursing her loose tongue. *She* forced her feet to remain rooted to the floor as he stopped before her.

Barely a handbreadth of space divided them, the true divide between them far greater than any physical distance. He lowered his lips close to her ear. "Have a care, Elizabeth." The scent of him, a dry, earthy oak moss, was intoxicating and so different from the lemon and bergamot he'd once favored. It highlighted how very much they were strangers to each other now... in every way.

Her body, however, had no discretion. Elizabeth's belly fluttered. "A... a care?"

"With all this talk of kissing and the marital bed, I might begin to think you're eager for me to, at long last, consummate our vows," he whispered, his breath tickling the sensitive skin of her right lobe, knocking the air from her lungs.

Elizabeth knew with the same confidence she did every last lesson she'd delivered in this finishing school that a kiss from this man before her would bear no hint of the clumsy, wet joining of their youth. That Crispin, the Duke of Huntington, was a man who'd wield those lips with skill where seduction would ultimately prevail.

Another smile ghosted his lips, a knowing one that brought the world rushing back to clarity in a rush of noise and motion.

With a gasp, she abruptly backed away. "Of course I don't want to f-fornicate with you." She despised the slight tremble of that one word that made a liar of her. For she did, even all these years later, wonder what it would be like to know Crispin Ferguson's embrace, not as an experiment, but as a like yearning shared between a woman and a man.

"Fornicate, Elizabeth?" he drawled, that damned dimple in his cheek indicating he was enjoying this entirely too much. "Never tell me your stuffy views on making love are a product of the illustrious Mrs. Belden."

Making love...

Her mouth went dry, her tongue heavy.

She and Crispin had spoken on anything and everything, but never *this*, never words that conjured forbidden acts and passionate meetings. His rogue's grin deepened.

Elizabeth tightened her jaw. He was very much the rake Society painted him in the gossip sheets. "Do not be silly. Mrs. Belden does not permit discourse on..." A twinkle glinted in his eyes. "You're teasing me."

"Indeed," he replied, infuriatingly smug. His casual drawl doused whatever madness had momentarily gripped her.

"Say what it is that brought you here," she demanded, tired of his games and the back-and-forth debate that was going nowhere. "I've students to instruct." Angry, mocking, miserable students who despised her for what she was—a dragon come to crush their spirits. Unlike him, a former fellow and scholar instructing young boys at Oxford on scientific matters of import.

"I trust your distinguished headmistress will be quite forgiving of our stealing a handful of minutes," he pointed out.

Yes, the ruthless proprietress of this place loved no one and nothing, except the approval of the peerage. She'd order the building turned upside down if it would ease a ducal frown into a smile.

"I don't care whether she is or is not. I care about the young women who are missing their lessons." Young girls were certainly better off doing... anything but what they'd previously been attending to in this room. Guilt needled her.

"Very well." Crispin straightened, his bicep muscles rippling the fabric of his wool riding jacket. "I want you to return to London... as my wife." He flashed a cool smile. "That is, after all, what you are."

Elizabeth opened her mouth and closed it several times. This time, no words came spilling out. *Annulment. Divorce. Outrage.* All had been responses or words she'd expected from Crispin's lips, but certainly not... *return to London as my wife.* It was *impossible.* Her heart did a funny leap, and she hated herself for that reaction. After all, the rule of reason said that if something didn't make sense, there was a reason for it. He didn't wish to be married to her. He'd never truly wished it. She eyed him suspiciously. "*Why do you want me to return with you?*"

"It is essential that Polite Society sees I am married, that you are real, and then?" He flicked a stare around the classroom. "You may go back to living your own life."

How very perfunctory he was. A duke passing judgment on this place and the life she'd made for herself. In this instance, she couldn't sort out which stung more. "I... see," she said, unable to keep the bitterness from creeping in.

He'd never wished to marry her.

Not truly.

He was your friend, Elizabeth, and you betrayed him. You put your own needs and desires above his…

Yes, their marriage had been based only on charity and *friendship*.

"May we speak?" Crispin motioned to the settee, as comfortable as one who owned that ivory seating. "Please?"

Please.

That was why, as a girl and then a young woman, he'd forever been her friend. He'd not been one of those nasty boys to revel in the power bestowed upon him as a ducal heir. He had not been one who'd commanded or accepted the world as his due. And now, all these years later, as a duke who could order all but the sun for his pleasures, he'd not changed. And how much easier it would have been had that not been the case. Clenching her fists, Elizabeth slid onto the edge of the seat.

Crispin took the aged King Louis chair opposite her, his powerful frame making the seat small. Grabbing the sides of it, he positioned himself so they faced each other. "As I was previously saying, since my father's passing, I've found myself…" He grimaced.

"Sought after by ladies everywhere?" she drolly supplied. As a young man, he'd earned the sighs of every girl in the village. Yet, he'd preferred her company above all others'. Even now it filled her heart with a silly giddiness. The Oxfordshire Oddity the village folk had called her. Until her relationship with Crispin had silenced them.

Crispin tugged at an immaculate, crisp, white cravat. "Hardly everywhere," he mumbled, just as modest now. "And not for any reasons that matter." Were he the smug, self-important lord just a step below royalty, it would be so very easy to resent him. What must it be like for him now, a specimen of masculine perfection to rival a Da Vinci statue and in possession of one of the most venerable titles?

You're the only one, Elizabeth, who doesn't see a future duke. You are the only one who sees me.

Unbidden, her gaze fixed on the sapphire signet ring upon his left littlest finger. The coat of arms marked his influence and lineage that went back to William the Conqueror.

Despite his noble roots, he'd craved her friendship as much as she'd yearned for his. When no one had wanted a thing to do with the unusual, bespectacled girl whose casual village-side discourse consisted of talk about a mare's estrous cycle, he'd delivered an equally eccentric bit of knowledge.

It's why they'd been a perfect match—as friends.

Until they'd not been. They'd gone and ruined something that had been too good, too precious to alter.

"I know it was a mistake, but it is done... and it cannot be undone."

Her throat worked painfully.

"Elizabeth?" he asked quietly, interrupting her miserable musings.

She cleared her throat. "Forgive me. Continue."

"I've recently come forward with the truth about my marital state."

The direct, logical person he'd once been would have done so in the bluntest way possible. "Never tell me you took out a page in the London *Times*?" she asked, finding her footing once more.

His rugged cheeks went red.

Despite the shock of seeing him and the madness of this moment, she couldn't stop the snorting laugh that burst from her lips. She made a futile attempt to bury it behind her hand. "You did."

"I didn't issue a public notice," he groused, his color rising. "Rather, I *carefully* dropped the information to Lady Jersey."

One of the leading ladies of the *ton*, the older matron would have sung such a juicy morsel to anyone and everyone with ears that functioned.

His calling forth that revered hostess also served as a reminder of the great divide between them. "Even a mother desiring a duke for her daughter would balk at bigamy," she drawled. "Therefore,

I trust my assistance is not truly required." Elizabeth made to rise.

"Elizabeth..." Crispin rested a hand on her knee, and her breath lodged in her lungs. "It is not that..." His words trailed off. Together, their gazes went to his hand upon her. The shock of his fingertips burned through the scratchy wool fabric of her dragon's skirts, his hand heavy and hot in a way that her body had never felt, his touch having the intended consequence of staying her movements—but not for the reasons he thought.

Some wave of dark, indiscernible emotion glinted in his dark blue eyes. His fingers tightened reflexively upon her knee, a clenching and unclenching of those long digits that crunched the fabric of her dress, searing her through her skirts.

Elizabeth swallowed hard.

Don't be a ninny. This is Crispin. Formerly a friend. Briefly a husband.

Except, the human body cared not for logic. They were all primitive beings. It was an understanding recorded since the beginning of time. That evidential understanding did nothing to dull the heat settling low in her belly. "It is not?" she prodded, her voice throaty to her own ears, sultry in ways she'd believed a bookish bluestocking such as her incapable.

As if burned, Crispin jerked his hand back, the imprint of that accidental caress lingering still. "Simple," he croaked. "It is not that simple."

Elizabeth fought through the daze he'd cast. "And why not?"

Crispin unfurled to his full height and began to prowl at a steady pace on the ancient floral Aubusson carpet. She narrowed her eyes. Pacing had forever been the telltale gesture of his unease.

"I might have earned something of a *reputation*," he muttered, avoiding her eyes when his forward pace brought him back to where he could make direct contact with her stare.

"Indeed?" She well knew what was written about Crispin. Even though she'd left him, she'd picked through those scandal sheets, aged by the time they reached Mrs. Belden's, about tales of Crispin's exploits. And each blasted piece had struck like an arrow to the chest, because he'd taken a vow to her, and their friendship had been one where pledges had meant something.

She feigned wide-eyed innocence. "Tell me, Your Grace, what manner of reputation is that?"

CHAPTER 4

ELIZABETH TERRY-BRIGHTLY, OR WHATEVER SURNAME she now went by, was nothing like the girl he remembered… and yet, at the same time, she was everything like her.

One thing, however, was very clear—the minx was having a deuced good time at his expense.

She may have become a master of dissembling in the time that had passed, but the glee she found in his discomfort was there in each well-placed barb she cleverly masked as a question.

He forced himself to stop, facing her once more.

More than a foot shorter than his own six feet, four inches and seated as she was, she still managed to stare down the length of her slightly too-long nose. Challenging him. Daring him. And somehow, also, teasing him. Such had always been her way.

"I've earned the reputation of a rogue," he confessed bluntly. Another gentleman would likely feel a modicum of remorse or regret at making that admission to his wife. For all the gossip, however, Crispin had not a jot to feel guilty over.

Elizabeth gave no outward reaction to his admission. "Have you?"

He narrowed his eyes. "Why do I think, Elizabeth, that you already knew that detail about me?"

A pretty blush stained her cheeks. "How would I know anything of the sort?" She countered with a question of her own, her pitched voice marking her a liar.

Why… it was true. The longtime friend and brief bride who'd

left in the dead of night had followed mention of his name.

Elizabeth watched him with suspicion-laden eyes. "What?"

With a slow smile, Crispin resettled himself onto the seat opposite her. Her betrayal had ripped him up. But knowing she'd followed his goings-on meant he'd mattered to her, too. "Why, you've followed me in the papers, haven't you, love?"

She shifted in her chair. "Merely to determine that you were nowhere near Mrs. Belden's."

His earlier and all-too-brief triumph faded. She'd left him. He'd given her his name and offered her security, and she'd simply abandoned him. As such, there could be no doubting her feelings for him. Or rather, lack thereof. "I see," he said evenly. That understanding had dawned long ago, and yet, something in hearing her speak so casually about hiding from him stirred the turbulent emotions within his breast, a swirl of anger, hurt, and shock that he'd thought he'd mastered, but they remained deep within.

Elizabeth sat upright, her spine going erect, as though a metal rod had been inserted. The girl she'd been would have shot out question after question. This new, more controlled, somber version of her younger self remained stoically silent.

Crispin went on with his reasons for seeking her out. "The reputation I've... earned"—he stumbled over that word—"has cast doubt on the veracity of my claims of marriage."

Elizabeth puzzled her brow. "They believe you've *lied* about being married?"

"Indeed." Stretching his legs out, Crispin looped them at the ankles. "Young ladies determined to have the title of Duchess of Huntington suspect that I, in my desire to carry on my roguish existence, have fabricated a wife."

She made a tsking sound. "If only you'd had such an idea ten years ago, you would have found yourself unburdened with a wife."

He blinked slowly, and it took a moment for those words and the implied meaning to sink into his mind. Was that what she believed? That all this time, he'd spent regretting the arrangement they'd struck as friends? One that had not only been mutually beneficial, but had formed a bond far greater than any cold, empty union of the *ton* because of the friendship between them?

Anger rooted around his chest, severing the thin thread of his patience. "I'm not the one who ran," he snapped. That leached the color from her cheeks. His chest rose and fell with the force of his fury, and he leaned forward in his chair, shrinking the distance between them. "You were. So do not play the wounded party, *Your Grace*," he shot back, turning the title they shared on her. Mindful that any busybody could be about, he lowered his voice to a hushed whisper. "You left, Elizabeth. You did. Not me." And in doing so, she'd turned her back on a bond that went back to the earliest days of their youth.

Crispin waited, braced for her response.

She clasped her hands primly on her lap. Her death grip drained the blood from her fingers and made a mockery of her calm. "So you need me to act as your wife," she said quietly.

"Yes, for Polite Society."

What did you expect? An apology? Any hint of regret or shame?

And would any of it have made a difference, either way?

"How long would you require I serve in that capacity?"

They might as well have spoken of a hired servant and not a woman who, with her veneered title, could command any ballroom or household throughout England.

He fisted his hands so tight, his signet ring bit into the bottom crease of his finger. "As my wife," he repeated, needing her to hear it and acknowledge it, for she wasn't a housekeeper or parlor maid. She was the woman whose name was eternally attached to his own. "I must introduce you to the world, as my *wife*."

"For how long?" she repeated.

At what point had such a relationship with him become so anathema to her? And why should it bother him still, all these years later? Hadn't he accepted her betrayal and built an existence without her in it? Except, her indifference made a mockery of that very thought.

To give himself something to do, Crispin pulled out his gloves and beat them together. "I'll require your presence for a handful of days. We'll host a formal ball for members of the *ton*. Nothing more." There had never been anything more. *But there could have been.* There almost had been. And not for the first time since she'd left, he thought briefly about what these years would have been like had she stayed. Fighting back the useless, maudlin musings, he fixed on the task at hand.

Her frown deepened. "Planning a ball requires far greater circumspection." She proceeded to tick off on her fingers. "There is the menu to consider and musicians. And, of course, because of your station"—*your*, not *our*—"invitations must be handwritten and delivered."

Ah, Elizabeth. She spit forth each detail the way she had her findings about a butterfly flitting through his mother's prized gardens. As a girl, and then woman, who valued research, Elizabeth, however, didn't have the logic required for the nonsense of societal functions. As she continued her accounting, he sat back and studied her. "Of course, you'll no doubt already have candles, but you'll require those that burn for eight hours." She furrowed her brow. "I'd venture three hundred candles, and they'll cost upwards of…" Her lips moved as she completed her silent tabulations. "Fifteen pounds."

He opened his mouth to interject, but she continued. "And there are floral decorations—hothouse and those taken from your private gardens."

Setting down his gloves, Crispin picked up the small leather volume that rested on the table between them. He briefly studied the gold lettering etched along the spine and then flipped through the tome. As he fanned the pages, section headings drifted past.

Deportment…

Propriety…

Conduct…

Butterflies are polymorphic, you know. A useful skill and all to evade their predators. You'd be wise to employ a bit of that strategy at your mother's next picnic…

"How very different your reading and knowledge content is now," he murmured.

She avoided his gaze, training it instead on the dull bit of literary nonsense best used for kindling in his fingers. "Given the reason for your sudden visit, it appears there is, and always was, more relevance to that information"—she motioned to that title he still held—"than any useless fact about butterflies."

A pang struck in his chest. Is that what she truly believed? Or was that what the clever young woman who'd pored over scientific journals and periodicals told herself to ease the loss of those topics that had so fascinated her? It was on the tip of his tongue to ask as much, but something in the strain of her lips called back the questions.

Crispin redirected them to safer territory. "The ball has already been planned, Elizabeth." His mother, one of Society's leading hostesses, had leaped at the opportunity to plan a ball, until she'd learned the reasons for it. "The moment I secured confirmation of your whereabouts, I took the liberty of having the event organized and invitations sent out."

Fire flashed in her eyes. "You assumed my accompanying you was a given, then?"

No. He'd never known precisely what Elizabeth Brightly, as unpredictable as an autumn leaf winding a path to the ground, intended to ask... or do. That unpredictability was one of the first things that had so captivated him as a young boy meeting a girl with her head buried in a tattered copy of *The Aurelian*, the coveted text about moths and butterflies by Harris gifted to her by her father. "I had"—*hoped*—"expected you would join me."

"I see." Elizabeth stood and wandered over to the floor-to-ceiling window streaming in sunlight through the well-shined lead panels. She directed her gaze to the grounds below.

How could she see anything when he himself had been flipped upside down the moment he'd set foot inside this slightly out-of-mode parlor and found her here? All at once, a friend and a stranger.

She glanced briefly back. "You trusted you could simply order me back." Her voice rang with bitterness and regret.

Not for the first time, anger swirled in his chest because of this woman. She thought so little of him, when he'd always held her on a pedestal above all. She'd been his only friend, the one person who hadn't given a jot that he'd one day become a duke. Mayhap that was why her betrayal had most stung. Why it still did.

"No," he confessed in somber tones as he climbed to his feet. For the reputation of scoundrel that dogged him these years, he'd never been one to prevaricate or practice in the art of deception. "I won't order you. I'd ask you for your help, Elizabeth."

She sank her slightly crooked front teeth into her bottom lip, troubling that plump flesh, bringing his attention to her mouth.

A mouth he'd joined with his but once, and then when they'd been mere children conducting an experiment on "the kiss." It had been a quick meeting, over too quick for him, coming long before she'd been his briefly betrothed and even more briefly his bride.

Now he stared, transfixed, his throat dry, as he imagined her lips under his, not as part of any scientific study between children, but for reasons that had only everything to do with learning each other in every way. She'd be explorative and unabashed. As a woman, she'd kiss with the same abandon as she'd chased him as a child through the Oxfordshire countryside.

With a distracted pucker between her red brows, Elizabeth turned, and he swiftly schooled his features.

"Very well." She ran her palms along the front of her skirts.

It took a moment for those words to register. "Beg pardon?" What in blazes had they been discussing? It was all jumbled in his mind.

"I'll accompany you to London." Elizabeth paused. "And then, I have your word, I am free to return?"

"This is where you want to be?" he countered.

There was a minute pause he might merely have conjured from wounded male pride. "Yes," she murmured.

He folded his hands behind him. As a duke with a fortune to rival Prinny's, five country seats, two seaside properties, and jewels to bestow upon her that dated back to Henry VIII's first wife, it was humbling to find that the woman he'd married preferred a life of drudgery—in a place rumored to crush young girls' spirits, no less.

"As you wish." Needing some distance from the one who'd betrayed him, Crispin quickly rose. "Accompany me back for one ball, and you'll be… free." As she'd always wished. Pain sluiced through him, as cutting as a knife. "We leave tomorrow."

Before she might change her mind and withdraw yet another promise made, Crispin left.

CHAPTER 5

The following morn, Elizabeth and Crispin had come almost full circle, in an unexpected way.

Now they made a different journey than the one they'd taken to elope to Wilton before returning to his family's Oxfordshire ancestral estate. This time, they found themselves traveling onward, not to greet his regally powerful parents… but *all* of Polite Society.

Elizabeth's stomach flipped over. It was one thing instructing the ladies of London and sending them on their way, never to be seen again. It was altogether different to join their ranks.

"Enough," she muttered to herself. "You are no less than they are."

Reminding herself of her own worth did little to settle the pitch of her belly.

A moment later, the well-sprung black carriage with gold velvet seats sprang into motion, drawing Elizabeth away from the place that had been a home to her these past years.

And the place that would be a home to her in the years to come.

It was a fate she'd long accepted as fact, although logic said this reunion had been coming, that it had been overdue. A couple could not simply marry and then… part. Not without consequences and not without some closure. Especially when it involved a ducal heir.

Only, he was no longer a ducal heir. Crispin Ferguson was very much a duke, born and bred to the role. He exuded that masterful confidence and strength managed only by kings and those closest to him in rank and privilege.

But not all dukes were doddering, and in their time apart, Crispin had... changed. He'd added muscle to his once lanky physique and radiated a primal power that she didn't know what to do with.

Drawing back the intricately tailored curtains, she stared out at the modest country manor house where she'd served as a finishing school instructor. The gardens and greenery surrounding the perimeter of the stone structure provided a bright splash of color amidst an otherwise dreary scene.

Eventually, the nestled-away school faded from view and left only the rolling countryside in its wake.

Nay, that was not the only sight outside her window.

Elizabeth squinted, searching for a better glimpse of the figure riding ahead.

Her heart did a little jump.

Crispin sat tall and relaxed with his broad shoulders back, a masterful rider wholly in command of his mount. His gaze pointed forward, past the chestnut gelding's ears, and he maintained an expert focus and ease in the saddle.

That, however, had always been Crispin.

From archery and fencing, to every athletic pursuit in between, he'd been accomplished in any and every endeavor. And yet, when the village boys and those visiting his family's estates had been more engrossed in physical pursuits, Crispin had preferred to have an essay in hand. He'd fluently spoken Latin and Greek and debated the complex concept of metaphysics in those respective languages with the same ease with which he'd mastered other skills.

Whereas Elizabeth had always been rot at riding or swimming, he'd excelled in... *everything*, really.

She dusted a finger over the window, tracing a counterclockwise circle upon the sun-warmed pane, spiraling left of that central line. Her gaze fixed on the circular smudge left there.

"*Give me your palm, Elizabeth.*"

She hesitated before holding it out. Wordlessly, Crispin bent over her ink-stained palm and traced a delicate backward circle. She giggled at the faint brush of his fingers. "Th-that tickles." When he continued, attending to that pointed task, she leaned forward. "What are you d-doing?"

"*It's an ancient spiral. It speaks to the winding journey we must take if we are to truly know and love ourselves. And in that*"—*he completed the circle*—"*we return with more wisdom and power.*"

Elizabeth abruptly dropped her hand to her lap. Aside from her parents, Crispin had been the only person to never see her as just an oddity and nothing more. He'd engaged with her in discussions that would have scandalized Polite Society for the sheer intellect of them.

And because of it, she'd elevated him to a level no mere mortal could reach.

That was why she'd fled. That was why she'd hidden.

No. She dug her fingertips into her temples and rubbed. That hadn't been the only reason. There'd been so many more that, when tangled together, the only true course presented was her leaving.

As such, she'd not truly thought of it as hiding from him. *Hiding* suggested that another person wanted to find you. Ultimately, Crispin hadn't truly wanted to marry her. He'd done so out of friendship...

"It was a mistake marrying her. I know that, but there can be no undoing it."

Elizabeth's fingers curled into reflexive fists, noisily crinkling the fabric of her dull gray skirts. Odd that a handful of words could hurt so, even all these years later. Particularly ones she'd played and replayed in her mind in the hope that the familiarity of them would remove any sting.

But it wasn't just about the pain caused by his regret.

She again found Crispin with her gaze.

She'd left *for him*. She'd gone so he wouldn't have to be reminded daily of the mistake he'd made—and so regretted.

After all, many lords and ladies carried on their own existences apart from their spouses. They had pragmatic unions bent on lineage and carrying on ancient titles.

Eventually, Crispin would have required an heir. As one who attended to details, Elizabeth had known as much. She'd just not allowed herself to consider the proper time to reunite with him. Time had simply... passed, until ten years divided them.

He'd not, of course, given any indication that he *wanted* to bed her.

"That is not why I'm here."

Elizabeth cringed. Why, with his dimpled grin, he'd all but laughed at her for even suggesting he might have located her for the sole purpose of begetting an heir.

Except, for the very briefest moments in time in Mrs. Belden's parlor, as he'd stared at her mouth, something had passed in his eyes. Something dark and dangerous, and inexplicably enticing for it—desire. Even as it was foolish for her to think he desired her in any way, there had been a flicker of passion.

A sound of disgust escaped her. "You pathetic ninny."

He was a rogue. By the very nature of the reputation he'd earned, he seduced and bedded grand beauties and wicked widows all over London. Never once in any of the scandal sheets had she read of Crispin being paired with a reed-thin, uncurved, bespectacled miss. No, they'd been lush and earthy and... not like Elizabeth in any way.

And she hated it. And Elizabeth hated him for his reputation and all those women who'd known him in the one way she hadn't.

You left, Elizabeth. You did. Not me.

She caught the inside of her lower lip hard between her teeth and silently damned him for being correct.

She had left, and she'd left *him* behind. And not for the first time since that early morn departure by mail carriage through the English countryside onward to an uncertain future, she considered what life would have been like had she stayed. Would she and Crispin have remained friends poring over journals and attending lectures in London, debating topics as they'd always done?

"How very different your reading and knowledge content is now."

Elizabeth finally looked at the aged brown leather journal beside her on the bench, a title that she'd had little time to read at Mrs. Belden's, but had pulled free as soon as her meager possessions had been packed in Crispin's carriage.

He was correct. She'd undertaken a whole new school of learning, topics and matters they'd both despised and mocked, but had ironically proved the basis of Elizabeth's existence.

She hesitated, and then picking up the small journal, she proceeded to flip through the volume.

The pencil markings upon the pages, renderings made in her quick, eager hand, had been faded by time. Elizabeth smoothed her palm over one drawing, faintly smudging the butterfly sketched there. How many times had she sat side by side with Crispin on a hillside, completing each sketch, both silent, no words needed, as they'd studied those texts?

Elizabeth pored over each sketch, the beloved works that had kept her awake as she strained to complete them with nothing more than a lone candle's flame to illuminate her efforts. She, as Crispin had aptly pointed out, had missed these studies in ways she'd not allowed herself to consider—until now. Until him.

She lingered on each piece they'd worked on together.

Mayhap they would have carried on with that same enthusiasm for learning.

Or would they ultimately have been pulled apart anyway, by resentment and the weight of his regret?

Her throat bobbed. She'd been too much a coward to remain behind and find out what happened to a young couple born to completely different societal ranks and who'd rashly wed. Particularly when one of that pair regretted the miserable, uncomfortable journey to Gretna Green.

Elizabeth snapped her book closed and glanced out the window once more.

From up ahead, Crispin cast a look back over his shoulder. Their gazes briefly collided.

Her heart knocking hard against her rib cage, Elizabeth tugged the curtain shut, welcoming even that illusory hint of privacy.

I can do this. It's merely one ball and a handful of days. And then, from there, she could return to Mrs. Belden's and live the remainder of her life apart from Crispin.

Except, why, reunited as they were all these years later, did that realization make her suddenly want to cry?

With a groan, Elizabeth dropped the back of her head against the carriage wall. "Enough," she muttered to herself. She was not one of those woebegone sorts who lamented what might have been.

She'd not begin now.

And certainly not for the man he'd become: a rogue, a scoundrel, scandalizing Society by his attendance at wicked masquerades and the string of lovers he'd taken through the years.

Forcibly thrusting thoughts of him aside, Elizabeth grabbed her valise from the opposite seat and set the heavy bag on her lap. She grunted. Wrestling with the rusty brass latch, she forced it open and rustled through the meager contents.

Decorum for Dancing Debutantes.

"No," she muttered, shoving aside the small leather tome, searching the others for the best reading option to occupy her for the course of their journey.

Curtsying for a Queen… and Other Ceremonious Expressions of Greeting for the Peerage.

"Blah." She grimaced, giving voice to the annoyance she'd long been unable to share at Mrs. Belden's over the miserable topics and the even more foolish titles. Her fingers collided with *The English Dancing Master*. Elizabeth drew it out, briefly flipping through the pages, and then tossed it into the bottom of her valise. It landed atop the small stack with a satisfying *thwack*.

For the first time since Crispin had reappeared and her world had been tilted on its axis, Elizabeth found herself smiling. She paused and drew a deep breath into her lungs. Oh, this was a journey she made with Crispin, the scoundrel of a husband she'd abandoned days after their wedding who would see her thrust amidst Polite Society. There would be room enough for horror and unease for the remainder of the carriage ride—and then their arrival.

And yet, there was something… invigorating in all of it.

Leaving Mrs. Belden's.

She shoved aside another book.

Talking to herself if she wished.

Elizabeth dug around, rustling through her bag.

Uncaring if she was too quiet or too loud.

Humming a country reel from *The English Dancing Master*, Elizabeth reached the bottom of her bag and stopped.

She puzzled her brow.

That was it.

She rummaged again through her bag. There had to be… something she wanted to read there. And yet…

Elizabeth sat back in the plush squabs of her bench. There wasn't. Everything she'd read or studied or lectured on had been dreary topics required of her. They'd become such a part of her existence, as common as plaiting her hair or rising in the morning.

And you've despised every last moment of it…

As soon as the traitorous thought crept in, she sat upright.

"I didn't hate it," she muttered to herself. "I've enjoyed *some* of the teachings."

To prove it, if even to herself, she grabbed the book at the very bottom of her collection. *Proper Rules of Proper Behavior and Proper Decorum.* She groaned and then quickly caught herself. Snapping the well-read volume open to the first page, she proceeded to read.

It is an essentiality that all young women, regardless of station, birthright, or rank.

She pulled a face and turned the page so hard it tore in the corner. "Redundant," she muttered.

A memory trickled in. Those earliest days of her arrival, with false references crafted in the late Duke of Huntington's offices. She'd been young, alone, scared, and so very miserable.

"*Do you have a problem with the selected texts, Mrs. Terry?*" Mrs. Belden thumped her cane, hard, and Elizabeth jumped.

"No. No. None at all, Mrs. Belden. Your text is…"

"Perfect." She whispered to the page before her the lie she'd given the old harpy. There'd been nothing perfect or good in any of those dratted teachings. They'd simply been a routine that she'd eased into and accepted as the new norm of her life.

Her throat bobbed. How dare Crispin ride in all these years later and recall a different life? One where she'd read… whatever it was that she wished and had been wholly supported in those endeavors.

Tears blurred her vision, and she frantically blinked them back. "Dust," she said softly, swatting at her eyes. "Merely dust."

Giving her head a clearing shake, Elizabeth settled into her seat and, with the calm, rhythmic back-and-forth sway of Crispin's carriage, read.

It is a universal truth widely recognized by those of venerable birth that dignified norms must be honored and upheld by all those desiring an equally venerable match. The union of a nobleman and lady maintains centuries-old connections that pay homage to the greatest foundations of all the kingdom was built upon and—

Her lashes fluttered, and she jerked herself awake. Drawing in a breath, she found the place she'd left off.

…decorum, decency, deportment signify the d's by which all ladies should live.

The most important of all the d's where the text was concerned… *distressingly* tedious…

Elizabeth briefly closed her eyes.

When she opened them, she registered an absolute still.

In a bid to push back the blanket of darkness surrounding her, she blinked slowly.

Her surroundings were unfamiliar and blurred, with the errant chitter of insects her only sound. Panic pounded at her temples. *Where... what?*

Elizabeth fished around for her spectacles.

As her fingers collided with the cold, familiar metal spectacles on her lap, reality came flooding in.

Crispin.

His request that she return with him.

Scrubbing at her eyes, Elizabeth jammed her glasses back into place.

At some point, the carriage had stopped.

On the heels of that came a dawning horror.

We've arrived.

Except...

She peeled the curtain back and did a sweep of the rolling emerald hills. The rich shades of green lent a darker hue under the cover of the night.

What in blazes...?

She searched for a hint of Crispin, straining for anything, even the steady beat of his horse's hooves.

Elizabeth swallowed hard, fighting back the earlier vestiges of sleep. Mayhap they'd stopped for the evening? But here...? In the midst of nowhere?

Her mind raced.

Or perhaps there were highwaymen.

An owl hooted an eerie night song.

With a squeak, Elizabeth dived for the handle. Shoving the door open, she leaped out, her boots sinking into a thick puddle of mud that splattered her skirts and cheek.

She shot a palm out, resting it against Crispin's ducal crest, to keep her balance. The abruptness of her movements sent her glasses tumbling from her nose.

Elizabeth scrabbled with the metal frames, her fingers tangling with them before they sailed through her fingers.

Her heart plummeted, and she glanced down in vain at the

blurry, darkened earth.

"Blast and damn," she muttered, dropping to a knee. She winced as the ground squelched, dampening her skirts. If Mrs. Belden could see her now, there'd be no post awaiting her upon her return. Elizabeth felt around.

Crispin's dark-clad driver, Brambly, came rushing over. "Is everything all right, Your Grace?"

Her heart sped up, and she did a nearly blind search for Crispin.

The servant, with more gray at his temples than when they'd last met, doffed his hat. "Your Grace?"

Me. He's talking about me, you ninny.

"I'm quite fine, Brambly." She plastered on a smile that went unreturned. "Thank you for asking."

"Your Grace." He sketched a stiff bow.

Yes, because a duchess could run through the English countryside sans garments, and the world would simply ask if she required help in her travels. She and Crispin had alternated between jesting and rolling their eyes at the attentions given those of that exalted station.

As though he himself wouldn't one day find himself filling their noble ranks.

They just hadn't acknowledged it.

Or ever entertained that she, Elizabeth Brightly, a village girl, would find herself joining Crispin's ranks.

At last, her fingers brushed cool metal, and triumph filled her. "Ah." Wiping the damp frames on the front of her coarse wool cloak, Elizabeth stood. "Wait!" she called out, and the graying servant turned back.

The portly man who'd always been ready with a grin and a jest now met her with coldness. "Your Grace?" he asked as he returned. A palpable dislike poured off his round frame.

Elizabeth frowned, knocked off-center again. Everything had changed, even with the servants who'd once treated her as though she were a cherished member of the Ferguson family.

The driver stared back at her impatiently.

She cleared her throat. "Why have we stopped?" she brought herself to ask through his annoyance. Crispin had been clear that they'd ride without stopping. There was the ball to consider… and the fact that he wished to conclude their business together.

Brambly nodded, and she followed the direction of the gesture. "Problem with His Grace's mount."

Pressing a hand over her brow to tunnel her vision, Elizabeth peered off into the distance. "His mount?" A memory flickered of she and Crispin watching as that cherished horse was foaled. They'd been two friends joined in equal awe and joy at the wonder of that moment, when any other lord would have merely waited for the delivery of a prized mount, a material possession that would exchange hands.

"Is there anything else you require, *Your Grace?*"

"No," she murmured. "That will be all."

The gravel crunched noisily under his feet as he returned to his post atop the box.

After he'd gone, Elizabeth trained her attention in the direction Brambly had indicated.

It really wasn't her business. Crispin didn't want her underfoot… or even near him. As such, she should return to the carriage and wait.

Elizabeth warred with herself.

Alas, she'd never been one to sit idly.

She considered the long Roman road a long while, and then, even as any intimate exchange could prove only a folly where this man was concerned, Elizabeth started down the road.

CHAPTER 6

Elizabeth had said yes.

Given the fact she'd gone out of her way to avoid him for nearly ten years, he'd anticipated it would be a good deal more difficult to attain her capitulation.

At best, he thought she'd give a polite *no* and send him on his way.

At worst, he'd foreseen himself begging her to return.

Copernicus whinnied and danced about on three legs.

"Easy," he murmured, stroking his withers. "Forgive me. I was distracted."

The chestnut stallion tossed his head, snorting loudly.

"I know," Crispin mumbled. "You deserve my full attention. You have it now."

Even as he sank back to his haunches to resume his inspection of the abrasion on Copernicus' right hoof, he sensed the lie as much as the loyal horse who drew his injured hoof protectively closer.

Crispin had done his best to forget Elizabeth. Through the initial terror of imagining her off on her own, logic had prevailed. There had never been anyone more resourceful or capable than Elizabeth Brightly. What she lacked in brawn and height, she far surpassed in wits and cleverness. No, the same girl who'd managed to knock out, with nothing more than a pebble aimed at the bastard's temple, the village bully who'd been mocking the vicar's simple daughter, would always do just fine on her own. Those assurances hadn't erased his fear, but they had prevented him from spiraling into madness because of the perils she'd face as a woman on her own.

Crispin stared blankly at Copernicus' wound. It had been more than just fear that had gripped him in those days, it had been heartache at her betrayal. They'd quickly plotted and planned a future together, friends who'd become companionable spouses.

Bitterness twisted at his lips. It hadn't taken her but a handful of days to come to regret her decision.

Copernicus nudged at the top of Crispin's head.

"You're right. I'm being remiss." He glanced up at the massive creature. "Again."

Copernicus whinnied in equine agreement.

Yanking the crisp white kerchief from inside his jacket, he snapped the fabric open. He proceeded to carefully clean the gravel and dirt from around the wound, and then he applied the fabric to the lightly bleeding injury.

A circle of crimson immediately stained the scrap, and Copernicus rumbled through his nostrils and danced away from him.

"Easy," he murmured in calm tones. "I have to stop the bleeding."

Copernicus immediately stilled.

In quick order, Crispin tugged free his cravat and set to work making a makeshift bandage, pausing in midwrap.

He sensed her presence before he heard or saw her. It was an intrinsic sense of knowing when Elizabeth was close that had always been there.

Crispin finished his task and stood.

The half-moon hanging in the night sky cast a soft circle of light about Elizabeth, with her same loose, too-big spectacles and drab skirts.

When, as a duchess, she should be wearing the softest, finest fabrics. Even as that had never been her way, she deserved to be draped in them. Anything but the coarse, dreary articles that made up her new wardrobe.

Uninvited, she came over.

Copernicus' ear pricked forward, and he burrowed his broad snout against her chest.

"Poor dear. Up to trouble again, are you?" she murmured, scratching the mount between his eyes.

Crispin stared on.

"Can you not find other friends? Those of the noble sort? Male ones? The girl is an oddity, Crispin," his mother implored. "She speaks to horses."

He, too, had spoken with those loyal creatures, but never when anyone had been about. Elizabeth had been unrestrained and unapologetic in her affections for all creatures.

As if feeling his stare, Elizabeth glanced up.

She abruptly released Copernicus' nose and stepped back.

The horse bleated, dancing forward for another hint of her affections.

Just like me, the poor fellow.

"Brambly indicated he was hurt."

"It is a flesh wound. I've already bandaged him—" She dropped to a knee. "I'll return shortly. You'll be safe with Brambly—"

Elizabeth scowled up at him. "Let me see to his bindings." She was already unwinding the sloppy one he'd assembled.

Yes, she'd always been splinting wounded sparrows and rabbits and had been far more skilled at it than he… or anyone he'd known.

She disentangled the lightly stained cloth, and feeling around the wound, she inspected the injury.

Pulling off his stained gloves, he went to a knee beside her. "What is your opinion?"

Elizabeth continued to probe the slight gash. "He was scraped. See here?" she murmured, trailing a fingertip vertically, taking care to avoid the seeping wound. "There's bits of gravel and rock lodged within that are irritating him, but he'd not go lame from it." Elizabeth held her palms up for Copernicus, and he nudged her fingertips. "I need to see the underside, sir."

He bleated.

"Tsk, tsk. You're braver than that." She softened the chastisement with a soothing caress along his elbow.

Crispin stared on as she ran her fingers back and forth in a gentle touch, and swallowed hard. He and Elizabeth had known everything about each other, and yet… he hadn't known her in the way Copernicus did now. He hadn't known the feel of her fingers, the brush of her hand in a lover's caress. "That's it, love," she was saying softly, and there was a husked quality to her voice that hypnotized.

He gave his head a disgusted shake. It was a sorry day indeed when a man envied his horse for the attentions he received.

"Did you feel each hoof?" she asked, sparing him a quick glance.

"I didn't," he said, his ears going hot. He'd been too busy lamenting what might have been and nursing wounded feelings at her betrayal to properly attend his horse—his *loyal* horse.

Scooting around Copernicus' right side, she started her examination of the back hooves.

"Did you find any variations in temperature?" she asked. "To indicate a possible injury or abscess," she added, the way he had schooled countless young men at Oxford on astronomy.

What a bloody waste of her talents these years. "I didn't."

She'd spent so much time instructing girls on matters of deportment and decorum, and all along, she'd had so much more to teach them. He hated that truth as much for the students she taught as for Elizabeth herself.

"What is your opinion?" he asked, forcing himself to abandon the past and focus on Copernicus' injury.

"He is fine. At least, his rear limbs are." She moved the heels, tapping the hoof walls. "You check for yourself," she urged.

While Elizabeth moved her study to Copernicus' front legs, Crispin inspected the back hocks for himself. As he did, from under the enormous mount's legs, he studied Elizabeth.

She was almost ten years older than when he'd last seen her, and there was a greater maturity to her heart-shaped face, a restraint that hadn't been there in her youth, but served her well in her examination now. For those changes to her temperament, an even greater intelligence sparkled in her eyes. It was a feat he would have believed impossible. She'd already been more clever than anyone he'd known.

"Ah," she was saying as she sank back on her heels. Several curls fell across her brow, and she pushed them behind her ears.

Using that as an invitation to join her, as he'd wanted to from the moment she'd moved out of his reach—always out of his reach—he looked to the hoof she lightly held. "What is it?"

"It's not merely the scrape," she explained. "Here, see?" And with her long, graceful neck bent, hair drawn tightly at her nape, he caught sight of a pink birthmark at the center of her nape—heart-shaped with a jagged, arrowlike slash through it. For everything he remembered and knew about this woman, that enticing mark hinted at all the ways in which she remained a mystery. And all the ways he longed to know her. Desire stirred, a potent hungering filling him to touch his lips to that tempting mark and explore it with his mouth. "Do you see here?" she asked, not raising her gaze.

His throat bobbed up and down. *You. I see you…*

Elizabeth shot a puzzled glance up at him.

He coughed into his fist. "I don't." Because he hadn't been attending the lesson she doled out. Rather, he knelt there, lusting after her.

"It's not your fault," she reassured, entirely too forgiving. "It is dark, and as such, you would not have necessarily noticed in your earlier examination." Elizabeth gently lifted Copernicus' left hock, and grazing her fingertip just above the horseshoe, she drew his attention to the discoloration there.

Crispin cursed roundly. "Bloody hell." How had he missed the darker spot? *Because you've thought of only Elizabeth Brightly since you discovered her whereabouts.*

Copernicus danced nervously on his back legs, drawing the injured limb closer.

Collecting the reins, Elizabeth offered soothing words to the mount, and the horse immediately calmed. Once he'd settled again, she returned to her previous ministrations. She sniffed at the bottom of his hock. "There's no odor."

"And no discharge," he noted, finally giving his horse the attention he deserved.

She nodded. "I need to slowly clean off the abrasion and then bandage him." She offered Crispin the reins once more. Shrugging out of her cloak, Elizabeth gripped the collar of the coarse garment between her teeth and pulled hard.

Riiiiiiip.

The loud rending earned another nervous dance from Copernicus.

"Easy," Crispin whispered for the horse's benefit, patting his sweaty coat. All the while, Crispin remained riveted on Elizabeth as she shredded the fabric into long, jagged strips. Elizabeth saw to Copernicus the way a field surgeon might a wounded soldier in battle. "Here," she instructed, handing over the makeshift bandages.

Here was a command perfectly befitting a duchess. That word, uttered in confidence, was refreshing for its sincerity.

Crispin accepted the brown fabric and shifted his weight over his legs. "Did Mrs. Belden have you tending to her livestock over the years?" he asked, his query nothing more than a pathetically weak attempt to draw forth the secret that had been her life these years.

If she knew he was fishing for information, she gave no outward indication. Not pausing in her task, Elizabeth snorted and countered with a question of her own. "Did Mrs. Belden take you as one who'd allow any young woman to care for horses?"

He found himself grinning. "No." The old harpy, who had exuded an icy reverence for the existing social strata, would have sought to shape Elizabeth into the same pale shadow of all the ladies in London. His smile fell. And yet, his wife had preferred that existence to one with him.

Mayhap it was fatigue, or the shock of seeing her again, or mayhap it was simply the intimacy of caring for his horse with this woman, but the hurt he'd thought conquered reared itself. Sharp. Poignant. Stark.

Elizabeth passed dirtied bandages over and replaced them with new strips of her shredded cloak, until the blood flow slowed and then stopped altogether.

With a pleased little smile, Elizabeth sank back on her haunches and studied the neat bandage she'd expertly tied about Copernicus' hoof. Several tight curls had escaped the familiar knot she'd always worn her hair in and hung over her slightly damp brow.

His fingers ached to test the texture of those red curls in ways he never had before.

"There," she announced, brushing the back of her hand over her forehead. "That should keep until we have him in a proper stable where he might rest it."

We.

One word that joined them together.

Without hesitation, she placed her long, blood-marred fingertips in his. Any other woman would have wilted at even the prospect of dirtying her hands, let alone staining them with a horse's blood.

They stood, awkwardness setting in when there had only ever been an ease between them.

Elizabeth was the first to break the moment. She bent to rescue her cloak.

Crispin intercepted her efforts. Tossing it onto a nearby boulder, he shrugged out of his cloak, made of a fine wool and trimmed in velvet, as her own garments should have been.

She stared quizzically at him. "What are you—?"

"You shouldn't be going about in a shredded garment." She deserved better. And the evidence of how she'd been living set the muscles in his stomach twisting into knots.

"Pfft." She stepped around him and reached for the article in question. "My cloak still serves its purpose."

That had always been Elizabeth. Unimpressed by the material baubles and fripperies that enthralled the rest of the world.

She latched the button clasp at her throat, and her fingers trembled slightly. That slight quake indicated that, for her control, she was not as composed in this moment as she'd have him believe.

What's become of us?

There'd only ever been a comfortableness in their exchanges, an ease that he'd never known with another single person. Crispin cleared his throat and rocked back and forth on his heels. "I should lead him on to the inn." He motioned to the graveled Roman road ahead, and Elizabeth followed the gesture. "It's but a short walk to the edge of Hampstead Heath." And he needed time to collect his thoughts and resurrect the barriers he'd built in her absence. "I'll return shortly."

He glanced off to where Brambly sat atop the carriage. The servant caught his gaze from across the way.

"I can join you," Elizabeth ventured tentatively.

Crispin whipped around. She *wanted* to accompany him?

"That is… I don't have to." Elizabeth's gaze fell to the ground. She kicked a pebble with the tip of her scuffed boot, and it collided with the top of his foot. "If you'd rather…"

"Very well." He forced the response out in neutral tones. Except, as they started onward, a lightness spread in his chest. He was surely pathetic for the warmth that her simple request had wrought, and yet, he'd always had a weakness for Elizabeth Brightly.

He was just as weak now.

CHAPTER 7

*V*ERY WELL.

Crispin's response hadn't exactly been a resounding welcome.

Nor had it even been a mildly enthused one.

And why should it have been? They'd shared a bond over the years, but for him, it had never been a romantic one… whereas, for her?

Her mind shied away from any further exploration of what she'd felt for Crispin Ferguson, the Duke of Huntington. They were feelings and sentiments she'd never allowed herself to explore, for fear of the implications of them.

Facts were safer. They were concrete and indisputable, whereas feelings and emotions were open to interpretation and analysis and could be twisted and bent so that a person was no longer in possession of clarity over one's own feelings.

Walking side by side, so close their arms occasionally brushed, Elizabeth huddled within the folds of her cloak.

She shouldn't have asked to join him.

He would have been better off going out on his own, leaving Elizabeth behind with a disdainful Brambly as her only company. The sooner they returned to London, hosted that ball, and went back to the way things were, the better off they would both be.

Because every moment with Crispin put her further and further down a path of peril where she was forced to see all the ways he *hadn't* been altered by time, rank, power, or privilege. He was a titled gentleman still unafraid to kneel in mud and care for his horse, and where any other man, regardless of station, would have balked at a woman taking on that same task, Crispin had relinquished control and seen a woman as being as capable as anyone.

Whenever she'd thought of him, he'd always been changed in her mind. He was the rogue the papers purported him to be, who kept company with other like-minded rakes and had greater interest in the beauties he bedded than in the works he'd once read.

Her heart clenched, squeezing like one of those vises her papa had used when he'd built the rocker 'round their cottage, the pressure making it hard to draw a proper breath as jealousy swamped her.

There had been others in his life. Not village girls, but ladies he'd truly wanted... in the ways a man longed for a woman.

Elizabeth bit the inside of her cheek hard enough that the metallic tinge of blood filled her senses.

She stole a sideways peek at him. This broad, powerful figure was a stranger physically, and yet, despite those pieces of gossip she'd stolen about him over the years, he was unchanged in all the ways that mattered. Had he been the pompous duke who cared more for his own comforts than that of a loyal horse, it would have been easier to accept that he'd given his affections to other women. Lords weren't loyal to their wives. Her mama had always said as much, oftentimes in jest, as reasons she'd never have wanted anything more than her eccentric, failed merchant of a husband.

They were all the reasons she'd loved him as a friend.

Liar, you always wanted more with him.

She stumbled. *No.*

Retaining his hold on Copernicus' reins in one hand, Crispin caught her lightly by the forearm with the other, and electric heat just like the sizzling charges she'd studied went through Elizabeth. Magnetic and tingling and—

Crispin steadied her. "Are you all—?"

"Fine," she blurted, her heart threatening to beat a path outside her chest. He was her friend. He'd only ever been her friend. She loved him as that and nothing more. Her mouth went dry as fear needled in her belly. It couldn't be anything more. "I tripped." She swiftly drew back from his hold. "On a root," she continued on a frantic rush. Unbidden, her fingertips went to the place his firm but contradictorily gentle touch had seared her, even through the thin wool fabric. His brows dipped, and he glanced over his shoulder at the handful of steps they'd traveled since. "Or a rock," she finished weakly. The clouds overhead chose that inopportune moment to float past the moon and cast a damningly bright glow upon her blushing cheeks. "It might have been…" *Stop. You simply lost your balance.* He needn't know more than that. Elizabeth went close-lipped and redirected her attention to the bandage she'd wound about Copernicus' wound.

Heat pricked her neck at the feel of Crispin's eyes on her.

In the end, she was saved by the unlikeliest of heroes.

Copernicus nudged Crispin hard between the shoulder blades, knocking him slightly forward. Switching the reins to his other hand, Crispin did a quick search of the injured mount. "You're as skilled as you always were at bandaging up a wound," he noted.

Some of the tension went out of her. This was safe. This was a familiar topic that didn't involve recriminations about their past, or the yearning she'd buried in her heart. "I'm not completely out of practice. I've had many spirited students over the years who required the occasional patching up."

"Were they?"

She stared quizzically back.

"Spirited?"

"Yes. Of course." A wistful smile played at her lips. "Some more than others." Some of the more lively students she'd instructed flashed to mind. Those mischievous girls had marked a break from the tediousness that had come to mark her existence.

"And did the students leave your tutelage with that same strength?"

She stiffened as the insult rolled along her back, one she'd have to be deaf to fail to hear. The oak-paneled inn drew into focus. Elizabeth kept her gaze on the whorl of white smoke spiraling from a distant chimney and fought for the restraint she'd so desperately mastered over the years. "Not all of us can have the luxury of a fellowship at Oxford," she gritted out, hating the envy that had always been there at his securing one of those distinguished posts. "And certainly not a woman."

"No, but neither did you have to trade your honor for a post at Mrs. Belden's Finishing School."

Elizabeth gasped and jerked to a stop beside the slate boundary stone at the center of the gardens. "How dare you?" He'd pass judgment on her for having survived these years as she had? And on the place she worked?

"I dare because it's true," he shot back, releasing Copernicus' reins. The horse hobbled over to the edge of the road and proceeded to chomp on the wildflowers growing there.

"You know nothing about Mrs. Belden's." Elizabeth seethed, tasting her fury. "And you know nothing about me." Not now.

It was yet another wrong thing to say. Crispin stalked over, a predator on the prowl, his gleaming black boots grinding up gravel and dirt. "No, I don't, Elizabeth," he purred in the hated, gruff rogue's tones he'd used on so many others.

And I'm just as weak for him.

"But once, I knew everything about you," he whispered, as if he'd followed her unspoken thoughts. "I knew the way you dog-eared pages you read until you had each verse or sentence upon them committed to memory. I knew how you loved the rain because you could splash through the puddles afterwards."

Her heart worked. He remembered all that? All distant memories of her younger self that no rogue should dare recall.

A ghost of a smile played at the corners of his lips. "Yes," he said again, with an unerring accuracy. "I remember even that."

The backs of her knees knocked into a boulder, the sharp stone biting into the fabric of her skirts, knocking her onto her buttocks. "And yet..." He stopped and framed his hands on opposite sides of her, effectively trapping her. "There is so much more that remains a mystery about you." He hung that statement there as a temptation. His arms came about her like a prison that, God help her, she didn't wish to escape. Her pulse slowed and then quickly picked up a frantic beat. "Like the taste of your lips."

Her heart jumped. "W-we kissed one another."

"As children." His breath fanned the curls that had escaped her tight chignon. "Not as a man and woman. Not," he continued, like temptation itself, "a kiss driven by desire that shreds rationale thought and leaves in its place nothing but unadulterated feeling."

Swallowing hard, Elizabeth tilted her head back to meet his gaze. The movement sent her loose wire-rimmed frames slipping down her face.

Crispin raised a hand between them. His fingertips brushed the seam of her lips, the tip of her nose, before capturing the spectacles and sliding them into their proper place. "There," he whispered, lingering his touch upon her.

He surely used nothing more than a rogue's tricks to discomfit her, and yet, she proved herself far less logical than she'd ever credited. The passion burning in Crispin's eyes stole the breath from her lungs, searing her with the intensity of a gaze so palpable she could almost believe his was a genuine hungering—for her. "You're so very familiar now with heated embraces and stolen kisses?" she countered, more a reminder for herself that the man who'd pledged his loyalty had betrayed those vows with others. Nameless, faceless beauties who'd had the pleasure of the very embrace he now spoke of.

That green serpent slithered around inside, poisoning her with her own jealousy.

Crispin smiled slowly. "Ah, but we're not speaking about any embraces I've shared with others." He dipped his head. Their breath stirred puffs of white in the cool night air, the little wisps tangling and dancing together. "I'm discussing the ways I haven't yet known you."

"Y-yet?" she urged, barely recognizing the sultry quality of her query. For the word he'd used suggested far more.

Crispin's gaze darkened, and he palmed her cheek.

Their eyes locked, their chests rose and fell in a like rhythm, and then, with a groan, Crispin claimed her lips.

Heat—sizzling, electric, and as dangerous as the lightning currents she'd studied as a girl—burned her from within.

Elizabeth moaned, and then gripping the lapels of his cloak, she angled her head to receive his kiss, this union of their mouths unlike the hasty one they'd shared as children. Now, only a raw, unadulterated passion blazed between them.

"Elizabeth," he groaned. Her name, a plea, a hungry, desperate rumble, only stoked the flames of yearning that now spread through her. He licked her lips, tracing the seam, silently pleading for entry, and she let him in.

His tongue brushed hers like a brand, marking her, and she moaned, matching his movements.

Never breaking contact with her lips, Crispin guided her back until she lay prone upon the smooth surface of the weather-beaten boulder, laying her under him like a primitive offering to the gods.

His mouth left hers, and she keened at the loss, that incoherent plea giving way to a groan as he trailed his lips everywhere, from the corner of her mouth and lower to the lobe of her right ear. He caught that delicate flesh and lightly suckled, drawing another earthy moan from deep within her throat.

"So beautiful," he breathed against her neck, and with a long, wanton moan, she tipped her head sideways, allowing him better access to that place where her pulse beat wildly.

He placed his lips gently to the spot, nipping at it lightly with his teeth, like a stallion marking a mare. So primal, so raw that the ache at her center grew sharp.

As he worshiped that flesh, Elizabeth tangled her fingers in the lush strands of his neatly clipped chestnut waves, holding him close.

All the while, Crispin worked his hands over her, exploring her. Through the fabric of her skirts, he found her hips, sinking his fingertips into the flesh.

"Crispin," she moaned. Of their own volition, her legs fell open in an invitation as old as Eve. His shaft, thick and hard with his desire, prodded her through her skirts, and the ache at her center grew. Panting like he'd run a great race, he dropped his elbows on either side of her head and reclaimed her mouth, thrusting his tongue deep and mating with hers in a primitive dance.

He wants me.

It was a heady, unlikely truth, and yet, every stroke of his tongue against hers and every rasp of his breath bespoke of a like hungering.

He drew her skirts up slowly. The cool night air slapped at her skin, a balm to the fire he'd set. Crispin stroked her bare leg, as if familiarizing himself with the feel of her, a glorious massage that pulled incoherent, garbled entreaties from her throat.

Suddenly, Crispin tore himself away.

"No," she whispered.

Breathing hard, he stared down at her through heavy lashes.

He touched a fingertip to his lips.

In quick order, he had her on her feet, and as her skirts fluttered into place, he righted the loose tendrils, tucking them back behind her ears with an ease only a rogue could manage.

What? Why had he stop—?

Someone cleared his throat.

Oh, blast.

The sting of mortification burned away the chill left by the night air, and Elizabeth shrank behind Crispin. Of course, as one with a scoundrel's reputation, he'd be a master at assignations.

A lad with tired eyes and a heavily freckled face stared baldly at them. "Can I help you?" he offered, alternating a curious stare from Elizabeth to Crispin several times before ultimately settling on the more well-attired and influential of their pair.

Crispin straightened, and gone were all traces of anger from moments ago. In their place was the smooth, even, ever-charming gentleman. "My mount is injured and in need of care and a stable." He tugged out a purse and tossed it over. The boy easily caught it. "I'll need to stable him here until I can send someone to retrieve him. We'll also require two rooms."

The child paused in midstudy of the velvet sack's contents. "Don't have two rooms, sir. Me mum and da have only one room for the night."

Elizabeth curled her toes into the soles of her boots. Blast. Of course there was only one room.

"We shall take your remaining room."

The boy nodded and then, collecting Copernicus' reins, led the mount to the stables.

After he'd gone, Crispin glanced over. "This isn't done," he promised on a husky whisper.

As they started toward the inn, dread twisted in her belly.

For, God help her, Elizabeth proved how very weak she truly was. She didn't want to be done with Crispin Ferguson, and that truth sent terror clamoring inside her.

CHAPTER 8

THERE HAD ALWAYS BEEN LIVELY debates between Crispin and Elizabeth. And laughter and discourse.

What they had never suffered from, however, was silence.

Until now.

A thick, tense, uncomfortable silence hung in the air and grew with every passing instant.

Since their embrace, the never-shy Elizabeth had avoided his eyes.

With their belongings being taken up to their shared room and a bath being readied by the tavern keeper, Crispin and Elizabeth sat across an uneven oak table amidst a quiet taproom, two plates between them.

Elizabeth pushed her fork around her dish, attending her skirret pie with the same intensity she'd bestowed on every tome he'd sneaked from his family's libraries and turned over for her research.

Which, after a day of traveling and with this being her first fare, would not have been unusual… if she hadn't grown squeamish whenever her own mum had cooked with skirrets.

Crispin tightened his fingers around the pewter tankard in his hands.

Her discomfiture was now as great as it had been the last time they'd kissed. That previous meeting of their mouths had wrought havoc on his senses and haunted his six-and-ten-year-old self's dreams.

That exchange, to him, had been magical and wondrous and—

Yuck. That was as pleasant as a raw skirret. Can you determine what all the fuss is about?

That had also been the moment he'd had his pride badly beaten by the truth that the feelings he'd carried for the slightly younger girl had been wholly one-sided—and humbling for it.

In the past, he'd bolted shortly after their first kiss, too much of a coward to face any more of her grimaces, but now he sat across from her, studying her bent head over the rim of his glass.

The pursed-lipped distaste she'd worn as a girl had, this time, been replaced by a woman's desire. Her breathless moans echoed around his mind even now, her entreaties quiet as she'd clung to him like ivy. Unlike before, she'd wanted him as much as he hungered for her, and that realization steadied him.

Leaning back in his seat, Crispin stretched his legs out, the tips of his boots colliding with hers.

She stiffened but made no move to pick her head up.

"You've changed in many ways, Elizabeth," he noted, deliberately husking his tone.

Her fork scraped across the plate, knocking a boiled potato over the edge and onto the table. She battled herself. It was a fight she wore in the tense set of her narrow shoulders. She was no coward, though, and Elizabeth raised her head slowly, daring him with her eyes to go on.

Crispin curled his lips up. "You've developed a taste for"—her thin red eyebrows shot above her spectacles—"*skirrets*."

She didn't blink for a long minute, her impossibly large eyes forming perfect circles.

He winked.

Elizabeth's brows fell, returning to their proper place.

Crispin nodded at her plate of carved, but otherwise uneaten, pie. She followed his stare. Muttering under her breath, she grabbed her knife and carved one of the already cut pieces into several, smaller, minuscule bits.

His lips twitched. "What was that?"

"I like them just fine," she mumbled. Still, she made no move to raise the fork to her lips.

He winged an eyebrow up.

She uttered something that sounded very much like *infuriating spider brain.*

"It's really an unfair charge, you know," he said, and she paused, a forkful of pie halfway to her mouth. "It's all a matter of proportion, really."

"What?" she ventured, lowering her utensil.

"The spider," he elucidated. "Given their size, they are, in fact, *mostly* brain."

She blinked wildly, and the contents of her fork tumbled onto the table. "Indeed?"

He sat back, encouraged by her interest. "Albrecht von Haller—"

"The Swiss naturalist," she interjected with such excitement glittering in her eyes that it lit her face and bathed her cheeks in a delicate flush.

All the breath lodged in his chest.

She is magnificent...

Elizabeth cocked her head, knocking her spectacles slightly askew and bringing him back from his woolgathering.

"He wasn't just a naturalist," he said, clearing his throat. "His accomplishments also included anatomy and physiology."

She opened her mouth and then stopped. Suspicion darkened her gaze, and she held her fork out menacingly. "We never read any evidence outside of his works on herbaria."

Crispin gave her a pointed look. "No, *we* didn't." They could have, though. There was so much they could have shared.

Elizabeth faltered as understanding marched across her expressive features. She slowly lowered her fork to the table.

His fingers curled hard around his tankard. He didn't want to shatter the fragile bond with talks of their broken past. "His son, Gottlieb Emanuel, came to speak extensively at Oxford, offering lectures on his father's works."

The animated spark was lit once more within her clever gaze. She sat forward. "Which topics did he speak on?"

How he'd missed these exchanges. Crispin nodded and set down his drink. "Haller believed that as body size goes down"—he held his hands apart and shrank them together until the palms nearly touched—"the proportion of the body taken up by the brain increases."

Elizabeth wrinkled her nose. "Which would not mean greater brain function," she pointed out.

"No." His grin widened. "It does, however, go to the relativity of size."

"Hmm." She chewed at the tip of her index finger, her gaze contemplative. She abruptly stopped. "Have there been studies performed?"

"On whether or not I'm spider-brained?" he asked, pulling a laugh from her, the bell-like expression of mirth earning stares from nearby tables. He joined in, his chest rumbling from amusement he'd not felt in so long.

"On the spider," she needlessly clarified, wiping the mirth from the corners of her eyes.

Crispin shook his head. "Not that I've been able to discover." He winked again. "I just took the liberty of applying the principle to your insult."

Her lips twitched. "Fair turn."

They shared a smile, and just like that, they were restored to the same pair who'd spoken for hours about topics that had horrified his parents. When was the last time he'd enjoyed himself this much? None of the company he'd kept these years had cared a jot about anything outside of their own pleasures: balls, soirees, scandalous masquerades with the lone friend he'd made in Elizabeth's absence.

As quick as it came, however, her smile slipped, and reality forced itself upon them once more.

As if it could ever truly be gone. As if they could simply move past her abandonment. And how he despised himself for being shredded by her betrayal still. He swiped his drink off the table and took a long swallow of the vile, bitter ale. "I'll allow you to your skirrets, madam."

She lowered her crimson brows. "Is that a challenge?" She gave a toss of her disheveled coiffure, and several still errant curls bounced, bringing his attention briefly to the high neck of her hideous gray gown.

In his mind, he stripped away that coarse fabric and replaced it with a shimmering satin that molded to her slender frame with her every movement. Lust bolted through him, replacing all earlier brevity and ease, as he was filled with the hunger to taste her once more. The fires of his desire blazed all the stronger as she tipped her chin up at a defiant angle, parted her lips ever so slightly, and popped that small flake of crust into her mouth.

A trace of powder lingered on her full lower lip. She darted her tongue out, that pink flesh trailing over the seam, and he fought back a groan.

"Sir?"

Crispin dragged a reluctant stare over to the serving girl standing beside their table, and he silently cursed the interruption.

The plump beauty sauntered closer and flashed a smile that served as a bold invitation. "Is there anything more you'll require?" she purred, angling her body in a way that dismissed Elizabeth.

From the corner of his eye, he caught the frown that turned Elizabeth's lips. "Nothing," she snapped. The serving girl blinked. "*We* do not require anything." Fire shot from his wife's gaze.

Surely she wasn't... *jealous?*

Pursing her lips, the servant dropped a quick curtsy and sauntered off.

Just like that, the moment he and Elizabeth had shared was shattered.

His wife shoved back her seat with such alacrity that it toppled back slightly and then righted itself.

He quickly climbed to his feet.

"It was a long day. I am going to seek my room," Elizabeth said tightly. She hesitated, and for a moment, she looked as though she'd say more. For the span of that endless instant, he wanted her to ask him to accompany her.

But then, with a slight bow of her head, Elizabeth turned and did what she did best—she left.

CHAPTER 9

¶It was too hard.

There had been a certainty on her part that being with Crispin would be difficult.

But she'd never expected it would be *this* impossible.

Her skin flushed from the heat of her bath and rid of the grime of a day's travel, Elizabeth lay sprawled on her back, staring up at the mural a rudimentary artist had attempted on the ceiling.

Slapping her palms over her face, she groaned long and loud, letting the frustration boiling within all day free to bounce off the stucco walls. "Albrecht von Haller," she moaned, the name muffled by her palms. "Haller's rule on proportion and anatomy."

She shook her head, and her damp, loose curls splattered droplets of water over the white coverlet.

Then there had been the damned serving girl. Buxom and beautiful and blonde and all the things Elizabeth was not, nor had ever been, nor would ever be. Long, long ago, she'd accepted that some women were born stunning, and others… common and as plain as tea in England, as Elizabeth was.

And yet, seeing another so boldly throw herself at Crispin, Elizabeth's husband, who not even two hours ago had had his mouth upon Elizabeth's and had explored her like she was one of those mythical sirens who lured weaker men out to sea. The moment had served only as a reminder of the scoundrel's reputation Crispin had earned himself in the gossip columns and among the most scandalous widows in London.

The same jealousy that had roiled within her in the taproom reared its unwanted head once more. Fierce, sharp, and biting, it made a mockery of her attempts at indifference, for the fact remained that she'd never been indifferent to Crispin Ferguson. As a girl, she'd been in awe of him and his wit. And then, as a young woman, she'd fallen more than half in love with him for those very reasons.

"And now?" she whispered to the too slender cherub above her with his slightly fanged teeth.

She wanted him now, all these years later.

A long, miserable groan spilled past her lips. Elizabeth flung her arms wide, wrinkling the aged coverlet. Tiny motes of dust danced overhead, and she followed one speck's winding trail down until it disappeared over the side of the bed.

It was the height of foolishness to desire a man who had never truly wanted her and who, in her absence, had lived quite contentedly without her.

Elizabeth chewed at her lower lip.

Except, even as the buxom serving girl had invited him with everything but words, Elizabeth had searched Crispin for a hint of interest—an encouraging smile, a wink, even an appreciative eye. There had been nothing.

That disinterest, coupled with the scholar who'd discussed anatomical principles, didn't fit with the man she'd so closely followed in the papers who eventually found his way to Mrs. Belden's.

"Enough," she muttered, pushing herself upright. She was a creature of logic, and she clung to that very reason now to keep herself from descending any further into this madness. "You don't want him or I—" Her mind balked, and she tripped over that word, unable to so much as breathe it into existence, lest it be transformed into truth.

Elizabeth hopped up, the cold of the wide, planked floors penetrating her feet. She ignored the chill as she began to pace, ticking off on her fingers as she went.

Fact: She and Crispin had a shared history. They'd been loyal friends long before they'd become outraged spouses.

Fact: She admired his intelligence and scholarly pursuits, but she would appreciate anyone who had a like skill.

Fact: What she felt or did not feel for him was irrelevant in the scheme of their future.

There was nothing more between them. Anything she felt for him was natural, born out of admiration she would have felt for anyone.

The walls of her chest ached, making it hard to draw breath. Elizabeth abruptly stopped, and the hem of her white cotton night shift whipped about her ankles.

The assurances rolling around the chambers of her mind were nothing more than lies she told herself.

She stared blankly at the corner of the room where two trunks rested, those two material possessions as different as their owners. One had been handmade with love, time, and skill by her father's hand. The other was a French wooden piece with rosewood rods and brass studs and railings that still wore the gleam of newness.

Of their own volition, her legs carried her over. She sank to the floor and rested a palm upon each trunk. One coarse. One smooth. Similar in some ways and yet so very different.

Just as she and Crispin had always been.

"What is the alternative?" she whispered. *That you confront feelings you've long denied?* What good could come in that?

At no point had Crispin indicated any desire for anything with her beyond this brief sojourn to London, a presentation before Polite Society.

It is essential that Polite Society sees I am, married, that you are real, and then? You may go back to living your own life.

No, those words hardly bore any hint of undying devotion or an everlasting need to be with her.

"Because he didn't want to be with you, you ninny," she said aloud, the reminder ripping open a wound that would never truly heal. His life would carry on without her, whereby he was free to live the bachelor's life, without worries about matchmaking mamas, or young ladies scheming for the title of duchess.

They would become strangers once more.

But he did not seem different. Not in the ways that mattered.

Elizabeth bit her lower lip hard.

Her gaze fell to Crispin's trunk.

She hesitated, staring at the gleaming rosewood lid.

It was the height of wrongness to even consider it.

Elizabeth glanced over her shoulder to the doorway as the need to know and explore shifted to Crispin's belongings. She warred with herself for another brief moment and then caught the bilateral clasps. The smooth hinges gave a satisfying click. Lifting the lid, she peered inside.

Her breath caught loudly.

She'd gone to heaven.

A blissful, glorious, never forgotten, but still distant heaven.

He traveled with books.

He always had. Even when making the journey from his family's ancestral estate to her family's modest cottage, he'd had a text in hand.

Leaning in, she surveyed the volumes all resting in piles in the corner of the trunk.

Her gaze flew over the gold, embossed titles.

Henry Thomas Colebrooke's *Essay on the Vedas*, *A Guide Through the District of the Lakes*, *Conversations on Chemistry*, *an Anonymous Work*. Elizabeth stopped.

Her heart missed a beat. Unable to breathe, or move, she simply stared at the frayed and aged text that was more pamphlet than anything. So very familiar… and forgotten.

With fingers that shook, Elizabeth picked up the cherished little copy of *The Child's Natural History in Words of Four Letters*. She caressed her palm over the pair of children painted on the front cover, the little girl staring intently over the shoulder of a little boy.

"It is us, Crispin. You must have it. I want you to have it, to remember me when you go to Eton."

The day she'd handed it over and watched the Duke of Huntington's carriage draw him away had been the most heartbreaking moment in her lonely, young life.

And the day she'd found him returned for good had been the happiest. It remained so, even all these years later. He, a duke's son, had managed the impossible—he'd persuaded his father to allow him to study in Oxfordshire under the tutelage of leading tutors.

A wistful smile played at her lips.

Of course, it hadn't really been impossible. Nothing ever had been truly beyond Crispin, the Duke of Huntington. With the skillful way in which he wielded words, he could have brought Lucifer and the Lord himself 'round to a truce.

She hugged the frayed book close, cradling it tenderly against her breast, mindful of the age and wear of it. And he'd kept it. All these years later, he'd not only held on to the child's volume, but he traveled with it, as well.

"Why would he do that?" she whispered. Why, if he didn't care? Even in some small way?

Footfalls sounded in the hall.

She glanced up, momentarily frozen.

The steps drew closer, confident, measured.

Bloody hell, she mouthed. Elizabeth yanked the top of the trunk closed, wincing at the damningly loud click as the lid fell into place. She scrambled to her feet just as the steps came to a halt outside her rented room.

Bloody, bloody, bloody hell. Elizabeth curled her fingers tight around the small children's book she still held, and horror went through her.

She briefly contemplated the trunk.

The faint rasp of a key sliding into place propelled her into movement.

Elizabeth dived for the bed, the rumpled mattress groaning loudly as she struggled under the covers. She stuffed her book—nay, his book—under the pillow and flopped down on her back, squeezing her eyes shut just as the door opened.

Eyes closed as they were, she still felt Crispin's gaze upon her like a physical touch. It lingered, hovering on her person sprawled in the center of the bed.

She made her tense lips go slightly slack, forcing the muscles of her face to relax.

The ungreased hinges groaned as Crispin shut the door behind him and moved about the room.

Alone.

They were alone.

Granted, she was sleeping, albeit pretending, and they'd been alone in other bedchambers when no one in the world had known.

But they'd been children, and he, the master of sneaking about, had found his way into her room so they could read by the candle's glow some scientific text he could not wait until the next day to show her.

Now, they were man and woman, who just a handful of hours ago had explored each other's mouths with a greater enthusiasm than they'd shared for any scientific topic.

At the absolute stillness of the room, Elizabeth forced one eye open ever so slightly.

With his broad back presented to her, Crispin stood beside the English oak settle bench. He rolled his shoulders, his muscles rippling the fabric of his riding coat. Crispin's hands came up, and she stared on, unable to look away, riveted, as he slipped the buttons free.

Shrugging out of the garment, Crispin laid the wool article neatly over the back of the settle bench and stood before her in only his shirtsleeves, trousers, and boots.

She swallowed hard. *Breathe. Breathe.*

Evenly. Deeply.

Because that was what sleeping people did.

Her attempts were futile. She was transfixed by the sight of him in dishabille. There was something so very forbidden about watching Crispin while he was unawares and shedding each article of clothing.

Crispin tugged his white lawn shirt from the waist of his trousers.

Oh, sweet Lord in heaven.

Hers was a silent prayer whispering around her muddled mind.

Crispin drew the garment over his head. The fire still dancing in the hearth bathed his body in a soft glow, and her mouth went dry.

Don't be a ninny. You've seen him in a state of undress countless times. Without a shirt. Without boots. Why, you even swam naked with him.

Granted, she'd been five years to his then eight, almost nine.

But naked was naked was—

A lie.

For she'd never seen him like *this*.

His back was a display of raw power and masculinity, all corded muscles and strength, with a proudly erect spine. He was such a study in contoured, chiseled perfection that an artist would ache to memorialize him in stone.

Crispin stretched his arms out before him and, gripping his bicep, drew that olive-hued limb toward his opposite shoulder.

Oh, my goodness, she silently mouthed.

No man, nay, no person had a right to be in possession of such beauty that it made mere mortals weep and stare. And there could be no doubting that, with her slender hips and even more slender waist and bosom-less frame, she epitomized the words *common* and *unremarkable* in every way.

While Crispin was... *clear?*

Elizabeth stared unblinkingly at the shadows dancing along his back.

He was too clear.

Bloody damn.

Holding her breath so tight her chest ached, Elizabeth inched one hand up slowly. Not taking her eyes from Crispin, she plucked the damning glasses from her nose and...

She angled her head, staring with blurred horror at the wire-rimmed spectacles.

Now, what was she to do with them?

And he's already seen you sleeping here, ninny.

Mayhap he'd not noticed her. Elizabeth jammed her glasses into place, and the bed squealed at the abrupt movement.

She rolled onto her side and drew in a false, shuddery snort. Silence fell, safe and reassuring, and she counted the passing seconds.

The wide-plank floorboards groaned, indicating Crispin had moved.

Do not be silly. He's hardly paying any attention to you sleeping here—albeit pretend sleeping.

And why should he? When she'd left him, the buxom beauty had been making eyes at him, one of the scandalous sorts his name had been tangled with through the years. With her back to him, Elizabeth abandoned her pretense of sleep and stared blankly at the shadows dancing on the walls. She had left him and had no right to any resentment—or any feelings, really—about the manner of women he kept company with.

And yet, she hated that a man who'd reveled in books and higher learning had filled his days and evenings with empty pursuits.

What would you have rather it been? That he'd found another peculiar bluestocking with whom he shared something even more meaningful?

She caught her lower lip.

She was as selfish as the day at Mrs. Belden's was long. For she wished there'd never been *anything* between him and... *any* woman. She wished there hadn't been roguish friends for him to keep company with in depravity and that he'd missed Elizabeth as much as she'd missed him.

And that isn't your only wish. Scandalously, you yearn to know him in the same way those faceless beauties have.

The urge to flip over and steal another peek at his masculine physique gripped her.

Of course, why shouldn't she casually roll over onto her opposite side? It would only make the illusion of her slumbering state all the more real. Concentrating on drawing in steady breaths, Elizabeth turned over.

She snored lightly.

Through her lashes, she peeked over. Seated on the oak bench, Crispin tugged off a black boot trimmed in a chestnut leather; the pair of them worth more than all the shoes she'd ever pulled onto her feet at Mrs. Belden's.

He set the boot parallel to the bench and then reached for his other foot.

She let her eyes open, and wistfully, Elizabeth studied him as he bent his head over his task.

All the ladies at Mrs. Belden's had tossed their garments or articles haphazardly about their chambers. They'd littered the floors and left the tidying to the respective maids. And if the chambers weren't set to rights in a manner to please the impossible headmistress, it hadn't been the young ladies who'd been chastised, but the servants. Too many of them had paid the price with the loss of their position.

Because that had been the world Mrs. Belden had striven to maintain, one where lords and ladies didn't even have the responsibility of looking after their own garments.

Crispin removed his other boot and rested it neatly beside its mate.

Just then, he glanced up.

Heart racing, Elizabeth slammed her eyes closed.

And snored.

CHAPTER 10

She snored.

Crispin compressed his lips into a line to keep from giving in to the smile tugging at the corners.

Elizabeth sucked in a shuddery, bleating breath through her nose.

And she *pretended*—poorly. She'd never been one to put on an act, though.

Unlike the ladies of Polite Society whose company he'd suffered through these years, who'd manufactured everything from their smiles to their seductive come-hither stares, Elizabeth had lacked artifice. And until he'd entered this hired chamber and spied her with her glasses on, staring at him from between her crimson lashes, he'd forgotten just how much he'd missed that candor.

Shoving to his feet, Crispin angled his neck first left and then right, stretching muscles stiff from a long day of riding. He stared contemplatively at the weak fire in the stone hearth. "Fire's dying," he muttered.

Crossing over to his trunk, he lifted the unlatched hood and drew out a handful of books. Crispin tucked them under his arm and carried the small pile across the room.

He drew his arm back and made to toss one forward.

"No!" Elizabeth cried, exploding from the bed. Her feet hit the floor with a noisy thump. The white bedsheets tangled around her long limbs, tripping her up. She cursed and pitched forward before quickly catching herself on the edge of the mattress. Frantically ripping the blanketing from her legs, Elizabeth surged across the room and planted herself before him. "I said 'no,'" she repeated. She glowered up at him with a stare belonging to a woman who'd been born to the role of duchess. "What do you think you are doing?" she cried, settling her hands on her hips, the subtle movement accentuating the slight curve to them, stalling his mind, and stealing his words.

Planted as she was before the fire, the soft glow pierced the fabric of her night shift, and through that thin, cotton fabric, he caught the dusky hue of her—

Elizabeth plucked the book from his hands and then made quick work of taking the others from him.

"The fire is dying," she muttered to herself, giving her head a hard shake. She stole the last volume from Crispin and grunted under the added burden.

Crispin folded his arms at his chest. "Sleeping, were you?"

Elizabeth went owl-eyed and held the pile protectively close.

He winked once more. "You make it entirely too easy, love."

Her mouth worked, and then with a toss of her wet curls, she stepped around him. "You are insufferable," she muttered, returning to the trunk. Lowering herself awkwardly to her knees, she restacked the coveted leather volumes with such tenderness, he scowled.

Who would believe it possible that a man could be envious of a damned book? With feigned disinterest, Crispin dropped an elbow atop the mantel. "You were awake," he said into the quiet, as a reminder that the moment he'd stepped into the room, she'd been as attuned to his presence as he was to hers.

She'd followed him with her eyes, surreptitiously taking in his every movement. Had it been her natural curiosity that had kept her gaze on him? Or was it something… more?

There was a slight pause before Elizabeth set the last volume down in his trunk. "I could not sleep."

What accounted for her restlessness? Was he the reason? As soon as the wondering slipped in, he squashed it. What a pathetic fool he proved himself still to be that he wanted that to be the truth.

Elizabeth caught the sides of the lid in her long-fingered grip and made to lower it into place.

"You forgot one," he said solemnly, briefly halting her efforts before she completed the movement and closed the trunk. Crispin pushed away from the mantel and strode across the room.

She faced him, watching him with guarded eyes.

He stopped at the bed she'd hastily abandoned. Not taking his gaze from hers, he reached for the pillow and removed it.

The small children's book lay there, the faded crimson cover vividly bright against the white sheets.

Her fingers tangled with the fabric of her night shift.

Crispin rescued the book from the bed and stared at the familiar cover of a book he'd taken out countless times through the years just so he could feel closer to her. Mindful of the worn binding, he opened the small book. "Nothing to say?" He directed that at the interior page where her name had been memorialized in her child's hand, with his below it.

"You kept it," she whispered.

"I'm not spitting in your hand, Crispin. Nor am I cutting my palm to make myself bleed. Here, take my book..."

He glanced up and held her stare. "Did you think it didn't matter to me?" It had been a gift from her. The first she'd given him. "*You* mattered to me." And she'd left without a by your leave.

That statement sucked the air from the room and laid bare the unspoken words that had needed to be spoken for years.

Setting the book down, he took a step toward her. "And you abandoned"—*me*—"our friendship," he substituted, "to serve in that place. You deserved better than that through the years, Elizabeth." How he hated that she'd chosen that.

"You would disparage the life I've made for myself?" she demanded. "The work I've done?"

"I would," he said automatically, without inflection. Whipping around, he stormed over to the oak bedside table and grabbed the neat pile of books set out. "*Decorum for Dancing Debutantes?*" He tossed the small leather volume back down.

"Stop it," she gritted out, stalking over. "I'm not having this discussion with you. Not again."

"We didn't have a discussion," he went on relentlessly. "*Curtsying for a Queen... and Other Ceremonious Expressions of Greeting for the Peerage.*" He tossed the next book onto the table. He made to hurl the last book and then stopped, studying the tome. *Proper Rules of Proper Behavior and Proper Decorum.* Crispin lifted it, turning the cover out so the title stared damningly back. "This isn't the life you wanted," he said softly to himself as he lay the last incriminating title atop the others.

She compressed her lips into a hard line. "You don't deny it."

"What do you want from me?" she entreated, turning her palms up.

"More than you want for yourself." He wanted her to engage in the scientific pursuits she so loved and engage in discourse with those who appreciated her mind and the depth of her spirit.

Elizabeth angled away from him, presenting her heart-shaped face in profile as she stared at the door.

Crispin closed the small space between them, and stopping before her, he brushed his knuckles along her jaw, forcing her eyes back. "Don't," she begged, but as he dusted his fingers over her silken skin, her eyes briefly closed.

Crispin, however, had waited years to say his piece, words that had shifted when he learned where she'd been and how she'd spent her life without him. "You were the one girl in Oxfordshire who lived life unapologetically, Elizabeth Ferguson."

She shook her head. "My name—"

"Is Ferguson," he supplied. For whatever regrets she carried, they were and would be husband and wife, until death did part them. How was it possible for two names to be paired so perfectly together, and yet the owners of them were forever divided? "You were learned and well-read, and you didn't give a jot about"—he slashed a hand at the cluttered table—"balls and soirees." All those affairs that were so important to his mother and the harpies she called friends. "And for you"—he roved his gaze over her face—"to simply leave me and our friendship and the life we might have known..." Crispin clenched his jaw. "I thought our friendship was greater than that."

A sad smile curved her lips. "It was always about friendship."

"Of course it was," he shot back. "And you squandered it."

"We should have never married," she whispered, and his body jerked. She might as well have run him through.

Ice dusted his spine, and he clung to the far safer fury. "It is too late for those regrets, madam."

"Yes." Elizabeth jutted her chin up. "We were doomed the moment we crossed into Wiltshire and said 'I do' before a drunken vicar." The hasty ceremony had been over so quick, he hadn't even known it had officially begun.

"You are wrong," he sneered. "We were doomed the day you left, Duchess. You destroyed the friendship," he charged. "Not me."

Her throat worked. When she spoke, her words barely reached his ears, and yet, attuned as he'd always been to Elizabeth Brightly, he heard them anyway. "You were better off, Crispin."

He drew back. "I was better *off?*" he repeated, shock pulling the query from him. Without her in his life? "*That* is what you believe?" In her leaving, the one happiness he'd known had been yanked from him.

All earlier hint of fragility lifted, leaving in its place a tensely proud Elizabeth. "It's what I know."

It's what I know.

Warning bells rang in his mind. Faint, but there and refusing to be ignored.

Elizabeth's lower lip trembled, and she forced her gaze away from his, belying her aloofness.

"Why did you leave?" He drew his arms back, flexing his fingers, more than half fearing her answer, but at last he had spoken the words he'd uttered to himself alone in the privacy of his rooms when the rest of the world slept. Now, he voiced them to the one who'd left a ripped, ragged hole in his heart.

"Oh, come, Crispin," she said quietly. "You can be bitter and resentful, but at least be honest. Do not pretend my leaving mattered to you." She made to step around him, but he slid himself in front of her, blocking her escape.

"How can you even say that?" he whispered. "You were my best friend, Elizabeth. You were my *wife.*"

With a soft cry, she tossed her hands up. "I was the wife you never wanted." Her voice pinged around the rooms, robbing him of his indignation. Several night birds slumbering in the oak outside went into panicky flight, abandoning their nests in favor of the night sky.

"What?" He stared at her, trying to make sense of that statement. How could she think—?

"You didn't want me," she charged, hurt dripping from her tone.

Crispin scoffed. "Of course I wanted you." She was the only person he'd truly yearned for in his life.

She laughed, the sound pitched and devoid of mirth. Warning bells went off; filling him with unease. "'I know it was a mistake, Father,'" she tossed back.

His breath lodged in his chest as understanding dawned at last.

Just like that, the past came whirring back in a rush of sound in his ears. His own carelessness was now laid before him as a sin. Elizabeth, the woman he'd held to blame all these years, was exonerated, and he was left the guilty party, deserving of her rage. *My God.* He scraped a shaky hand through his hair.

"*It is done, Father. And regardless of how you feel about her or our marriage, it will not... It cannot be changed.*"

Crispin's stomach lurched. Those had been words meant to appease his furious father and godfather. There'd never been even a hint of truth buried in them. "I didn't mean," he began hoarsely. "I didn't," he tried again.

"'I know she's not the ideal bride,'" she went on, relentless. "'That I'd be better served by a match with Lady Dorinda.'" He flinched. With every word she repeated, he stared down his own treachery. Telling her they'd been empty assurances meant to appease two powerful dukes ready to come to blows over Crispin's decision would change nothing. They only marked him for the coward who'd sought peace at all costs—including at the cost of his friendship. "'There can be no undoing it.'" Elizabeth's voice faltered, and she breathed into existence the hated words he'd uttered long ago. "'It is done.'"

He shook his head, his lips moved, but no words came out. "I didn't... I don't..." He stretched a hand toward her, but then let it fall to his side. "How...?" What was there to say? That he'd merely sought to preserve peace between his family and the Duke of Hardwicke? Neither had been more important than she was, but he'd allowed her to believe as much.

Elizabeth hugged herself in a lonely embrace. "I heard you," she said tiredly. "So do not pretend you wanted"—she slashed a hand between them—"*this*. Or anything more, Your Grace."

Crispin sank onto the edge of the bed. The lumpy mattress squeaked under the burden of his weight. "I did," he whispered. All these years, he'd blamed her. He'd yearned for her. Only to find, in the end, that his own cowardice and folly had cost him the future he'd desperately longed for with her.

It had only ever been her.

With his stricken expression and his ashen skin, Elizabeth could almost believe the lie.

She could believe he'd missed her and wanted a future with her. And mayhap she would have if she hadn't overheard the argument between him and his father.

With the fight leaving her, Elizabeth sank onto the mattress beside him. Drawing her knees up, she looped her arms around them. Her skin burned from the piercing intensity of his stare upon her.

Elizabeth dropped her cheek atop her knees. She'd not thought of that night in so long. She'd not allowed herself to.

"What I said to my father, Elizabeth," he said hoarsely. "I didn't mean any of it. I didn't feel those things."

"And yet, you said them, Crispin." Elizabeth looked at him, holding his gaze. As a woman who'd first set off on her own, she'd been filled with resentment. Now, she was a woman grown, and his rejection hurt still, but she could not hold him responsible for what he'd felt... or rather, what he'd not felt for her. "Within every statement made, there is a shred of truth," she said gently.

He flinched. "There was no truth in what I said," he said again.

Elizabeth gave him a sad smile. "You've changed so much." At that unexpected shift in discourse, he stiffened, and a question glinted in his eye. "Your hair"—she briefly brushed those locks she'd once shorn with a scissors when they'd been experimenting children—"is longer. Your frame..." Her gaze went to the swath of naked skin, his broad shoulders, the light mat of tight black curls upon his muscular chest. She swallowed hard. "Is different. You're a rogue." With legions of lovers all over London. Her foolish heart spasmed. "And yet, so much about you is unchanged." Lest he spy the misery that realization cost her, Elizabeth glanced over at his trunk. "Your reading is the same. And the way you neatly organize your articles by color, with those articles a cushion for the books that are really your prized possessions."

They shared a wistful smile. For whatever had come to pass, their souls would always march in the same time. "You always sought to please and protect... everyone." His biceps strained. "I do not speak that as an insult, but as a matter of fact," she hurried to assure him. She wasn't so petty and vindictive that she'd let her own hurts surpass all the good he'd done and tried to do. "You didn't want to displease your father." Which had been the inevitable outcome when he'd wed Elizabeth instead of the flawless Lady Dorinda. And what must it have done to him that he'd made an enemy of an ally of his family? That a decision he had made had visited pain upon his father? Elizabeth covered his hand with her own. "And you didn't want to marry me." He made a sound of protest, but Elizabeth pressed her fingertips to his lips, silencing him. "You sought to protect me. It is who you are. It is what you do." She drew in a breath, for the first time taking full ownership of that day. "I knew that and married you anyway." It was why she'd go back with him even now, as he requested, and enter a world to which she'd never belong.

He dropped to a knee so he could better meet her stare. "I married you because I *wanted* to."

"You married me to avoid an unwanted match with Lady Dorinda," she gently reminded him.

A muscle jumped in his jaw. He might—they might—have played around with that memory in each of their minds over the years, but no matter how they tweaked or twisted the facts, their past could not be changed.

"I heard it all, Crispin." His mother had delighted in escorting her belowstairs. All the while, she'd known precisely what Elizabeth would hear when they arrived outside that door.

"My mother?" he asked, his tones hollowed out.

"They were your words," she pointed out, and his ravaged gaze moved past her shoulder. Elizabeth drew in an uneven breath, but he was deserving of the whole truth. "She wanted me gone. She had the hope that your father could find a way to dissolve our marriage." Given the concessions Crispin had made to his father, she knew that would have been a resolution he would have gladly accepted. "But if I was underfoot..." She glanced down at her bare toes. After all, it had been simple enough to explain away Elizabeth remaining a handful of days following the deaths of her parents. Their fathers had been great friends.

A long, dark, vitriolic curse exploded from his lips and heated her ears.

Just another change. He'd never been one given to curses.

"What did she say?"

Of course he was too clever. He knew there was more there.

She met that query with silence, battling with herself, weighing the good to be had in him knowing everything.

"Elizabeth," he urged.

She'd brought enough turmoil, and yet, he was entitled to the truth.

"Your father threatened to end your fellowship at Oxford if I didn't agree to an annulment."

The quiet statement doused the room in a heavy silence.

"What?" he asked, his tone as blank as his stare.

Termed an indulgence, no different than a young lord's appreciation of horseflesh and carousing, the late Duke of Huntington had failed to see that, for Crispin, the thirst for learning had driven him. It had never been a mere diversion or pursuit where his interest would one day fade. "They needed me gone as quickly as possible, so they could begin the proceedings for an annulment." She briefly closed her eyes. "Except, there was no guardian." Elizabeth and Crispin had both known as much. That freedom was what had allowed them to marry without requiring approval for her then-seven-and-ten-year-old self.

"They knew where you were," he said, each syllable stretched out by horror, fury, and shock. "At Mrs. Belden's?"

"Dissolving a marriage, it turns out, is a challenge for even an all-powerful duke. When that became apparent…" She still hadn't returned, recalling that unexpected visit.

The ducal carriage. The golden crest upon it.

And the too brief hope about who would step out of that conveyance, only to be swamped by a crippling disappointment.

His face twisted in a ravaged mask that squeezed her own heart. "That is why you left," he said, his voice stark, his cheeks draining of the last of their color. "To protect me."

Elizabeth forced a tight nod, maintaining a thin grasp on all control of her emotions.

"It was the least I could have done for the sacrifice you made. You gave me your name, your hand, your protection. I'd not take your happiness, too."

Crispin pressed his palms briefly to his face "It wasn't their life to interfere with."

What must it do to Crispin for him to learn his life had been manipulated by those who'd given him life?

Her parents had only ever supported her. They'd indulged their aberrant bluestocking daughter. There'd never been conditions attached to their acceptance and love of her. But then, they'd not been born with the blood of nobles flowing in their veins. Who could say what they might have done or become had their circumstances been different?

Emotion blazed to life in Crispin's eyes. "It wasn't your decision to make."

That charge took her aback. "I did it for—"

"For me," he gritted out, surging to his feet. "You made a decision for the both of us, without any discussion. I was your husband." Elizabeth leaned back, unsteadied by the volatile emotion pouring from his frame. "And more than that, you were my friend, and never once did you ask me what I wanted."

"I *heard* what you wanted." She squared her shoulders, bringing them back. "Rather, I heard what you didn't want." *Me.*

That hung between them, throbbing with a life force of emotion.

Crispin's cheeks leached of color. "That was never true," he whispered.

And yet, it had been spoken.

Elizabeth pressed her fingertips into her temples and rubbed. They could run around in circles debating each decision, word, action, or inaction, and nothing would change. The past would remain unchanged by regrets. Letting her arms fall, she swung her legs over the edge of the bed. "Crispin," she said gently. "You never made me promises of anything more than a marriage of convenience. Freedom for the both of us from uncertain futures." Hers, which would have always been precarious. His fate and future, however, had been set. She hugged her arms to herself. "It would have been wrong of me to expect anything more." And so… she hadn't. Instead, she'd left.

His gaze blank, Crispin started on unsteady legs for the front of the room. He stopped with his fingers on the door handle.

She stared after him, wanting him to stay, wanting to return to the easy friendship they'd once shared. But one could not turn back time to undo regrets and heartache.

He glanced over his shoulder. "I did not mean to hurt you. I would lop off my own arm before I would ever bring you suffering."

She swallowed hard. "I know." Her voice emerged whisper-soft to her own ears.

His heated gaze seared her, and for the span of a moment, she thought he'd say more... about her... about them, together.

But then, without another word, he left.

CHAPTER 11

THE FOLLOWING MORNING, CRISPIN SAT at a corner table in the increasingly crowded taproom. He rolled his shoulders. His entire body ached from several days of uninterrupted riding. And of course there had been a sleepless night spent on the hard floor after he'd returned to his and Elizabeth's shared rooms.

Though, in fairness, there'd been little indication that she had found rest last evening either.

And how could they have?

With a cup of coffee cradled between his fingers, Crispin stared across the establishment to the fire blazing in the hearth.

Around him, laughter echoed off the cracked plaster ceilings while patrons raised their voices over one another, competing to be heard in the noisy din. The cheerful ease of this place stood in contradiction to the tumult Elizabeth had unleashed last evening.

All time had ceased to matter, blurring under the weight of realization.

She'd heard the words he'd uttered long ago to the thunderous Duke of Huntington.

The carefully crafted words—meant to assuage a displeased father so Crispin could maintain his fellowship and set himself and Elizabeth on a smoother path as husband and wife—had been heard… by her.

He tossed back a long swallow, his throat muscles working quickly, the warm, bitter brew stinging his throat, a welcome discomfort.

They'd been words uttered in cowardice when he should have told his parents to go to hell if they weren't content with his decision. But he'd always sought to minimize conflict and maintain peace. And that one instance shattered the special bond he and Elizabeth had shared and sent her into flight.

All these years, he'd been filled with resentment and questions. Always questions and more questions. All unanswered, with everything going back to Elizabeth's senseless betrayal.

Crispin swirled the remaining contents of his cup in a slow circle, studying the cyclonic twist.

Now, everything made sense. Too much. A once murky situation was now vividly bright in its clarity, and Crispin was the one truly guilty of treachery.

Frustration roiling in his chest, he set his drink down hard.

Surely she'd known he'd not truly regretted taking her as his bride. They'd been each other's perfect counterpart, balancing each other and bringing out their best, while knowing laughter and happiness.

He'd not properly appreciated that joy until she'd gone, and taken every reason to smile along with her.

How would they go on now? Together… or each of them alone?

She wants nothing to do with you, in any way. Her disdain was *so* strong that she preferred living at Mrs. Belden's, imparting lessons on topics she'd always despised.

And why should she? She'd married a damned coward.

Shame pitted low in his gut.

It didn't matter that he'd only just turned one and twenty when they married. He hadn't been a boy, but rather, a man who could have fought his parents on the union they sought between him and Lady Dorinda. Ultimately, however, that mutually beneficial agreement he'd presented to a then-seven-and-ten-year-old Elizabeth had come from an actual yearning to have her as his wife.

He'd wanted to spend forever with her, because there'd never been anyone whose company he'd craved more.

Elizabeth, however, hadn't expressed any romantic feelings for him, so he'd appealed to her logic.

And last evening, when she'd revealed the truth of his parents' machinations, he'd wanted to tell her everything. Wanted to tell her that she'd always owned his heart, but to give her those words now would have rung hollow and false. Nay, she had no reason to believe a single statement uttered from his lips.

A shadow fell over his table, and he looked up.

Brambly bowed his head. "The trunks are loaded in the carriage, Your Grace."

Crispin glanced over at the stairwell. "Thank you, Brambly." The servant nodded and hurried off.

Soon, they'd depart and make the rest of the journey to the beginning of the end of their relationship.

That realization left him empty inside. *Nay, you've been empty since she left.*

Crispin made to return his attention to his drink when a lone figure in the corner of the tavern caught his notice.

Head bent over a book, the lad could not be more than two-and-ten years of age. With his crimson curls unevenly cropped at the nape of his neck and a pair of too large round spectacles perched on his nose, he drew forth images of a child who could have been. A boy or girl several years younger, but no less devoted to his or her books and studies.

A child who would not be.

But he or she could…

That enticing thought whispered around his mind, and he clung to it, entertaining the possibility.

Why couldn't they begin again? With the past now laid bare between them and the secrets explained, they could renew the friendship they'd once cherished and start anew as husband and wife.

Elizabeth had left to save him. She'd spoken of their friendship. She'd not ever indicated there was anything more between them. Not even last evening. But her kiss had hinted at more.

"You empty-headed arse." The shout cut through the din of the tavern and his own musings. Crispin sharpened his gaze and found the innkeeper hovering over the bookish boy. "Enough with those books." He brought a hand up and thumped the boy on the back of his head.

Fury pumped through him, bringing Crispin to his feet. "You there," he barked.

The room fell silent as several serving girls stepped aside, allowing Crispin a wide berth.

His brow wrinkled with confusion, the innkeeper glanced around. The rail-thin lad behind him dropped his gaze to the floor.

"What is this about?" Crispin demanded, stopping in front of the pair.

The balding proprietor shoved the boy between the shoulder blades. His cheeks blanched of color, but then, he quickly found his footing. "Nothing to worry after here, your lordship," he assured, before directing his annoyance again at the child. "Off with you," he mumbled, swiping up the forgotten leather book. Its pages yellow, its bindings fraying, the book had been well-read and showed its age. "I don't tolerate idle ones about." He slapped the small tome against the back of the child's head.

Crimson rage descended over Crispin's vision.

Shoulders hunched, the child made to step around him.

"That will be all," Crispin commanded on a frosty whisper.

The innkeeper's enormous Adam's apple moved.

Settling a gentle hand on the boy's small, narrow shoulder, Crispin guided him to a stop. "Is this the manner in which you treat your children?" he demanded of the proprietor.

"He i-isn't my boy, your l-lordship," he stammered. Doffing his hat, he dusted it along his damp brow. "He's my wife's nephew. We took him in. He's a mouth to feed, and he'll do his part. Everyone who wants a bed and place to rest does. He'll not have a—"

Crispin raised a silencing hand, effectively cutting off the other man's ramblings.

He trained all his attention on the young boy. Except now, up close, he recognized his earlier assessment had been off. There was the hint of fuzz on the boy's upper lip, hinting that he was on the cusp of manhood.

"Look at his lordship," the proprietor barked.

Crispin shot him a hard look, and the other man instantly fell back. Shoulders slumped, the child lifted his eyes.

Tired. Downtrodden. Fearful.

They were Crispin's eyes… but long ago.

"A duke's son, are you? If you're so powerful, then this shouldn't hurt."

Crispin's gut clenched in remembered pain from the fists that had pummeled the breath from his lungs. He'd cried in a corner when everyone at Eton had slept on. Longing for home. For family. For Elizabeth. "What is your name?" he asked quietly.

"Neville Barlow, Your Grace."

The innkeeper's brows shot to his receding hairline. "A duke?" Spreading his arms wide, he dropped a deferential bow suited for the king.

Ignoring him, Crispin focused on Neville's latter words. "How did you ascertain I am a duke?" Unlike his mother, who insisted on displaying her status in her travels, Crispin had always preferred the anonymity afforded a simple "lord," to the fawning and pomp and circumstance that met a duke's every movement.

Neville lifted his thin shoulders in a shrug. "Your driver, Your Grace, referred to you as such earlier."

The lad was clever and perceptive... and his spirit and soul would be as crushed as Crispin's had been at Eton if he remained here with his uncle.

"Give Mr. Barlow his book." He issued the directive without so much as a glance for the innkeeper. When it was passed back to the boy's hands, Crispin motioned to it. "May I?"

Neville hesitated and then gave it over.

Crispin examined the gilded title.

"*The Present Practice of Justices of the Peace and a Complete Parish Library*," the boy murmured, his voice cracking.

"His Grace can read it for himself," the proprietor snapped.

"That will be all," Crispin clipped out.

Neville turned to go.

"I was speaking to your uncle."

Splotches of red suffused the innkeeper's cheeks. Then, with a bow, he shuffled off.

The other man forgotten, Crispin lifted the book. "You are interested in law?"

"My father was a barrister," he explained, his voice threadbare.

Crispin perched his hip on the edge of the table and examined the brown leather copy. "The book belonged to him, then."

Neville shuffled back and forth on his feet. "He insisted I read it."

"Is that why you're doing so now?" He waved the book lightly. "Because you were expected to do what your father did? *Or* is it because you enjoy the topic?" Such had served as the basis of Crispin's own existence. It had been broken up into his eventual ascension to the Huntington title... and everything else. Elizabeth had fallen into that hated latter category, when she'd deserved so much more... including a husband who would have cherished her and fought for her, if need be, in ways that Crispin had not.

"The former, Your Grace," Neville said.

"Is there a specialty you enjoy more than another?" he pressed, returning the book.

The boy's shoulders straightened, and for the first time since he'd observed him in the corner, his eyes glimmered, showing something other than the earlier misery. "I enjoy it all. Tort law. Public law. I, however, rather prefer land law." He fell silent, a blush staining his cheeks.

"Peculiar ninny-hammer is what you are. Born to a dukedom, and you'd rather be reading than having yourself any real fun."

He stared at the child's bent head.

That was me. I was Neville. Conditioned to feel shame for his scholarly interests. His mother had lamented those pursuits. His father had tolerated them. Only Elizabeth had fully celebrated Crispin's interests—and reveled in them alongside him.

"There's no shame to be had in academic interests." Crispin echoed the long-ago utterance that Elizabeth had shot back at two nasty boys in Oxfordshire who'd taunted her for her studies. How much braver and prouder she'd been than he. Elizabeth had taught him to find pride and power in his love of knowledge. "Would you wish to pursue a career as a barrister?"

"I had hoped to follow in my father's footsteps, Your Grace," Neville said automatically.

Crispin smiled. "I wasn't speaking hypothetically. My solicitor is getting on in years." Old Chadwick had served the previous duke and been only ever married to his position. The faithful servant had at least a decade more of service before he put down his quill. "If you are interested in pursuing work as a barrister, I will arrange an apprenticeship with him. And from there, you might continue on to Oxford. If that is something you wish."

The boy's mouth worked. "Are you funning me, Your Grace?" he whispered.

Crispin's lips quirked up at the corners. He didn't mention that a sense of comedic humor was an attribute he was sorely lacking. "If you wish for the post"—he slapped him on the back—"it is yours. And if you do not—"

"I want it," the boy croaked. "I do. I want the post."

"Gather your things. We leave this place shortly."

As if he feared Crispin would change his mind and renege on the offer he'd just made, Neville bolted off, knocking into several patrons as he went.

Several shouts went up.

Then Neville stopped. Slightly out of breath, he rushed back. "Forgive me, Your Grace." He sketched a deep bow.

Crispin waved a hand. "There's no need for that. See to your possessions."

With a wide grin, Neville darted off once more. There was a speed and determination to his steps that had matched Crispin's when he'd been freed from the hells of Eton.

He made to look away when his gaze caught on the willowy figure several paces away.

And, just like it always had when she was near, the world melted away so that only they remained.

Except, in light of the day's revelations and unlike the past, when words had always flowed freely, he was left with—nothing. No adequate apologies or words, or even coherent thought.

Abandoning his spot, Crispin joined her. "Good morning," he greeted quietly. "You are—"

"I heard what you did for that child," she blurted.

His ears turned red, just as they'd done when he was a boy of nine bested by her in matches of spillikins. She'd unnerved him. That, however, had not been her intention.

He'd come to the boy's aid. Nay, he'd not only offered his ducal assistance, he'd pledged the child a future, should he desire it.

"I did not do anything." Adjusting the knot of his cravat, Crispin started for the door with Elizabeth falling quickly into step beside him, easily keeping up.

And refusing to abandon her observation. "Why did you do that?"

"Do you take me for an ogre now?" he asked dryly as he drew the door open. Cheerful sunlight spilled into the tavern.

Elizabeth made no move to leave. "Of course not." She angled her head, studying him the way she once had the albino butterfly that had fluttered for several short days in her mother's gardens. "But neither do dukes go about and simply offer posts or an education at Oxford to strangers."

A patron started up the cobbled walk, springing them into movement. Elizabeth stepped outside.

Crispin paused to hold the door for the patron before joining her.

"You know very many dukes, do you?" he countered.

"I know a duke's daughter." A soft breeze caught her hem and whipped it lightly about her ankles. "And through that, her father." The Duke of Ravenscourt had left his miserable daughter, forgotten, at Mrs. Belden's. And according to the not-so-discreet whispers that had filled the halls, the distinguished duke had also littered the whole of England with his bastards. "I've also had enough interactions with noblemen through the years to know they do not simply do anything without expecting something in return."

She registered his silence and looked over. At the frosty set to his features, a chill scraped her spine.

"Did someone... harm you in any way?" There was a lethal edge to his query that promised death to any person who had.

And then the implications of what he'd asked registered. "No," she said quickly. Her cheeks warmed. Of all the worries she'd faced over the years as a woman living on her own, fending off unwanted advances had fortunately never been one of them.

Some of the tension eased from Crispin's broad shoulders.

They reached the gated fence, and Elizabeth stopped. "You didn't answer my question," she pointed out, staying his hand.

Crispin let his arm fall back to his side. "Sometimes, a person requires some help. It's important to offer that when one can and to accept that when one needs it."

She'd have to be deaf as the post before them to fail to hear the recrimination there. Elizabeth frowned. "I've never been too proud to accept assistance." Their marriage was proof enough of that.

A smile ghosted his lips. "I didn't refer to you, Elizabeth." He unlatched the gate and waited for her before falling once again into step beside her. As they walked the remaining length to the carriage, he kept his gaze trained on the gleaming black conveyance. "My years at Eton weren't kind ones." He spoke the way a skilled lecturer imparted essential facts to his charges, rather than the way a man would speak about an experience that had so shaped him. "I was regularly mocked, pummeled, and spoken about because of my singular interests in pursuits."

Of their own volition, Elizabeth's feet drew to a slow stop. "What?" she whispered as he continued on toward the carriage.

Moments ago, he'd not disparaged her, but rather—himself. He'd been speaking about *his own experiences*.

Crispin continued walking and then turned back. Reaching into his jacket, he drew out brown leather gloves and proceeded to draw them on. "My father had such hopes for my time at Eton and then Oxford. Above all, I didn't wish to disappoint him." Because he'd always striven to please everyone. It had been an impossible feat that, to this date, he likely could not realize, still. "One of my instructors took the liberty of writing the duke to share about my"—his lips pulled—"experience. He arrived himself and escorted me off." And Crispin had never returned.

All these years, she'd built him up as one who was larger than life in every way. The sun had risen and set to the mere thought of Crispin Ferguson. As such, she could have never contemplated a world in which he wasn't revered for the brilliant mind and kind friend he was. "Oh, Crispin," she managed, her heart aching.

He held her gaze. "My father was wrong in failing to accept our marriage, but he wasn't a complete failure as a father." The incident also highlighted a greater reason for his devotion to the late duke.

No, any other lord would have left his son to suffer through the horror of his schooling, a rite of passage of sorts for all future noblemen. After all, how many young ladies had been sent to Mrs. Belden's and had their spirits and souls crushed, with the blessing and permission of their respective families?

She stuffed her hands inside the pockets of her cloak to hide the faint tremble. "Why didn't you tell me?" As a friend, she should have known.

He quirked a black eyebrow up. "Tell you what? That I was a scared, bullied boy who ran away from Eton because I'd tired of finding myself beat up day in and day out?"

Pain lanced through her. For all the ways in which she had known him, there were so many more ways in which she had not.

"Did you believe I'd find you somehow less?"

Crispin clasped his hands behind his back and stared out at the rolling expanse of hills in the distance. "It was enough that I found myself lacking, Elizabeth," he murmured.

She stared at him. With his back presented to her, he was an immobile, proud figure. And shame filled her. As children, she'd been the one whispered about and mocked around Oxfordshire for being an oddity. Her world had been small, and never having set foot outside of it, she'd been unaware that life for Crispin, revered in the village as the ducal heir, could have been different from what she'd assumed. She could never have foreseen that he too would have been ridiculed for that which set him apart.

"I didn't know." She spoke the sad truth aloud.

"No." He sighed. "And you wouldn't have. I didn't want you to see that."

Elizabeth took a lurching step toward him. "But I wanted to. You were my best friend."

He'd remained a mystery. *And I want all his stories. I want his secrets and the pain he knew, and…*

The ground lurched under her feet.

I love him.

She'd loved him first as a friend and now, all these years later, as the intellective boy who'd grown into a man. A man who wanted her to pursue her studies as she once had, and still, even though he'd been named a duke, didn't give a jot about balls or soirees and found them as tedious as she did.

Crispin lifted a shoulder in a half shrug. "It is of no matter." A door slammed in the near distance, and they looked over at the boy sprinting down the cobbled path. "And if I can help prevent someone from feeling that same shame that I myself did, then I'll do so." The boy skidded to a stop. His gaunt chest heaved from his run. "Neville," Crispin said. "May I present Her Grace, the Duchess of Huntington."

Neville bowed. "Your Grace," he panted.

She smiled gently at the bespectacled boy with curly red hair. "I am so very happy you are accompanying us to London."

Us.

How right that felt. And yet, with the past at last laid open and their secrets spread out, there'd never been mention of anything…

more.

Her smile froze on her lips, straining the muscles of her cheeks.

And as Neville scrambled onto the box to sit alongside the driver, Elizabeth entered the carriage. Crispin reached up to shut the door.

She shot a hand out. "You are not… riding with me?" she asked, regret pulling the question out. Her cheeks flamed. "That is…" She cleared her throat and finished lamely, "Your mount? I trust the journey would still be arduous for him."

"Indeed." Crispin touched his gaze on every corner of her face. "I have several horses stabled along the route."

Belatedly, she took in the servant standing off to the side, the reins of an unfamiliar mount in his fingers.

Of course Crispin would have horses stabled along the traveled roadways. It had been too easy to forget over the years that he was wealthier than Croesus and a future duke atop it.

"Oh," she said as she settled onto the bench.

He paused, and her body arched forward, waiting for whatever words were on his lips.

"Elizabeth."

With that parting, nothing more than her name, Crispin closed the door behind her, stealing the sunlight that had bathed the carriage.

She sat back against the comfortable squabs, and her eyes snagged a pile of books on the opposite bench.

Wetting her lips, she leaned forward.

Her heart quickened.

Elizabeth gently reached for the pile, neatly tied with a long velvet ribbon. Loosening the tie, she freed the article, until the leather tomes stared back.

Emotion threatened to overwhelm her.

Essay on the Vedas, A Guide Through the District of the Lakes, Conversations on Chemistry, an Anonymous Work.

Tears blurred her eyes.

He'd left the books here for her.

The carriage lurched into motion, and she hurriedly caught the pile close, cradling it lovingly against her chest.

She'd been so determined to forget Crispin Ferguson, the Duke of Huntington. She had set up barriers to keep herself from hurting again, but with every exchange, he made it impossible.

It was easy to keep walls up against the rogue who'd left scores of broken hearts about London. But this Crispin? The tender, considerate gentleman who'd hand over treasured texts to her?

Elizabeth closed her eyes.

She loved him.

And she always would.

CHAPTER 12

IN THE DEAD OF NIGHT, they arrived in London.

It marked the beginning of the end of his time with Elizabeth.

"We've...arrived."

Neville's awe-coated statement pulled Crispin back from his musings. Crispin glanced over at the previously slumbering boy perched alongside his driver. "We have." And there was no place *less* Crispin would rather be. He forced a smile for the child's benefit. "You'll find the staff kindly," he promised, as he jumped down from his mount.

A groom hurried over to accept the reins just as the double doors of Crispin's Mayfair residence were thrown open.

Dutiful servants poured out of the white stucco townhouse like mice after a careless cook left out the cheese. Of course, regardless of hour, the world stood on alert, anticipating the wants and needs of a duke. It was an obsequious fawning his mother had reveled in, his late father had tolerated, and Crispin himself suffered through.

Crispin motioned to the youngest of the footmen. The livery clad servant shifted his path, and hurried over to Crispin. "Your Grace," he murmured, bowing.

"We will have a guest for the evening," he explained, squeezing Neville's shoulder. "May I present Mr. Neville Barlow. If you can introduce the young gentleman to Mrs. Willoughby and see she shows him to guest chambers, along with a meal, and anything else he requires.

He might as well have handed over a king's fortune for the

grateful look cast his way by the boy.

"This way, Mr. Barlow," the footman urged, and relieving the child of his burden, he escorted him off.

With the pair gone, Crispin returned his attention to the servants scuttling about...young men stealing curious glances at the carriage.

Crispin followed those stares.

Of course, this was no ordinary return. This was the return of the Invisible Duchess, as the gossip columns had recently taken to writing of her. All the household had likely waited with bated breath for a glimpse of the mysterious lady.

His driver reached for the carriage door, but Crispin waved him off and strode over. As he opened it, he did not know what he expected to find. Elizabeth sleeping, perhaps? Pale? Her eyes heavy from sleep after a long day of traveling?

As clear-eyed as she was at the rooster's first crow, she peered past his shoulder and climbed her gaze up the two-hundred-foot structure. Behind her oval lenses, her eyes formed perfect circles. *Heavens to Hades*, she mouthed, never taking her gaze from it as he helped her down. Transformed into one massive residence by the purchase of neighboring townhouses by his late grandfather, the Huntington London townhouse was expansive enough to rival most noblemen's country manors.

And she'd never before laid eyes upon it.

They'd shared nearly everything and every part of themselves, and yet, it was a reminder that they'd also been divided by their stations.

After she'd looked her full, Elizabeth wordlessly accepted his hand and allowed him to help her down.

Her legs swayed slightly under her, and he shot a hand out to steady her. His fingers curved against her slender waist as he gripped her, the feel of her against him right.

Elizabeth's breath caught audibly, and she wet her lips, drawing his focus to her mouth.

He ached to explore those lush contours once more. To spar with their tongues until their breaths melded into one.

"Crispin," she whispered.

"Hmm?"

And why should they not? They were husband and wife, and...

A carriage rattled by, the rapid churning of the conveyance's wheels snapping the fragile moment.

He glanced up in time to catch the curious passersby peering at them until their conveyance disappeared from sight.

Elizabeth followed his stare.

"Come," he said tightly and led her on.

Her steps, however, were unhurried. Her alert stare took in everything, touching on the lit grounds of Mayfair.

Crispin followed her stare. Clouds hung heavy across the London sky, blotting out the fingernail moon and smattering of stars that could find space among the London fog and dirt.

Elizabeth stopped and stared at the lamplighter at work, a young child assisting in his efforts.

Crispin had always despised Town. As a boy and then young man who'd been forced to visit, he'd silently envied Elizabeth staying in Oxfordshire and counted the days until they were reunited. "It is miserable, isn't it?" Artificial light doused the streets.

He turned to go, but Elizabeth remained fixed to the pavement, watching the portly lamplighter as he lifted his brass-tipped staff to the crystal box. "On the contrary." Crispin slowed his steps. "I've never seen anything like it."

Awe coated Elizabeth's words with such reverence, he squinted, attempting to see what it was that held her so fascinated.

"What is the hour?" she demanded, her voice animated. She whipped her gaze briefly from the pair working across the street.

Crispin fumbled for his watch fob and consulted the timepiece. "Nearly five minutes past one o'clock." And his wife was as alert as if she'd just arisen, fresh and ready to face a new day.

"Remarkable," she murmured and then spread her arms wide as the lamplighter descended the ladder and walked a handful of paces to the next post. "They've managed to turn *night* into *day*." She stared at Crispin, clearly expecting *something*. Tossing her hands up in exasperation, Elizabeth quit his side and rushed off, all but sprinting to the nearest lamppost.

The hovering servants exchanged glances, shifting on their feet.

Crispin dismissed them with a slight nod, wholly riveted by Elizabeth's palpable excitement. She brushed her gloveless palm over the metal post. "Do you know, gas lighting first appeared in Pall Mall in 1812, but they used wooden gas pipes?"

"Did they?"

She sighed. "Crispin."

He shook his head.

"Wooden gas pipes," she repeated. "There were numerous explosions and a few deaths."

He removed his hat and beat it against his leg. "Hence the perils of metropolitan living."

Elizabeth scoffed. "Nonsense. How many times did we sit with only the benefit of a single candle to light our books? Why, if we'd had this…" She spread her arms wide. Her eyes twinkled with her excitement, and at the sight of her in such an unfettered state of joy, he felt something shift in his chest. "The day is longer, and there is so much to see, and…" Her chattering drew to a stop. "What is it?"

Drawn like a moth to the flame, he drifted over. "It is you."

"Me?"

He dusted his knuckles down her satin-soft cheek. "I'd never considered it in that way." London had always represented a cage, a hated place he was expected to spend time because of his station and role in Parliament. What would it have been like sharing this place with her?

Elizabeth smiled, dimpling her cheeks. "Well, you should. There is good to be found in everything. If you simply look."

Another carriage rattled by. "It is late," he murmured.

"Yes." Yet, they stood there anyway.

For when tomorrow came, so would the ball, the one night he'd requested of her before he set her free, and there would be her eventual return to Mrs. Belden's.

Hollow at the thought, Crispin returned his hat atop his head. Taking the unspoken cue, Elizabeth fell into step beside him. This time, as they drew before the handful of limestone steps leading to the black double doors, only Aldis, the recently hired butler, stood in wait.

"Your Graces," he greeted, dropping a deferential bow as they entered.

With it, reality intruded, as it invariably did in this rotted place. "Aldis." He did a sweep of the foyer.

The blessedly empty foyer.

He clenched his teeth so hard his jaw ached. His faithless, single-minded mother, was nowhere in sight.

"Her Grace has not yet returned for the evening, Your Grace," the butler murmured.

Some of the tension went out of him. That meeting would come later.

Crispin looked up the stairwell where Mrs. Willoughby, made her descent.

"Good evening, Mrs. Willoughby," he greeted the plump, white-haired older woman. "Mr. Barlow—?"

"Has been shown to his rooms," she supplied, with a curtsy and a wide smile. She turned her focus to Elizabeth.

Crispin performed introductions between the two. "Will you show Her Grace to her chambers?" he asked, feeling Elizabeth's stare on him.

"Of course, Your Grace," Mrs. Willoughby said with her usual cheer. "If you will follow me, Your Grace."

Elizabeth lingered her gaze on him. Looking as though she wished to say something. Did she want him to follow her? Did she wish to continue their discourse on London? What was it?

In the end, silent in ways she'd never been, Elizabeth followed the housekeeper.

Crispin stared after the departing pair as they climbed abovestairs and then continued down the intersecting hall at the entrance of the landing.

When they'd gone, he turned to Aldis. "I require one of my mounts readied."

If he'd asked the man to fetch the king's crown, he couldn't have appeared more shocked. Aldis, wide-eyed, took in Crispin's rumpled garments, and he sniffed the air momentarily before mastering his perfect composure. "As you wish, Your Grace."

He shook his head. Yes, because Crispin was nothing if not predictable. No one would dare expect him, immaculately attired and not steeped in scandal, to venture out at this ungodly hour with his garments in their currently sorry state.

And so it was, not even thirty minutes later, Crispin found himself striding through the crowded floors of Forbidden Pleasures. Raucous laughter rolled around the floors of the gaming hell, punctuated by the intermittent squeal of a whore and the clinks of coins hitting coins.

Doing a sweep of the room, Crispin settled his gaze on the gentleman seated at the center back table. Occupied as he was with a cheroot in one hand and a tumbler of whiskey in the other, Hugh Madsen, the Earl of Fielding, still managed to perfectly balance two blonde whores on his lap.

As Crispin wound his way through the crowd, greetings went up, but no one gave more than a passing look at his presence here. A crimson-haired beauty stepped into his path, halting his determined march. "Are you looking for company this evening, Your Grace?" she purred. Her husky greeting carried over the din.

"Not at this time." And certainly not with this woman or any other present. Crispin tossed several coins to the young woman to soften the blow and then continued on. The only one whose presence he craved in every way was now tucked away in his London townhouse. *It is where I should be... with her...*

And yet, his mind and emotions were all jumbled, and he could not be under the same roof with her. Not until there was some clarity.

He reached Fielding's table.

His friend glanced up lazily, and then the other man's patent boredom was transposed into wide-eyed shock as he took in Crispin's garments.

The earl dismissed the pair. "I'm afraid we'll have to continue our discussion later, loves."

They pouted. "We can entertain you *and* your friend," one of the pixielike beauties invited. She drew the scandalously plunging bodice of her gown lower, putting her enormous breasts on full display.

It was an all-too-familiar carnal offering found in this den of sin, more common than a bow or curtsy among Polite Society. Forbidden Pleasures was a place where honor was left at the door and sin triumphed over all.

"I'm afraid business calls." The earl lifted his knees up and down, dislodging the two women from their perches.

The pair hadn't even completely sashayed off before Crispin was reaching for a seat. "I need help," he said without preamble.

The other man saluted him with a nearly empty whiskey. "You *need* a bath, and if one wishes to be truly precise..." He flicked the diamond stickpin at the center of his immaculately tied snow-white cravat. "A new valet."

With a sound of impatience, Crispin tugged out the chair and waved off the servant who rushed over with a glass. "It is—"

"Never tell me." Fielding waggled his brown eyebrows. "Your wife?" he ventured with a cynical drollness that contradicted the earlier brevity. "You did not find her?"

"On the contrary," Crispin said under his breath.

Other than his parents, the only one who knew of Crispin's hasty elopement and the bride who'd taken flight was the man before him. It was a secret he'd kept, but through the years, he'd made no effort to hide his disdain of Elizabeth.

"Ah, you found her, and that is the problem." Fielding tossed back the remainder of his drink. "That makes *far* more sense."

No. Nothing made sense anymore. Crispin dragged a hand through his hair.

"Oh, this is bad indeed," his friend muttered. "You, smelling like horseflesh, in dusty garments better fit for kindling, and now messing your hair?" His mouth hardened, and he set his empty glass down. "Let me assure you," he said, dropping his elbows atop the rose-inlaid mahogany tabletop, "whatever she's done to have you so tangled up, she is not worth it. Never was." Grabbing the half-empty bottle, he splashed several fingerfuls into his glass. "Never will be." He paused with the glass at his mouth. From over the top of it, Fielding grinned. "Though, in fairness, none of them are."

"She is," Crispin said quietly. "I want you to help me win her."

His friend choked on his swallow, drawing in great, gasping breaths.

Crispin leaned across the table to slap him between the shoulder blades, but the other man waved him off.

"M-mad."

Yes. He'd always been more than a little mad for Elizabeth Brightly. She was one who could speak circles around any scholar and was passionate in every pursuit she took on.

After his paroxysm faded to a lingering cough, Fielding dragged his chair closer. "You want to win *her*. The woman who left you, without so much as a note."

"I know what she did." Now, however, and more important, he knew why she'd done what she had.

His friend carried on in a furious whisper. "The same woman

who made you a subject of the *ton*'s scrutiny." When the last thing any gent, particularly an unfortunate one saddled with a ducal title, needed was more attention.

"She left to save me." And ultimately, in her absence, he'd been broken.

That effectively silenced Fielding.

Crispin explained his parents' roles in manipulating both him and Elizabeth, including everything from the threat of his lost fellowship at Oxford to the miserable place she'd been forced to call home the past nearly ten years.

When he'd finished, the earl was quiet.

Grabbing the decanter, he topped off his glass and pushed it across the table.

Crispin shook his head.

"It's one damned whiskey, and if this doesn't merit a drink, then nothing else will. Drink." His friend clipped out the order.

Crispin took the glass and downed the whiskey in a long, slow swallow. The liquid burned a scorching trail down his throat. He grimaced and set the empty tumbler down.

"I said to take a drink, not finish the contents in a single gulp," Fielding drawled. Reclaiming the glass, he poured another and pushed it across the table once more.

"I'm not looking to get soused," Crispin muttered, but nonetheless, he accepted the offering and took a sip.

"Some moments call for a good sousing."

Despite the reputation he'd earned these past years, Crispin had never been one of the carousing sorts. But yes, in this, Fielding proved correct. If there had ever been time for a gent to drink, this was it.

They sat in a companionable silence that was eventually broken by the other man.

"Now"—the earl leaned back in his seat—"as you are the more logical in our pair, let us speak this through rationally. A fellow does not simply abandon ten years of resentment." He shot a hand up, and a servant came forward with a glass.

"He does if he finds out he's been the bloody arse, guilty for crimes he accused another of." Crispin directed that utterance into the amber contents of his glass.

"Ah, but you've managed an arrangement any gent would

envy you for." As he enumerated a list of points, he lifted a finger. "You're leg-shackled." Fielding shuddered. "But to a woman who is… invisible. You're free to carry out your own pleasures without a nagging wife underfoot. And then when the time for an heir comes?" He poured himself a drink. "Then you don't have to bother with a *simpering* virgin."

A simpering virgin? There'd never been anything simpering about Elizabeth, and there never would be.

"Fielding," he warned.

His friend sighed. "Very well. But I would not be a friend if I did not point out that your union is perfect as it is."

For most lords, yes. They were self-absorbed gents who preferred bedding their mistresses and wagering away their fortunes at the club he and Fielding even now frequented. "Help me," he repeated in grave tones. Crispin curled his fingers around the cold glass. It was not every day a man humbled himself, but pride had cost him Elizabeth once before. He'd be damned if he let her go this time without attempting to woo and win her.

"You don't need my help, Huntington." Fielding shoved his chair back onto its hind legs and balanced the mahogany seat at a precarious angle. "You've managed to charm every last dowager and eager widow in London."

Crispin's ears went hot.

"Ahh, I take it Her Grace has heard tales of your… *exploits*," the earl surmised.

"They weren't…" Crispin scrubbed a hand over his face. "Fielding," he warned. It was late. He had, at most, twenty-six hours before the terms of his latest agreement with Elizabeth were satisfied, and then she'd be free to go on her way. Panic sent his heart into a triple beat. "Tell me *what* to do."

"Fine. Fine. You want to know what to do?" He brought the chair back into a steady, fully upright position. "Go home. Because arriving in Town with your wife in tow, and then abandoning her that same night while you dally with a whore at your club, is hardly going to endear the lady to you," Fielding said dryly.

"I'm not dallying with whores."

"I know that. And you know that." The earl flicked a hand out toward a nearby hazard table. The two dandies observing them immediately averted their stares, training them on the velvet table. "But the stories, as they invariably are, in London will be spun with only the most scandalous thread. And after you return home?" Fielding grinned. "Make love to your wife."

He exhaled his frustration. "It is not that… simple." It never was. "I want to woo her."

Fielding widened his smile. "It is always that simple, Huntington. You want to woo her, then make love to her."

He remembered their kiss in the countryside. The taste of her. The heat of her. The feel of her so right in his arms. Like they'd been born for each other's embrace.

Crispin reluctantly shoved to his feet. "She wants more than seduction," he said, his voice hoarse to his own ears.

Fielding chuckled. "If you believe that, then you know your wife even less than you credit."

With the earl's obnoxiously amused laughter trailing after him, Crispin quit his club and started home.

One that was no longer empty, where Elizabeth even now slept.

A lightness settled around his chest. How very right that felt. Sharing a household with her, one that would be a home if they were together. And how it would steal his happiness again if she left.

No. The deal they'd made, of one night together, would never be enough. He wanted her in his life—forever.

CHAPTER 13

He'd gone out.

The housekeeper had just taken her leave, and when Elizabeth had sought out the floor-to-ceiling double windows that overlooked the Mayfair streets, she'd spied him.

He'd not bothered with so much as a change of garments or a bath, but instead, had climbed astride a different mount and ridden off.

And he'd been gone for two hours since.

It shouldn't bother her.

He'd expressed remorse for the great misunderstanding that had divided them, but he'd never indicated there was anything... more. Between them, that was.

There *had* been the kiss.

Elizabeth pressed a callused fingertip to her lips, and they tingled from the memory of his mouth on hers.

Seated at the window seat in her temporary chambers, she dropped her head back against the wall and knocked it lightly. "You are a fool." The old clippings scattered on her lap, their content committed to memory long ago, were proof enough of her foolishness.

For there had been kisses between Crispin and... *many* women.

And because she was a glutton for her own suffering, Elizabeth picked up one of the yellowing pages she'd torn out at Mrs. Belden's nearly eight years ago.

The recently widowed Baroness Norreys was discovered in a scandalous state of dishabille leaving the Pleasure Gardens of Vauxhall. The gentleman to follow shortly from that midnight rendezvous...

"Was none other than the Marquess of W and future Duke of H," Elizabeth whispered into the empty room.

Jealousy lanced through her, suffocating in its intensity. Embers popped and hissed in the hearth in an echo of her own blasted misery.

For surely the hundredth time since he'd gone off, Elizabeth stole another glance out at the empty streets below.

She would sit here, while Crispin did... whatever it was that rogues did. For what purpose? With sleep eluding her, Elizabeth stuffed the neatly snipped articles back inside the valise at her feet and set out to explore Crispin's residence.

The heavily padded carpet, warm under her feet, muted her footfalls as she took leave of her rooms.

Or rather, the duchess' chambers, as the housekeeper had referred to them. For Elizabeth's weren't simply guest apartments for any mere stranger, but ones reserved for the lady of the household. Intimately aligned with Crispin's, they remained separated by a wall and two walnut-veneer doors.

Elizabeth wound her way through the halls.

Every other Empire-style crystal and bronze swan sconce remained lit, with the candles' glow illuminating the wide corridors and the wealth and grandeur of this place. The rosewood pedestal held a gold urn that gleamed from the efforts of the dutiful servants who looked over these treasures. An oil painting hung in a large oval frame, the lone piece of artwork in the length of the corridor.

Elizabeth briefly considered the framed scene.

According to the lessons she'd been forced to conduct on the proper décor for a nobleman's residence—and Mrs. Belden and the books on the subject had all been abundantly clear—the artwork on display was to be of the distinguished ancestors and the family who dwelled at the property, as a reminder of their power and greatness. Elizabeth had always scoffed at the pomposity of that, but Crispin had none of those figures on display. Instead, the single work was of a bucolic country scene.

Adjusting her spectacles, Elizabeth lined herself up before it and took in the small cottage, bent trees, and rolling hills that could have been any English countryside.

"It is miserable, isn't it?"

Elizabeth tried to reconcile that wistful regret with the same man written about in the papers, who'd dashed off the moment he returned, likely to visit one of the scandalous clubs he frequented.

Oftentimes, it was as though Crispin were two very different people—the tempting scoundrel and the scholarly gentleman—and both held her enthralled.

Drawing the belt of her wrapper tighter about her middle, Elizabeth resumed her exploration of his home.

What might have been their home together had she stayed.

"I want you gone. We will find a way to secure the annulment Crispin so greatly desires."

Elizabeth jutted her chin out. "And if I refuse to leave?"

"Pfft. I always thought you were more clever than that."

Heat rushed to Elizabeth's cheeks.

"Why would you stay? You've heard yourself, Miss Brightly. My son regrets wedding you." The duchess sent her a hate-filled stare. "And he'll regret it even more when we cut him off without funds and sever his fellowship at Oxford."

The duchess' long-ago threat squeezed at Elizabeth, filling her with the familiar hurt, but now there was something more—a biting, vitriolic fury for the one who'd manipulated both her and Crispin.

Forcing the memory of that day and that woman into the furthest chambers of her mind, Elizabeth wandered in and out of parlors, located the Portrait Room where Crispin's ancestors had been all neatly organized, until she reached the farthest recesses of the townhouse.

A pair of painted, white lead-light doors stood as a vibrant contrast against the dark of the hall. The stained-glass perimeter of the frame had been adorned in…

Her breath caught audibly as she was drawn on silent feet closer—

"Butterflies," she mouthed.

She stretched a hand out and trailed her fingertips over the crimson wings of one of the glass renderings.

It was a coincidence, and nothing more.

Her throat worked. Only—

"They live just a handful of weeks." Sprawled on her stomach, the dewy grass dampening her dress, Elizabeth followed one monarch as he fluttered from flower to flower. "How very sad their existence is."

"On the contrary," Crispin murmured in soft tones, his gaze taking in the delicate creature's every movement. "It isn't how long one lives, but what one does with one's time while they are here."

From that moment on, her love of the winged creatures had been forever linked to Crispin and that summer day in her family's gardens. She'd studied the butterfly, learning every detail from every book Crispin had sneaked off from his tutors to feed her insatiable thirst for a greater knowledge of them.

Elizabeth pressed the handle, and a warm heat filled the hallway, a soothing balm against the night's chill.

Hurrying inside, she closed the door behind her and leaned back against the glass panel. And promptly exhaled her whispery surprise.

The expertly designed room trapped and retained all the earlier warmth of the previous day. Lit gilt brazier stands set around the conservatory added a layer of heat to the gardens.

Elizabeth drifted deeper into the grounds, her tread silent upon the plush lawn. Holly and ivy climbed trellises artfully placed throughout, while Eucryphia and glossy dark evergreen created the illusion of an outdoor scape.

A pale blue hanging snagged her notice from the corner of her eye.

Wandering over to the neatly tended holly tree, Elizabeth contemplated the unusual piece that dangled from a thin branch. Nearly two feet long and several inches wide, it had the look of a house her papa had once constructed for the warblers that inhabited the poplar outside her chamber windows.

Going up on tiptoe, Elizabeth peered inside each of the narrow slots, trying to make something out of the darkness.

Above the tops of the tree, a holly blue flitted about, and Elizabeth went absolutely motionless as the butterfly drifted lower and then slid effortlessly into one of those side slats.

"It is—"

"A butterfly house," Crispin called out from over her shoulder.

Elizabeth gasped and spun about.

Crispin stood at the front of the room, his arms folded across his chest. At some point, he'd discarded his jacket and cravat, but remained in the same wrinkled lawn shirt and mud-splattered boots he'd worn for his ride that morning.

"You're not abed," he noted, strolling over with lazy, languid steps.

Damn him for being so captivating… even just *walking*. It was infuriating that he should take ordinary and transform it into spellbinding. She focused on drawing in an even breath. "No," she acknowledged. "I was unable to sleep." He sharpened his gaze on her face. Elizabeth hurried to clarify. "I was awake so long that my body has moved beyond rest." Did he sense the lie? Did he gather that her own tortured imaginings of him with one of his lovers had robbed her of all hope of sleep?

"I see."

And though there was not even a hint of arrogance or conceit contained in those two words, something told her that he very well knew. With his instincts and insight, he saw more than she wished to share.

Disquieted, she reexamined the wood structure. "I've never heard of a butterfly house." He came over and took up a place beside her, standing so close their arms touched. Her pulse pounded, and she struggled to make her suddenly heavy tongue move. "I-it is like a birdhouse, then?"

"They are different," he said, so even and pragmatic in that pronouncement that it effectively doused the haze he'd cast. "Birds require a sheltered place to raise their young. Butterflies don't."

"No," she murmured, peering deeper into the darkened recesses. "They are delicate, but far more resilient." A wistful smile tugged at her lips.

He lowered his lips close to her ear, and little tingles danced along her lobe, pulling a breathless laugh from her. "How many nights did we spend searching the grounds with nothing but a lantern to light our way, peering under leaves for slumbering butterflies?"

"Countless ones." He'd been an unjaded boy, free with his smile, his garments as mud-stained as her own.

Whenever they'd been together, he hadn't bothered with the constraints of a jacket or cravat. How singularly odd that he should be in a similar state of dishabille and yet with wholly different pursuits bringing him to that point.

Her smile faded.

It was a sobering reminder about the new divide between them.

"Tsk, tsk. I am disappointed, Elizabeth."

Elizabeth drew her brows together. "I don't—"

"The girl I recall never had fewer than a dozen questions on any topic. You possessed even more for those discussions on the butterfly."

"I was different then." *We were different.* "I've learned to be more measured. More restrained." Her livelihood at Mrs. Belden's had relied upon it. She gave him a meaningful look. "More careful."

Crispin dropped a hip against the carved stone sundial and hooded his gaze. "I know you," he insisted in the melodious, rogue's murmur that conjured seduction and sin. "You might present one way for the world, but you're the same girl you always were. Inquisitive. Eager to know and explore... everything."

Her heart thumped an erratic beat.

Somewhere along the way, they'd shifted course, and they were no longer two adults speaking of butterflies or forgotten memories. She was a woman, and he was a rogue who, with his words, whispered of the forbidden.

"You presume much," she said for her own benefit. Elizabeth wetted her lips, and his gaze homed in on that gesture. His thick lashes swept down, barely concealing the desire in the sapphire depths of his eyes—for her.

"Do I?"

"You do. I've changed." She looked him up and down, lingering her stare deliberately on his wrinkled garments. "We've *both* changed." In ways that made any hopes of any future impossible. Because she could not, even if he wished for her to remain here, do so if he were going about at all hours of the evening... visiting wherever it was he'd been. It would break her in ways their first separation hadn't managed.

He narrowed his eyes. "Why do I believe that was intended as an insult, Elizabeth?" Frustration rippled off his frame.

She'd offended him. Why should he care? If he was an unrepentant rogue, happy for his freedom, what should it matter what she believed about him?

"Not an insult," she said, shaking her head. "Rather, it was stated as a matter of fact. I don't have time to run around hillsides and ponder a butterfly's wings for the length of the day. I'm a finishing school instructor, Crispin. I'll leave, and there won't be room for endless hours of discussion on anything but those topics you rightly disparaged." She could at least own the truth of that. He'd been correct. There was nothing honorable in the lessons she doled out. All of that, her future, her work at Mrs. Belden's, left her bereft.

"You can stay here," he said quietly.

Those four words, a suggestion and a question all rolled together, shrank the air between them.

"What?" she whispered.

Crispin straightened, unfurling to his full height. He closed the handful of steps between them, and capturing her chin in a delicate grip, he ran his thumb down her cheek. "Stay."

Stay. Her breath stuck somewhere between her throat and lungs, trapped there as she stood stock-still, afraid to move, to breathe.

"You don't have to have that life you described," he continued in somber tones stripped of the earlier rogue's murmur. All the while, he continued that delicate caress. Soft as the butterfly's wings, it brought her eyes briefly shut, and she leaned into his touch, his offer, desperately yearning for both. "We can have a future together."

And there it was. The dream she'd pined for in silence for ten long years, laid out. As a tender offering.

Crispin lowered his mouth to hers, and Elizabeth tipped her head back to receive the kiss, but the scent of whiskey wafted over her lips.

She turned her head, and his kiss grazed her cheek. Reality came rushing in. "You're a rogue." She drew in a breath and stepped out of his reach. "You smell like spirits and cheroots."

His cheeks flushed. "I'm not ape-drunk, Elizabeth. And I wasn't smoking. The smell is merely attached to my garments."

"It is the places you go," she entreated, needing him to understand. "It is the people you keep company with." She paused. "It is the life you've lived since we've been apart."

He opened and closed his mouth several times, but no words emerged.

Elizabeth scrunched her toes into the soft lawn. Oh, God. She silently begged with the earth to open up and take her under. "I do not begrudge you for… taking a lover… lovers," she amended lamely. *Liar. You hated him for it. And you hated them even more for having earned his affections.* Even as it was her fault for leaving him and their marriage.

"Look at me," he commanded with a quiet insistence that brought her gaze up to his. "I met with a friend this evening, Elizabeth. When I was broken with your leaving, the Earl of Fielding was the only one there for me."

He'd had another friend in his life. He hadn't been alone. How was it possible to feel joy and an aching sadness at the same time? When she'd been miserable and missing him at Mrs. Belden's, Crispin had found another.

Her shoulders sagged. "You don't owe me any answers, Crispin," she said tiredly. "As you pointed out… I left. You were free to live your life, as you wished." And as he would when she returned to Mrs. Belden's.

Elizabeth pressed the frames of her spectacles back behind her ears and, bowing her head, started for the butterfly doors.

"You believe I was unfaithful to you?" he called after her. The annoyance and hurt wrapped around the question froze her midstride.

Elizabeth completed the step and turned slowly back. "I…" There had been the papers and his own relish several days past in throwing his reputation in her face.

The pale glow of the moon played off the chiseled contours of his face and illuminated the spark of regret in his eyes. "How low your opinion of me is," he noted, and where there'd been anger before, now there was acceptance. "I gave you no reason to doubt my devotion." He strolled over, the bulge of his corded biceps making a lie of any feigned casualness. Crispin roved his eyes over her face. "There has never been any other woman, Elizabeth."

That statement brought to a cessation the flow of all logical thought.

He quirked his mouth in an irreverent half-smile. "The papers?" he supplied for her. "The gossip? The world is content to see what they want to see. A bachelor duke, friends with a scoundrel, must be a rogue." The knot in his throat moved rhythmically. "There was only ever one woman I wanted. One woman I desired."

"Who?" she asked, giving him nothing more than that single, breathless syllable.

A pained chuckle rumbled from his chest. "Oh, Elizabeth. How is it possible for a woman to be so very clever and to know nothing all at the same time?" He dropped his forehead atop hers. "It is you, Elizabeth. There has only ever been you."

And just like that, the world ceased spinning on its axis.

Elizabeth fluttered a hand about her breast. "You've never...?"

Crispin pressed his fingertips against his brow and rubbed. And he wished in this instance that he was the rogue the world had proclaimed him to be. For then he would have all the charming words expected of him. But so much of his life had been lived fulfilling expectations—those his family had of him, those the *ton* had for a duke. "I realized I loved you when I was six and ten, but I've loved you forever."

She emitted a soft, whispery gasp.

And before she might again reject him, he covered her mouth with his and kissed her. Crispin kissed her as he'd dreamed of since a long-ago kiss stolen under the crisp Oxfordshire skies. Kissed her as he had just a day earlier, but this time without the restraint, giving himself over to the hunger tearing through him.

Filling his hands with Elizabeth's slender hips, he drew her close, pressing her body to his.

Moaning, Elizabeth melted into his embrace, and parting her lips, she allowed him entry.

Crispin swept his tongue inside, sparring with hers. And on her lips and every breath she drew and exhaled, he tasted his own desire.

Through the thin fabric of her night shift, he searched her slender body with his hands. Reaching between them, he cupped her right breast, tweaking the tip through the fine cotton. Over and over. Until Elizabeth dropped her head back on an incoherent half plea, half sob.

Desire pumped through him, and with a primitive groan, Crispin guided her garment lower until her breasts lay bared before him and the London night sky.

He drew back slightly, and she cried out at the loss. Tangling her fingers in his hair, she tried to guide his mouth back to hers, but Crispin resisted.

His breath rasping in the quiet, still but for the errant breeze and the trickling water of the Grecian fountain, he worshiped her with his eyes. A handful of freckles dusted the column between her breasts, her large nipples a pale pink hue. The gentle swell of her cream-white breasts had been made for his palms, and he filled his hands with her.

Elizabeth bit her lower lip. Her lashes fluttered, and through those crimson lashes, she followed his every movement the way she'd contemplated any scientific study she'd launched.

Between his fingers, Crispin rolled the pebbled tips of each mound, teasing them with little flicks, and Elizabeth dropped her head. "Crispin." She moaned his name, an entreaty.

"You are so beautiful," he breathed against her skin. Bending his head, he drew a nipple into his mouth and suckled.

Elizabeth cried out.

He caught her as her legs went weak and shifted his focus to her other breast, lavishing it until keening moans echoed around the gardens.

"I have wanted you long before our first kiss," he panted, his breath rasping against her flushed skin. He pressed a kiss to the place where her heart beat wildly. "I have dreamed of this..." Long after she'd gone. He hesitated, drawing back. "But you deserve more than being made love to out here on a—"

"Don't," Elizabeth ordered breathlessly, catching him by the shoulders. "This is how it should be." Her fingers came up to clasp his head, and she drew his mouth back to hers. "This is how I *want* it to be."

With a groan, Crispin claimed her lips. Never breaking contact, he guided Elizabeth to the grass so that they knelt there. He stroked his tongue over her lips, tracing their plump seam and then finding his way inside once more.

And she let him in. Welcomed him. Turned herself over to him with a searing fierceness that sent a stabbing ache of need to his shaft, fueling his hunger, raising the heat of the blood coursing through his veins. When he shifted his attentions to the delicate shell of her right ear, Elizabeth moaned. "Th-this is c-certainly d-different than our last em-embrace." Her voice broke on a moan as he suckled at that lobe.

"Which 'last kiss' do you refer to, sweet Elizabeth?" he whispered against her ear, pulling a breathless laugh from her. "Outside the inn only last evening?" Not pausing to wait for an answer, he worshiped her previously neglected breast.

Her hips arched reflexively as she ground herself in a primitive dance against the hard ridge of his manhood. "N-never last evening's kiss."

"And here our first kiss left me ruined for any other woman," he teased. And then all words, laughter, and pain of the past melted away, superseded by only their mutual hungering to taste passion with the other. Crispin wrestled with the buttons along the back of her night shift. It hadn't been enough to simply worship those perfect swells. He wanted to see all of her cream-white skin, only flushed red from her desire, bathed in the soft light of the moonlit sky.

Crispin blazed a trail of kisses over the column of her neck to her jaw.

Elizabeth tipped her head sideways, allowing him complete access to her, opening herself to him in ways he didn't deserve, but he was too much of a bastard to ever deny himself.

"So many damned buttons," he gasped. He'd believed it wholly impossible to so despise an inanimate object such as a button.

"M-Mrs. Belden believes the button preserves a lady's—" *Riiiip.* The tiny buttons rained down about them. "Virtue," Elizabeth finished. Through the thick haze of passion swelling between them, they shared a brief smile. Crispin collected the hem of her night shift.

Then all humor faded away as he exposed inch by inch of her satiny, soft flesh.

All the air stuck in his chest, lodged there painfully. And he allowed himself that which he'd yearned to do—he caressed her with his gaze, touching his eyes upon every enticing freckle and delicate curve. Through his search, Elizabeth knelt there, proud as Athena.

As the seconds tripped by, she brought her arms up almost protectively about her breasts.

Crispin caught her arms in a delicate but firm grip, staying those attempts.

Indecision raged behind her smudged spectacles.

How could she not know her own beauty?

"There is no one more magnificent than you, Elizabeth. In mind, spirit, and beauty."

Her lips parted, and she exhaled a soft, shuddery sigh.

She held her arms open for him. "Make love to me."

It was a command, belonging to a woman who knew what she desired. Blood pumped to his shaft, and that organ sprang harder from his need for her.

Crispin guided her down so that the lush, emerald patch of earth served as their mattress.

And in this, she'd been correct. There was something only right that this moment should come here, like this… in this make-believe Eden.

Crispin sat up, and Elizabeth lifted her heavy lashes, watching him, a question in her eyes.

Not taking his gaze from her, he pulled his shirt from his trousers and over his head and tossed it aside. Next, he pulled off his riding boots, throwing them onto the forgotten pile of garments.

Elizabeth pushed herself up onto her elbows, and with wide eyes brimming with desire, she took in his every movement.

Crispin shoved down his breeches and kicked them aside, and then he stood naked before her.

Unabashedly, she worked her passion-heavy gaze over him, leaving no swath of his skin untouched. There was an infinitesimal pause as she fixed on his abdomen, and then she proved as fearless and beautifully unashamed as she'd always been.

Her eyes fell to the organ that stood proudly erect, the crown pressed to his abdomen.

"You are magnificent," she whispered in an echo of his very own thoughts about her. She stretched her arms up in a siren's invitation, and he was as lost as those sailors at sea.

Groaning, Crispin came over her. Propping himself up on his elbows, he took her mouth in another kiss, and as she wrapped her arms about him, she met every lash and stroke of his tongue.

Crispin reached between them and found the downy patch of curls shielding her femininity.

A hiss exploded from her lips, lost to his mouth.

He palmed her, pressing the heel of his hand against her sensitive flesh.

"Please," she whimpered, bucking into his touch. She let her legs splay in an invitation, and he slid an answering finger inside her wet channel.

An incoherent sound—neither moan nor groan, but rather, both rolled into one—soared to the glass ceiling.

"I want… I didn't know…"

"Neither did I," he managed to squeeze out, his voice hoarse as every nerve and fiber of him strained under the overwhelming need to lay himself between her legs and plunge deep. He teased her nub, explored the plump folds that shielded it. Crispin reveled in the feel and heat of her.

Sweat beaded on his brow, and a lone drop wound a path down his forehead.

Elizabeth stretched a trembling hand up and caught that moisture. She brushed his hair back behind his ears in a tender lover's touch.

Crispin continued to tease and touch her, until Elizabeth's hands fell away and wrapped about him once more, until she was scraping her nails down his back, gripping him tightly, pleading for him.

He settled himself between her thighs, nestling his shaft against her moist curls. An agonized groan ripped from him, and he waged a battle for control.

"Please," she begged, testing his every last shred of strength and resolve.

Dropping his brow to hers, Crispin slid slowly inside, filling her tight core inch by inch. He stopped. It was too much. "Oh, God." He squeezed his eyes so tightly shut that pinpricks of light danced behind them.

"Marmoream relinquo, quam latericiam accepi. Nil ego contulerim iucundo sanus amico. O mihi praeteritos referat si Iuppiter ann—"

"Are you quoting Latin?" she asked on a breathy laugh.

"No."

She arched her hips, urging him.

"Yes," he rasped, the one-syllable utterance dissolving into a groan.

Elizabeth smiled wickedly up at him.

"You minx."

Her smile froze in place as he found that delicate nub once

more. "Mmmmm." And with words lost for both of them, Elizabeth wrapped her legs about him and rotated her hips.

"Forgive me," he whispered and then plunged the remaining inch inside, filling her.

Elizabeth's cry rang about the room before Crispin covered her mouth with his and swallowed the remainder of that shattered yell.

His heart thundered in his ears, beating hard against hers. They remained motionless, neither moving for different reasons. One suspended by want, the other pain. And it was that pain that allowed Crispin mastery over his desire.

He pressed a kiss against her temple. "I'm so sorry," he said softly, his breath stirring a loose curl.

Elizabeth opened her eyes, her spectacles askew, her smudged lenses reflecting his hungering for this woman. "Make love to me," she urged.

He groaned and then began to move inside her. Slowly at first and then faster. His hips bucked frantically. And with every thrust, the thin thread of control he had strained under the weight of his own desire. Elizabeth matched his movements, holding him close. Whispering his name. Pleading with him.

Oh, God. *Tantae molis erat Romanam condere gentem...*

Elizabeth's hips took on a frantic, undulating rhythm. Her breath came fast.

I cannot wait... "Come for me," he pleaded. He battled with himself. Wanting her pleasure to come before his. Before all else. *"Nostri coniugii memor vive, ac vale."*

Elizabeth's entire body stiffened. And with a glorious scream, she came.

With a groan, Crispin let himself surrender, pouring himself inside her, coming so fast and hard that light flashed behind his eyes, and all he saw, breathed, or felt... was Elizabeth.

He collapsed, catching his weight on his elbows to keep from crushing her.

One night would never be enough. He wanted forever with her.

Elizabeth.

CHAPTER 14

THE FOLLOWING EVENING, ELIZABETH STOOD before a floor-length bevel mirror as maids bustled about her chambers and helped prepare her for the ball.

Half of her curls had been upswept, held in place by gleaming butterfly combs, while the other strands had been left loose about her shoulders.

She cocked her head, hardly recognizing herself.

For in this instance, she could almost believe she was beautiful.

"There is no one more magnificent than you, Elizabeth. In mind, spirit, and beauty."

Her body warmed in remembrance of the words he'd rasped against her, a flush stealing over her pale skin.

Crispin's embrace had shown her that she was beautiful. That he desired her.

Three servants came rushing over, a satin sapphire gown held out between them, pulling her back from her wicked thoughts.

"Here we are, Your Grace," Calista, the cheerful young girl who'd been assigned the role of lady's maid, announced.

Elizabeth lifted her arms up, and they drew the article into place, knocking her glasses forward on her nose. The satin settled about her ankles in a noisy whir and a remarkable fit.

As the other maids rushed off, Calista hummed the haunting melody of *Scarborough Fair* and made quick work of the pearl buttons down the back of the gown.

Elizabeth pushed her spectacles back into place.

And then froze.

"Oh, my," she whispered, her voice breathless.

Butterflies made of diamonds adorned each softly puffed sleeve of her gown. The crystalline creatures had been intermittently affixed along the pleated skirts of the satin masterpiece. The delicate creations glimmered in the candle's glow, casting a prism of rainbow light off the satin wallpaper.

With reverent fingers, Elizabeth grazed the lone butterfly along the deep, lace-trimmed bodice.

"Beautiful, is it not?" Calista remarked. Her eyes twinkling, she leaned forward, holding Elizabeth's gaze in the mirror. "His Grace had it commissioned himself. He brought in only the best modiste and instructed her on how the gown must be designed. Insisted on butterflies."

Emotion wadded in her throat. "It is beautiful," she agreed, a sheen of tears glossing her eyes. All these years, she'd believed she hadn't mattered to Crispin. That he hadn't remembered the memories they'd shared and had instead replaced them with newer ones, with newer women. And he'd remembered... everything.

"There has only ever been you."

A lone tear wound a trail down her cheek. All the gossip, all the stories, had been just that, nothing more than stories.

Calista's smile slipped, and she paused in midbuttoning. "Here, Your Grace. None of that," she chided. "Can't have you marring the kohl under your eyes." Humming a more cheerful tune, she resumed buttoning the back of Elizabeth's gown. "There," Calista announced and backed away, beaming like a proud mama. "You are ready."

There were never less-true words spoken than those three. A village merchant's daughter-turned-finishing school instructor, she was more suited to serve trays to the assembled guests than welcome them as their hostess.

Elizabeth eyed herself in the crystal mirror, angling her head sideways as she considered her reflection.

And yet... with the Ferguson diamonds heavy about her neck and the ethereal masterpiece Crispin had designed, she might as well have been any other debutante who'd left Mrs. Belden's Finishing School groomed for the role of duchess.

It was something that, as a girl of seven and ten, she'd never fully considered the implications of.

But with Crispin at your side, and you both happy, filling each other's lives with love, your future can be anything you wish it to be.

"I swear I'm going to marry you one day, Elizabeth Brightly."

Laughing, Elizabeth didn't pick her gaze up from the lone ant carrying a crumb larger than his own size. "You're silly, Crispin Ferguson," she murmured, pressing her face closer to the earth. "You cannot marry me."

"And why not?" he demanded, the affront in his four-and-ten-year-old voice bringing her gaze up. "I can marry whomever I wish."

Elizabeth rolled her eyes. "No, you cannot. Your mother wouldn't let you. You have to marry a fancy lady like Lady Dorinda, who curtsies real nicely and doesn't track mud through your halls."

"We shall see, Elizabeth Brightly."

In the end, the child she'd been had also seen the impossibility of what he'd ventured. But why had it been impossible? She stood stock-still, unbreathing, unmoving, as she confronted her own cowardice. For she had allowed the duchess to dictate their future. Elizabeth had been told her worth was nothing, and Crispin's future and happiness had been hung upon her shoulders. But ultimately, Elizabeth had left. Ultimately, she'd made a decision, for them both, that had affected both their futures. Oh, all these years, she'd assumed the role of the wounded party because of what she'd overheard... and the threat made by the then duchess.

But that did not take away from the truth—she had run.

All the air left her on a dizzying whoosh, and she briefly closed her eyes and fought for her bearing.

Crispin had been correct. They had been husband and wife and friends. And as such, she should have communicated to him what she'd heard so they could decide on their future—together.

In this moment, she acknowledged the truth she'd long denied herself—she'd been afraid. Afraid of what decision he would make, and so leaving had been as much for her as for him.

In her leaving, she'd robbed him of a decision and spared herself the possibility of hearing his rejection.

"Your Grace?" Calista's hesitant whisper slashed across her musings, bringing Elizabeth's eyes snapping open. "The duke is ready belowstairs."

"Of course," Elizabeth acknowledged, her tongue thick.

She drew in several steadying breaths. The past could not be undone. Only their future remained now, and what came of it was what they would now decide as husband and wife—just as it should have been decided in the past.

After pinching her pale cheeks in a bid to bring color back to them, she smoothed her palms along her skirts. It was time.

A short while later, Elizabeth found her way through the Huntington halls and belowstairs to where Crispin waited.

One hand resting on the stair post, Crispin reclined against it with a regal languidness, his other hand cradling his timepiece.

She paused, and all the earlier pain and frustration eased from her chest.

And how very good it was to again smile without fear of recrimination or scolding for having a smile that was anything but the carefully measured polite one insisted upon by Mrs. Belden.

Crispin looked up. The chain slipped from his fingers and sent the watch fob twisting back and forth, forgotten. "Elizabeth," he whispered.

Nervously clasping the rail, she glided down the steps, her skin heating several shades as he watched her descend.

How singularly odd to share the most intimate parts of oneself and to lay bare before another, only to find oneself wholly uncertain in the light of a new day. "Crispin," she greeted when she reached him.

"You are…" His gaze worked a path over her like an intimate touch. "Breathtaking."

He extended his elbow, and Elizabeth slipped her arm through his, joining them and allowing him to lead her to the ballroom. The crystal chandeliers, all lit with long, tapered candles, illuminated the white Italian marble floors and Doric columns. As they walked, all the fear left her, replaced with a feeling of absolute rightness in being with him.

"My mother is not attending," he announced in somber tones.

Of course, reality invariably intruded.

Elizabeth stiffened.

"I am sorry," she said softly as they took their place at the top of the sweeping double staircase that overlooked the ballroom.

"I'm not," he said simply, drawing her knuckles to his lips, and they tingled under his fleeting caress. "If she cannot accept you as my wife, she has no place here."

Warmth swept her at that devotion, along with a stinging regret. For she'd never wanted to come between him and his family or his dreams. But she'd also always proven selfish where Crispin was concerned—she loved him and wanted him in her life.

Nearly three hours later, the last of a long line of guests had been received and announced until the once cavernous space was filled to overflowing with satin-clad ladies and elegantly attired gentlemen.

Around the ballroom, wistful ladies covetously eyed Crispin, women of all ages but born to Crispin's station who'd gladly trade her for the role of duchess.

None had given her the cut direct.

At best, she'd been received warmly by some guests.

At worst, bald curiosity had been her other greeting.

For all intents and purposes, the evening should be… nay, could be considered a success.

And yet…

A frisson rolled along her spine. The unshakable unease had dogged her the moment she'd descended the stairs to find Crispin waiting, replaced only by a brief calm.

Her fingers tightened reflexively upon the crystal flute, and she took a sip of the warm brew.

"You never asked how I found you," Crispin murmured at her side.

The melodic baritone rose above the din of the orchestra's lively reel. Blinking slowly, Elizabeth glanced up.

"I figured if you'd truly wished to find me, a runner could have easily managed the task."

He chuckled. "Is that what you think?" Crispin teased a finger down her jaw. "You underestimate your ability to hide and my ability to find you, madam."

They held each other's eyes over her glass.

"I hired runners and private detectives. You were gone without a trace, Elizabeth Ferguson." His expression darkened. "And you would have remained so had it not been for a chance meeting between myself and a young woman." Crispin glanced to the front of the ballroom.

Puzzling her brow, Elizabeth followed his stare to the striking couple who wound their way down the stairs and through a throng of guests. Peers and servants melted aside in an indication of the couple's wealth and power.

Elizabeth squinted, focusing not on the tall, powerful gentleman in full command of the ballroom, but rather, the woman at his side. There was something so very familiar. Something…

She gasped, dimly registering Crispin's rescue of her champagne flute as the late-to-arrive guests stopped before them.

"Elizabeth, may I present Their Graces, the Duke and Duchess of Hampstead."

She pressed a hand to her mouth, and with a loss of proper salutations and deference for the distinguished guest that would have given Mrs. Belden a fit of the vapors, Elizabeth fixed on the woman at his side.

"Rowena?" she asked, a question in her own voice as she touched a hand to her breast. She quickly found her footing and dropped a belated curtsy. "Your Grace," she greeted the chestnut-haired nobleman at her husband's side.

Lord Hampstead flashed a crooked grin and gave a wave of his hand. "My wife has that effect on people."

"Elizabeth," Rowena greeted with the composure of a woman born to her station and not one who just one year ago had toiled alongside Elizabeth at Mrs. Belden's Finishing School. Rowena looped her arm through Elizabeth's and then hesitated, casting a glance over at her husband. "Will you gentlemen be all right without us for a bit?" she asked, the teasing in her tone contradicted by the worry in her gaze.

The Duke of Hampstead bowed his head.

As both gentlemen fell into easy discourse, Rowena led Elizabeth off, steering them past nosy guests straining for a glimpse of them.

Rowena steered them to the farthest corner of the room. The floor-length arched windows at her back overlooked the London streets, the pillar a barrier that offered some privacy.

All earlier hint of her smile faded. "I am so sorry," Rowena whispered, gathering Elizabeth's hands in her own. "We all have our secrets, and I inadvertently revealed yours to…" The other woman glanced back over her shoulder, peeking around the column in the direction of Crispin and Hampstead. "Your husband." Her voice faded to a barely there whisper that Elizabeth strained to detect above the noise of the room.

"It is fine," she assured. Four days earlier, she would have had a very different response to the other woman's worry. "How...?"

"I accompanied my husband's ward on a lecture at the Royal Museum given by His Grace. He spoke at length on the domestication of a butterfly." Rowena wrung her hands together. "Many scoffed at the idea of such a feat." She held Rowena's eyes. "But I'd seen it done once before."

A memory trickled in.

"No!" Elizabeth cried. Rushing through the gardens, she put herself in front of a circle of students. "Do not crush it. The butterfly is quite resilient. He or she can live even outside of their natural habitat...

"Me."

"You," Rowena confirmed. "You'd rescued that injured monarch from Mrs. Belden's gardens and kept the creature in your rooms, under a glass." The other woman had known that. "After the lecture, when introductions were performed, I mentioned your efforts... and His Grace asked for your name."

Her heart sped up.

That was what had brought them back together—a matter of chance, and fate. An exchange between two members of the peerage that had come not in a ballroom, but at a lecture hall, when the unlikeliest of presenters, a duke, should be approached by a duchess.

Rowena wetted her lips. "You are... certain you are safe? You wish to be here of your own volition?"

In other words, had Crispin forced her cooperation? "Crispin is never one who'd force any person to do something they do not wish," she said quietly for the other woman's benefit. Even as he'd sought her cooperation, he'd not threatened her future to bring about her agreement.

Rowena smiled wistfully. "You love him."

Elizabeth's gaze went across the ballroom to where Crispin stood conversing with the Duke of Hampstead. "I do." She always had.

As if he felt her eyes on him, Crispin looked up. From over the heads of the twirling dance partners, he winked.

She grinned, a giddy lightness suffusing her breast and making her look away. As she returned her attention to the lone friend she'd made at Mrs. Belden's, a pair at the entrance of the ballroom snagged her notice from the corner of her eye.

All moments of seeming perfection ultimately ended.

Oh, blast.

"The mother?" Rowena murmured.

Elizabeth started, realizing she'd spoken aloud. "You know something of it?" she asked, her stomach churning.

"I know a lot of it," the other woman confessed. "In my case, 'the father.' He... sent me away." Rowena hugged her arms about her middle.

"Isn't that the way of it?" Elizabeth murmured. There were expectations for vaunted heirs, and never did the world allow for an interloper.

The dowager duchess swept down the staircase with the regality of a queen gracing the company of her lesser subjects. For the first time, Elizabeth allowed herself to consider the gentleman at the dowager duchess' side.

"Oh, my God." It slipped out a strangled prayer. There could be no mistaking the Terry crimson curls, the spectacles, and pale skin. Just as there could be no doubting that the gentleman's presence on this particular night, of all the nights before it, signified only one thing.

The duchess and her guest reached Crispin and said something.

A moment later, he was following the pair back up the stairs and disappearing from the ballroom.

Unwittingly, she reached out and found purchase in Rowena's fingers.

"Elizabeth?" her friend urged, squeezing Elizabeth's suddenly moist hand. "What is it?" The query came as if down a long, empty corridor.

"It is my uncle," she managed, her voice faint. The absentee guardian, returned from the grave and on the arm of Crispin's mother, could only ever mean one thing, and that would never be good.

With Rowena calling after her, Elizabeth started quickly across the room, this moment feeling very much like another night nearly ten years ago.

CHAPTER 15

His mother was smiling.

And history had shown that nothing good could ever come from that smile. Particularly when it was issued on the heels of a directive, and in the midst of a ball, while Crispin had been in discourse with a fellow duke, no less.

Unease tripping along his spine, he motioned the pair to enter his offices.

"I trust whatever it is that demands my presence is of vital importance," he drawled, a warning layered in steel.

The dowager duchess' lips formed a tight moue of displeasure. "You should be more pleased to see your dear mother, Crispin," she decreed as he closed the door behind them.

"I don't have time for your games this evening, Mother," he bit out, sparing a warning glance for the somehow familiar gentleman at his mother's side.

"No games, Crispin," she countered, pressing an affronted hand to her chest. "You know games are beneath my dignity."

"Indeed." Such had been the lesson learned firsthand as a boy when asking her to join him for a game of spillikins. He might as well have asked for the king's head in a basket, as scandalized as she'd been. Folding his arms at his chest, he nudged his chin up. "Given that, say whatever it is that could not be said amidst polite company, but was also too vital to wait until the end of the evening's ball," he instructed. Striding past the still silent stranger, Crispin found a place at his desk.

His mother's lips curved up into the closed rendition of a smile that she'd managed in the whole of his life knowing her. Strained. Uncomfortable. And better suited for one with gas. "I've solved our problem."

Crispin perched his hip on the edge of his desk. "I wasn't aware we had a problem."

She wrinkled her nose. "Very well, I've solved your problem."

Too proud to suffer so much as a wrinkle in her silk skirts, the dowager duchess would never dare to admit a weakness in front of a stranger, as she now did.

Crispin narrowed his gaze on the painfully thin, lanky gentleman. With his shock of red hair and pale cheeks, he was of indiscriminate years. The stranger swallowed audibly and looked between mother and son. "I... might I suggest introductions are in order?" he said, struggling a bit with his intricately knotted cravat.

"Introductions are a splendid idea," his mother exclaimed with a buoyant clap of her hands. "May I present Mr. Dalright Terry."

Terry.

Crispin sat upright.

"You recognize the name." It wasn't a question spoken by his mother.

An uncharacteristic joy glimmered in her eyes that only increased the ominous foreboding. Crispin alternated a stare between the two members of this unlikely pairing. "What is the meaning of this?" he demanded on a seething whisper.

"That is no way to greet a gentleman who is, by order of marriage, family."

Mr. Terry stood up all the straighter, puffing his chest out.

"It is when said gentleman should have proven absent for more than ten years," Crispin snapped, deflating the other man's inflated pride.

His mother moved in a whir of skirts. "Tsk, tsk, Crispin. As a scholar, I expect you of all people would understand that Mr. Terry is an avid explorer who's contributed greatly to..." Her lightly wrinkled brow furrowed as she stared expectantly over at her guest.

Elizabeth's uncle coughed into his hand. "The binomial naming system for animal and plant species."

The dowager duchess turned her nose up. "Er... yes... well... I trust you see the importance of... that."

No, he didn't. Not when the other man's exploration and studies had superseded his niece's well-being. "You had an obligation," Crispin clipped out.

Mr. Terry bristled. "I was traveling."

"Your niece was an orphan."

The gent wisely took a step back.

Crispin's mother placed herself between them. "Do cease this instant, Crispin. You are not a bully." Nay, he'd been the one bullied. As such, he'd never beaten, bloodied, or mocked a single soul. But this, this man, who'd abandoned Elizabeth and hadn't bothered to show his damned face when she'd found herself grief-stricken and alone in the world, reemerged more than a decade later.

"Get out."

"Crispin!" his mother exclaimed. "I expect more from you than that."

A growl worked its way up his chest. "Very well," he said in measured tones that challenged the thin grasp of his control. "Get out, before I have you thrown out on your arse."

Except, Elizabeth's uncle proved far braver than he'd credited, or than his nervous Adam's apple bobbing up and down made him out to be. "I-I cannot do that." He glanced over at Crispin's mother in the quickest of exchanges that, had he blinked, Crispin would have missed. But he saw it.

The warning bells roared in his ears. "And why is that, Mr. Terry?"

"Because I do not approve of the union."

"Pfft," Crispin scoffed. "Your time for approving or disapproving was ten years ago." He started quickly across the room and reached for the door handle.

"You misunderstand," Elizabeth's uncle said quickly. "As her guardian, my approval was *necessary*."

Crispin abruptly stopped, and he stared, his eyes locked on the paneled oak door.

"Valid unions between wards who haven't yet reached their majority require the approval of a guardian." Terry's words were delivered as if he'd been hand-fed them in a stage production.

And in this... he had.

His heart knocking against his rib cage, Crispin turned around. "What are you saying?" He winged a brow up, fighting to retain calm. "And I would advise you to proceed very carefully, Mr. Terry," he suggested, lending an icy frost to the warning.

Mr. Terry faltered, but then he looked at the dowager duchess. She gave a slight nod.

Elizabeth's uncle spoke on a rush. "I am saying that Lillibet—"

"Elizabeth," Crispin corrected. His wife had always despised the moniker assigned to her by her family.

"—could not have legally wed without my consent. As such, the union is... the union can be challenged and an annulment granted."

The silence between the three of them lengthened. The clock ticked. The faint rumble of carriages sounded in the streets below.

Crispin's mother preened. "I have managed what your father could not." Her nostrils flared. "What your father *wouldn't*. You made him feel such guilt over your actions that he could not bring himself to end it." She gave a flounce of her ringlets. "Well, I've managed what your father did not."

"And what is that?" he asked impatiently, tired of her ramblings and Elizabeth's uncle's presence.

"Why, I've secured peace between our family and the Langleys."

"That is an impossible feat," he muttered. The Langleys had burned with their hatred of the Ferguson's since Crispin's marriage, and Lady Dorinda's subsequent one shortly thereafter to a cad who'd drank, whored his money away, and then found himself shot dead by an irate husband across a dueling field at dawn. Familiar guilt sat like a pit in his gut.

"An impossible feat for some." His mother swatted his arm. "But not for your mother."

"And how have you managed that?" he asked tiredly.

The place between her brows puckered. "You are usually far more clever than this. Your marriage is invalid, Crispin. Don't you see? You are free." She beamed. "Free to right a past wrong...and finally marry Lady Dorinda."

Long ago, Elizabeth had learned the perils of listening at keyholes.

More than ten years earlier, she'd had her heart broken for it.

Now, she had it broken all over again.

"You are free. Free to marry Lady Dorinda…"

Elizabeth gripped the edges of the door, curling her fingers so tight into the wood that she left crescent marks upon it. And she focused on breathing.

Quiet, even breaths that wouldn't reveal her place outside, while mother and son, and now Elizabeth's errant guardian, discussed Crispin's future—without Elizabeth in it.

She squeezed her eyes tightly shut.

He loves me.

He always has.

He'd missed Elizabeth when she'd gone.

But their marriage had also broken a familial alliance between him and his parents' godchild. A ducal daughter. Groomed to be a ducal bride. And that relationship had been severed with Crispin's marriage to Elizabeth.

And now, what his mother and Elizabeth's guardian presented made something that had once been impossible possible.

Elizabeth forced her eyes open, and perhaps she was a glutton for her own self-misery. She strained her ears, searching for any hint of reply, or sound, or discourse from the trio behind the panel.

There was something so very much worse in Crispin's silence.

Say something, she silently pleaded. *Tell her that your love for me is far greater than any obligation you have to the Huntington line.*

When still no reply was forthcoming, Elizabeth reached for the handle, intending to let herself in and this time force her presence upon the room, an interloper in a discussion they'd not have her be a part of. As she hadn't done in the past.

To what end? To influence… whatever Crispin would, or would not, say?

She lowered her arm back to her middle and hugged herself to keep from throwing the door open.

She'd not have him. Not that way. Elizabeth wanted him, but she would not insert herself into the midst of the offer with which his mother had presented him.

Freedom.

She scrabbled with her lower lip.

How she wished she could be selfish enough.

Elizabeth had turned to go when Crispin's low baritone shattered the quiet and froze her in her tracks.

"Get out."

Her heart stalled.

"Crispin?"

"You enter my household on the evening I'm presenting my wife before Polite Society and threaten me with the dissolution of our marriage."

Elizabeth's heart resumed beating, pounding a frantic beat against her rib cage. She pressed a hand to her chest, certain the arguing pair in that room could hear it. That she'd reveal her presence on the fringe as she listened in.

"You yourself said it was a mistake, Crispin," the dowager duchess exclaimed, exasperation rich in that reminder. "You indicated that if you could do things differently to preserve the connection with Lady Dorinda, you would." There was a pause. "And now you can."

"You'd have me do that, without a thought of what it would mean for Elizabeth's future?"

"Bah, the girl is resourceful. She's managed just fine without you, Crispin, and she will continue to be fine when she leaves."

It was the closest his mother had ever come to paying Elizabeth a compliment. How very ironic that it should be given only with the hopes of sending her on her way.

"Do you require assistance, Your Grace?"

Elizabeth cringed at the unexpected interruption and looked to the butler.

He stared back, a question in his eyes.

Elizabeth gave her head a jerky shake and, with careful steps, strode over to the waiting servant. "There is something you can do." He inclined his head. "Will you see that a carriage is readied?"

"Now?" His brown eyebrows shot to his receding hairline and then swiftly descended.

Yes, it was certainly in bad form to flee one's own ball, leaving the household altogether in the dead of night with a houseful of guests expected to remain for another six hours at the least. "Yes, as quickly as you are able."

The servant dropped a brow. "As you wish, Your Grace." As he took himself off, rushing in the opposite direction, Elizabeth continued briskly onward, not breaking stride until she reached her rooms.

Her lady's maid glanced up. Her already wide eyes went round. "Your Grace," she exclaimed, rushing over.

"Calista." Elizabeth started over to her dressing room, and bending down, she grabbed the handles of the trunk crafted by her father and dragged it from storage.

It scraped noisily along the floor as she went.

The girl glanced at the trunk, following Elizabeth's every move as she wandered to the armoire, tossed the doors open, and pulled out an armful of her garments.

"Your Grace?" the girl croaked.

"I don't require any assistance," she assured, not taking her eyes off her task.

Elizabeth dropped the neatly folded undergarments into the bottom and then returned to the rose-inlaid armoire and fetched her dresses. Nay. Dragon skirts were what they were.

"And did the students leave your tutelage with that same strength?"

Elizabeth jerked to a stop and clenched and unclenched the fabric in her arms. She drew the garments close. How many years had she spent justifying the work she'd done at Mrs. Belden's? She'd been… surviving. Only, it wasn't until Crispin had challenged her existence that she'd acknowledged the harm she'd done to others, all in the name of… survival.

Securing her own future didn't pardon the lessons she'd doled out. The spirits she'd crushed. The dreams she'd quashed.

Gritting her teeth, Elizabeth tossed the dresses into the bottom of the trunk and stalked over to gather the remaining garments, burying her head in the armoire. At her back, there was the faint click of the door opening.

Calista quit her position at the armoire and hurried from the room.

A moment later, the door closed behind her.

"My mother arrived a short while ago," Crispin said quietly from the front of the room. "With… a guest. Your uncle."

"I am aware," Elizabeth acknowledged, yanking at her cloak with its shredded collar. The mangled article remained caught on a gold hook. A loud rending filled the room as she at last managed to free the wool garment.

"You are aware," he echoed.

Elizabeth carried her cloak over to the trunk and dropped it inside. She made to turn, when Crispin said, "You overheard"—he grimaced—"what was said, then."

Finally, Elizabeth stopped and met his veiled stare across the room. Eyes that had seared her with unrestrained passion and love last evening now revealed nothing.

"I heard enough," she said quietly.

CHAPTER 16

CRISPIN HAD BELIEVED THERE WASN'T a greater pain than what he'd suffered after finding Elizabeth gone all those years earlier.

Just as he'd been wrong about so much, he found himself proved wrong once more.

With a hollow numbness, he took in the frenetic movements with which she collected those heinous garments and stormed across the room, stuffing her belongings into the trunk made by her father.

I am losing her all over again.

Only this time, it would rip his heart apart in ways it hadn't before.

Because this time, when she left, the thread that held them together would be severed by their families… and as his mother had said, Crispin would be free.

Nay, Elizabeth would be free.

A cinch tightened about his lungs, squeezing off air flow, straining the muscles until they ached.

"Your uncle is contesting our marriage," he said, not recognizing the strained quality of his own hoarse voice.

"I heard as much," she muttered and resumed her packing.

How in blazes was she so collected? How could she be so bloody casual when his existence had been yanked out from under him?

Crispin took several steps and then stopped. And then took another, and another, until he stood at the edge of her trunk. He stared down at the contents she'd already piled inside.

"I told my mother I love you." As he should have told both of his parents when he and Elizabeth had eloped. She'd deserved a husband who'd been unafraid for her. Who'd battled the world and hadn't sought to mollify those unwilling to accept their union. "I told her that I've always loved you."

Elizabeth hovered at the armoire. "Did you?"

God, how he despised the hesitant surprise in those two short syllables. He nodded once. "I explained that you've always had my heart and that I admire you above all others. That your spirit and strength and intelligence mark you greater than any other woman she'd have me wed—regardless of station."

The long column of Elizabeth's throat moved up and down.

Encouraged, he took a step closer. "I made a mistake in rejecting my feelings for you before, Elizabeth," he said softly, the avowal echoing around the room. "It is a mistake I'll always carry, but I own every feeling I carry for you now." He crossed to her and took her hands in his, and the gray dress she'd been holding fluttered into a forgotten, whispery-soft pile at their feet. "And I don't care about familial alliances or the scandal that will follow when your uncle disputes our marriage." His throat worked painfully. "I want you, Elizabeth." He slashed a hand at the trunk. "And I'll be damned if I let you run this time"—his chest rose and fell—"unless that is what you wish." Because even as it would shatter him to let her go, he loved her that much, where her happiness and her future meant more than his own.

Elizabeth opened her mouth. But no words came out. And then…

"Is that what you believe?" She raised a tremulous palm to his cheek. "That I'm *leaving*?"

He blinked slowly. "Generally, that is what packing suggests," he said dumbly, glancing pointedly at her trunk.

Her lips turned up in a watery smile. "Oh, Crispin. Yes, that is precisely what it means. I am packing. But I did not intend to go alone."

His mind stalled. "I don't understand."

"I trusted that… given the state we find our marriage, an elopement was in order."

"An elopement." She hadn't been leaving. Or rather, she had been… but she'd intended to go, this time, with him.

"That is, I assumed you would wish to accompany me to Gretna Green." Her smile fell. "Unless you'd rather not…"

She still did not know. It was surely a mark of his own failing that she did not know, all these years later, just how much she meant to him. That his life was fuller for her in it. And empty with her gone.

"I lied to you." At that quiet confession, Elizabeth stiffened. "The day I found you at Mrs. Belden's, I was angry. I'd been angry for so long." Anger had been safer than the agony that had come with her abandonment. "I asked you for a day." He chuckled. "But a day was never going to be enough. I knew that the moment I set foot inside that harpy's school and saw you scrambling about for your spectacles."

Elizabeth pressed her fingertips to her lips.

Crispin dropped to a knee. "Marry me," he whispered. "Again. Marry me, this time, forever."

Elizabeth's body remained stock-still, and then with a half laugh, half sob, she launched herself into his arms, toppling him backward. "Forever," she promised.

And with their laughter melding as one, Crispin wrapped her in his arms and claimed her mouth in a kiss that promised just that—forever.

THE END

COMING SOON!

Enjoyed His Duchess for a Day?
Pre-Order Christi Caldwell's August 2018 release,

The Vixen

USA *Today* bestselling author Christi Caldwell pits a fiercely independent beauty against a devilish investigator.

Set apart by her ethereal beauty and fearless demeanor, Ophelia Killoran has always been a mystery to those around her—and a woman they underestimated. No one would guess that she spends her nights protecting the street urchins of St. Giles. Ophelia knows what horrors these children face. As a young girl, she faced those horrors herself, and she would have died…if not for the orphan boy who saved her life.

A notorious investigator, Connor Steele never expected to encounter Ophelia Killoran on his latest case. It has been years since he sacrificed himself for her. Now, she hires orphans from the street to work in her brother's gaming hell. But where does she find the children…and what are her intentions?

Ophelia and Connor are at odds. After all, Connor now serves the nobility, and that is a class of people Ophelia knows first-hand not to trust. But if they can set aside their misgivings and work together, they may discover that their purposes—and their hearts—are perfectly aligned.

Pre-Order at Amazon!

OTHER TITLES BY CHRISTI CALDWELL

HEART OF A DUKE
In Need of a Duke—Prequel Novella
For Love of the Duke
More than a Duke
The Love of a Rogue
Loved by a Duke
To Love a Lord
The Heart of a Scoundrel
To Wed His Christmas Lady
To Trust a Rogue
The Lure of a Rake
To Woo a Widow
To Redeem a Rake
One Winter with a Baron
To Enchant a Wicked Duke
Beguiled by a Baron
To Tempt a Scoundrel
The Heart of a Scandal
In Need of a Knight—Prequel Novella
Schooling the Duke
Lords of Honor
Seduced by a Lady's Heart
Captivated by a Lady's Charm
Rescued by a Lady's Love
Tempted by a Lady's Smile

SCANDALOUS SEASONS
Forever Betrothed, Never the Bride
Never Courted, Suddenly Wed
Always Proper, Suddenly Scandalous
Always a Rogue, Forever Her Love

A Marquess for Christmas
Once a Wallflower, at Last His Love

SINFUL BRIDES
The Rogue's Wager
The Scoundrel's Honor
The Lady's Guard
The Heiress's Deception
The Wicked Wallflowers
The Hellion
The Vixen
The Theodosia Sword
Only For His Lady
Only For Her Honor
Only For Their Love
Danby
A Season of Hope
Winning a Lady's Heart

THE BRETHREN
The Spy Who Seduced Her
The Lady Who Loved Him
Brethren of the Lords
My Lady of Deception
Memoir: Non-Fiction
Uninterrupted Joy

BIOGRAPHY

CHRISTI CALDWELL IS THE BESTSELLING author of historical romance novels set in the Regency era. Christi blames Judith McNaught's "Whitney, My Love," for luring her into the world of historical romance. While sitting in her graduate school apartment at the University of Connecticut, Christi decided to set aside her notes and try her hand at writing romance. She believes the most perfect heroes and heroines have imperfections and rather enjoys tormenting them before crafting a well-deserved happily ever after!

When Christi isn't writing the stories of flawed heroes and heroines, she can be found in her Southern Connecticut home with her courageous son, and caring for twin princesses-in-training!

Visit www.christicaldwellauthor.com to learn more about what Christi is working on, or join her on Facebook at Christi Caldwell Author, and Twitter @ChristiCaldwell!

For first glimpse at covers, excerpts, and free bonus material, be sure to sign up for my monthly newsletter!

Printed in Great Britain
by Amazon